RAVINDER SINGH

PRESENTS

A Good Girl

Chandana Roy

Black Ink

Published by:
Black Ink
E 4/15, 4th Floor
Krishna Nagar, New Delhi 110051
E-mail: queries@blackinkbooks.in
Website: www.BlackInkBooks.in

First published by Black Ink in India in 2015

This is a work of fiction, Names, characters, places and incidents are either the product of the author's imagination or are used fictitiously and any resemblance to any actual person, living or dead, events or locales is entirely coincidental.

ISBN 13: 9788192982205

Typeset in Arpit Printographers, Delhi
Printed at YashPrintographics, Noida

To my parents, who raised me to be a
good girl and yet gave me the freedom
to choose who I wanted to be.
Thank you *Bapi-Maa.*

Part I

Chapter 1

July 2011,
Springfield, Virginia

Ellora is bored. She has not said much since she joined the group of women in the room. In a gathering like this, she always retracts into her shell and speaks only when spoken to. Not that anybody minds. They are all too busy sharing gripes and gossip and exchanging recipes and tips to pay attention to someone who has voluntarily chosen to be a passive listener. All except her elder sister Aparna, who throws an anxious glance in Ellora's direction every now and then. Now that she can see how lost she looks, Aparna feels slightly guilty for having dragged her reclusive sister to a party she had not wanted to attend in the first place.

"If in the next few minutes, Ellora continues to wear the same weary look, I'll have to take matters in my own hands," decides Aparna. Resolution made, she goes back to listening to her friend Alka Mehra, who is currently engaged in doing what she loves doing most: imparting nuggets of wisdom. Indeed, Ms. Mehra has lots of nuggets to impart. If so far, no one from the audience has opened her mouth to interrupt the copious, non-stop flow of words effortlessly rolling off her voluble tongue, it is only because most mouths are filled with the hors d'oeuvres served by the liveried waiters.

"Masala tea. Just what I need," says Ellora, as she readily accepts the bone china mug offered to her. Indeed, a pick-me-up cup of tea is just what she needs right now, for she can barely suppress her yawns. Thankfully, a few sips of tea help her to shake herself out of her torpor and become more aware of what is going on. However, now that she has sufficiently awakened to comprehend the inane conversation around her, she is even more desperate to go out and breathe some fresh air.

The large French windows offer an excellent view of the beautifully landscaped gardens outside. Ellora longs to take a walk on those flower-edged paths. Yet, despite the strong urge to leave the room, she hesitates to get up for fear of inviting unnecessary attention to herself. Fortunately, her sister Aparna reads her mind and comes to her rescue by helpfully suggesting that she check out the garden in the back.

"Ellora, why don't you go out and explore the backyard before it gets too dark for photography?" Then, turning to friends, she declares by way of explanation, "Ellora is into nature photography. In fact, some of her pictures have even won awards."

Ellora flinches, as she becomes aware of the heads that have now turned in her direction. They are all smiling at her encouragingly. She shyly smiles back, even as she silently wonders how many of these women staring at her with such frank interest are actually interested in knowing about the awards she has won for photography. *In fact, as soon as I leave, most of them will be more interested in asking Aparna-di why, despite being thirty plus, I've not bagged the most prestigious award of all: a husband," she cynically concludes.*

Ellora cannot help being cynical about people. She has lived most of her life being a subject of curiosity and a topic of conversations; conversations that have very little to do with her achievements and awards. She knows from experience that no matter how innocuously the conversation starts, it invariably leads to the inescapable question: "So when're you going to give us the good news?" People openly wonder why someone as beautiful as she is, has not yet found a good match (or a good catch, as some of them callously put it). It was a routine inquiry in India. Whenever she was at a social get-together, the inevitable question popped up without fail.

Fortunately, things are different, now that she is in the United States. Ever since she arrived here six months ago, the frequency with which she is confronted with the question has reduced considerably. Nevertheless, Ellora is uncomfortably aware that the question is bound to pop up one of these days and when it eventually does, it is bound to rake up her past, too. Now that she has made her first public appearance at a party comprising mainly Indians, it is just a matter of time before people start speculating why she has not tied the knot yet; speculations that may ultimately lead them to dig up her past and unearth all the dirt associated with it. Ellora does not know how much her sister's friends know about her scandalous past, but she does know that the day they get a whiff of it, she will once again become a hot topic of conversation. And for good reason, too.

However, for now, Ellora is happy to be in the company of the mute flowers and garden gnomes not inclined to gossip or ask inconvenient questions. She closes her eyes and takes a deep breath, filling up her lungs with the scented air. What a relief to have escaped the boring babble that had nearly put her to sleep! The garden, on the other hand, has awakened all her senses. A treasure trove of hidden delights, it is crammed with flowering trees and colourful annuals that bloom everywhere with a carefree abandon, creating a vibrant splash of colours all around. The place has a relaxed informality but Ellora can see that beneath the garden's carefree cheerfulness lies careful planning.

It is a warm July afternoon with the sun shining as if there is no tomorrow. Ellora sits down on a wooden bench and leisurely soaks in the sights, smells and sounds of the garden awash with colours, scents and movements. Birds noisily forage in the trees, their sonorous calls reverberating from the branches heavy with summer blooms and berries.

Cardinal birds feed upon the serviceberries that are as brightly red as their own feathers. Butterflies flutter and feast on the lilac panicles of a Buddleia bush. Nearby, orange dragonflies hover like toy helicopters over a small circular pond filled with dazzling water lilies. The courting pairs merrily indulge in aerial copulation, with the male swiftly lifting the female in mid-air and the female complying without a murmur of protest. They remain suspended in the air, their outstretched diaphanous wings with crisscross veins trembling in tandem.

The sight of the dragonfly pairs takes Ellora back to her childhood days when upon spotting one such pair during a school picnic, she had gleefully clapped her hands to draw everyone's attention to the fascinating drama taking place in mid-air.

"Look, look! A double-decker helicopter," she had squealed excitedly.

There had been a hushed silence following her dramatic declaration and then some girls had started giggling uncontrollably, at which their class teacher (a spinster in her late thirties) had given them a stern look that had silenced all of them.

Ellora smiles as she recalls the chain of events that her naïve comment had elicited. Over the years, 'double-decker helicopter' became a popular catch phrase among her classmates, many of whom used it in their conversations to bypass using the crude four-lettered word that good girls from good families were not supposed to utter in public, or in private, for that matter. Years later, Aditi, her best friend at school, grinned mischievously when she told her, "You were bang on, when you inadvertently coined that phrase. Do you know the etymology of the word helicopter? It comes from the word helix, which literally means a screw. Change the benign noun to a lewd verb and you know what I mean."

* * *

The dragonfly pairs that had transported Ellora to her

schooldays are now hovering quite close, impervious to her presence. She decides to click some pictures of the colourful courtship of the airborne insects. She will send them to Aditi, with whom she has recently started exchanging emails after a prolonged period of silence. It would be interesting to know if her childhood friend still remembers the 'double-decker helicopter' episode after all these years.

Ellora gets up to shoot the mating insects but the frisky dragonflies have no desire to be caught on camera in a compromising position. As soon as she starts focusing the telephoto lens of her camera on them, they quickly disperse, as if they have somehow sensed that someone is about to intrude upon their privacy.

With her airborne subjects vanishing into thin air, Ellora has no other option except to sit down once again and enjoy her surroundings. She makes herself comfortable on a rustic wooden bench under the canopy of a profusely blossoming Crepe-myrtle bush near the lily pond. She does not know it but draped in a turquoise-blue sari, she herself makes a very pretty picture against the backdrop of the heavy clusters of brilliantly pink flowers.

She had been reluctant to wear the chiffon sari, saying the material was too sheer, but her sister had dismissed all her misgivings with a categorical, "That's sheer nonsense! Nothing in my wardrobe is too sheer to wear!"

As someone who has been assigned the responsibility of finding a suitable match for Ellora, Aparna loves exercising her newfound authority from time to time to overrule her sister's silly objections. She is not the type of person who would let trivial objections from her younger sister come in the way of her serious objective, which right now is to present Ellora as glamorously as possible to as many prospective suitors as she possibly can. If it means dragging her to parties she does not want to attend and forcing her to wear clothes she does not want to wear, so be it. After all, as an elder sister who knows better, it is her birth right to counsel, coax and (if need be) even coerce her wilful sister, who indeed needs a whole lot of counselling, coaxing and coercion. Left to her own devices, Ellora would have come to the party in one of her dowdy handloom dresses.

If Aparna could have had her way, she would have made Ellora wear one of her latest acquisitions: an emerald green silk sari with intricate zari work. However, Ellora had balked at the suggestion.

"I wouldn't be caught dead in that glittering green sari on a hot July afternoon. Do you want me to look like an out of season Christmas tree?"

"Vicky Bhalla's anniversary bash is the much-awaited event of the year. Everyone is going to come dressed in shimmering silks and flowing chiffons. You can't go to a grand party like this in a dowdy cotton dress."

"Then let me stay home," Ellora had stubbornly insisted.

The sisters finally reached a compromise when, giving in to Aparna's persuasive pressure, Ellora reluctantly picked a plain chiffon from her sister's extensive collection of fancy saris.

Now, as Ellora observes her reflection in the nearby pond, she desperately wishes that she had worn something more sensible and less eye-catching. Not quite comfortable in her diaphanous sari and glittering ornaments, she yearns for the casual comfort of her rugged handloom dress. She frowns, as she critically scrutinizes her undulating image in the pond. The borrowed blue topaz around her neck and ears sparkle each time they catch a beam of sunlight, making her feel extremely overdressed, whereas her see-through sari reveals more than Ellora is used to revealing and makes her feel extremely under-dressed. What really frustrates her though, is the fact that even though she is dying to have a closer look at the water lilies, she is unable to venture near the pond because it is tricky to walk on the slippery tiles wearing her high-heeled shoes. Therefore, she resigns herself to sitting on the bench, which is the nearest she can get to the water lilies blooming in the pond.

Serenity reigns in this part of the backyard and yet, from her vantage point, Ellora has a clear view of the gathering without being spotted by anyone. The party has already started warming up with a stream of guests gathering on the sprawling poolside patio, but she is enjoying her solitude far too much to have any inclination to join the boisterous crowd. In her secluded corner, she is insulated from the outside world without being totally cut off from it. In fact, she has a ringside view of the circus in front of her.

As predicted by Aparna, most women have come dressed in heavily embroidered and brilliantly shimmering silks, chiffons and crepes. Even those who were splashing around in the pool in their swimwear a few minutes ago have now changed into their party clothes.

A new arrival, however, stands out among the flashily dressed crowd because of the casual way he is dressed. Wearing a pair of blue jeans and a crisp white, half-sleeved shirt, he looks confidently cool among the over-dressed people around him. Even from a distance, Ellora can make out that the man is handsome in a wholesome North Indian way. Tall and fair, he has the assured, yet laidback air of someone who knows he is good looking, but is not overtly concerned about it.

He seems to be very popular among the young women. They are all vying for his attention, notes Ellora. *How would've Aditi described this good-looking fellow? Delectably Handsome? Ridiculously Handsome? Mind-blowingly Handsome? Or Heartbreakingly Handsome?* she wonders.

It is an old, difficult-to-break habit with Ellora. She cannot look at a good-looking man, without first wondering how Aditi would have described him.

Not a day goes by when Ellora does not think of her childhood friend.

* * *

For someone who was just fifteen when Ellora first met her, Aditi Sharma was a tyrannical chit of a girl who had strong opinions about everything and everyone. And worse, she was never too unwilling to impose her opinions on others and never too shy to air her views. If her comments offended people, it was their problem, not hers. Aditi had many redeeming points but diplomacy was not one of them.

Ellora smiles, as she recalls the comments Aditi had made, when she had first shown her the photograph of her dancer mother.

"My mother was very pretty, wasn't she?" she had eagerly asked her friend. Actually, it was a statement rather than a question, for Ellora knew that her late mother had been a celebrated beauty of her time. Everybody, even the editors of famous celebrity magazines said so. That was why she was crestfallen, when Aditi had just shrugged her shoulders and bluntly replied, "No, she wasn't." Ellora was about to retort by saying something sharp and nasty to her opinionated friend but before she could open her mouth, Aditi had solemnly uttered, "Your mother wasn't just pretty; she was beautiful."

"What's the difference? She had asked, elated that her friend considered her mother beautiful, if not pretty and relieved that she was spared the ordeal of saying something nasty to her best friend.

"A lot, silly," her outspoken friend had replied. "The world is full of pretty women, but there are only a handful of women who can claim to be beautiful. Your mother was a beauty without a shadow of doubt. A classic beauty, no less. Look at her exquisitely chiselled features, her big soulful eyes and her high cheekbones. Not many women are born with such perfect features and such fine bone structure."

Then, examining Ellora's face critically, Aditi had added, "You've inherited some of your mother's features, but alas, not enough to be called a beauty. Your nose, my dear, is too blunt for that and sadly, it doesn't even hold the promise of shaping up into something sharper and shapelier in the near future." Then, seeing Ellora's dejected expression, Aditi had thoughtfully handed her a fruit gum, before nonchalantly continuing with her facial evaluation. "You can, at best, be described as pretty. But I'll hand this to you, Ellora Chatterjee; your eyes are almost as big and beautiful as your mother's. If you do something about that bulbous nose of yours and cultivate a little more attitude and poise, who knows, one day you too may bloom into a beauty like her," her forthright friend had prophesied.

* * *

Now, sitting under the Crepe-myrtle tree, Ellora absentmindedly takes out some chewing gum from her handbag and starts chewing on it, as she goes back to ruminating about a conversation which, though it took place many years ago, is still fresh in her mind. She wonders what Aditi would have to say about her present appearance if she were to see her at this moment; all dressed up in a borrowed chiffon sari and sparkling blue topaz.

Ellora's train of thoughts is interrupted by a pair of yellow goldfinches that sing in a happy, rambling twitter, as they fly down from a nearby tree to sit near the lily pond. She quietly watches the tiny birds, as one of them - presumably the male one, ventures closer to the pond to gaze at its own dazzling reflection.

"My my! Aren't you vain, Mr Narcissus?" says Ellora in a hushed tone.

Again, it is difficult for Ellora not to think of her childhood friend. It was Aditi, who had first introduced her to the story of Narcissus. The two of them were playing scrabble in Aditi's room, when her friend had looked out of the window and said, "Do you see those yellow flowers in the far corner of the garden? They are called narcissus after a good-looking boy who fell in love with his own reflection. So enamoured was the vain boy with his beautiful face, that every day he would kneel beside a pool and gaze at himself for hours. No wonder that he drowned one day. They say, when the boy's corpse eventually turned to dust, these flowering-bulbs sprang up from the earth."

Ellora had still been trying to digest the complex story, when Aditi increased her confusion by adding, "He literally pushed up the daisies."

"Daisies?"

"It's a figure of speech, silly. When someone is dead and buried, he is said to push up the daisies. In Narcissus's case, of course, it is more appropriate to say he pushed up the daffodils."

"Daffodils? But didn't he push up the narcissus?" Ellora was now more confused than ever.

"The daffodil, for your kind information, is also known as the narcissus," informed Aditi in an exasperated 'how-can-you-be-so-dumb?' tone.

There was no doubt that being a voracious reader, Aditi was precocious beyond her years. She knew a lot and liked nothing better than showing off her stupendous knowledge to her sweet and docile friend, who listened to her with the rapt attention of an obedient pupil. Another thing Aditi liked doing was using her sizeable vocabulary in describing people, particularly good-looking people. Under her clever friend's expert tutelage, Ellora too quickly learned to use innovative phrases to describe people's appearances. It soon turned into a fun game. Whenever they spotted a good-looking man, which sadly was not often enough, they would try to come up with an appropriate phrase to describe him.

At fifteen, the girls were just beginning to develop an interest in the opposite sex and were desperate to meet someone, anyone, who reminded them of the stereotypical romantic heroes of the Mills & Boon and Barbara Cartland novels they both devoured at night. The concept of a tall, dark and handsome man was fascinating to their adolescent minds, even though they were intrigued as to why a white man was described as dark. They lamented the fact that there were not too many broad-shouldered and square-jawed boys around them. Of course, they knew boys who were quite tall and very dark, but alas! None of them could be regarded as handsome by any stretch of the imagination. The only men they saw inside the gates of their girls-only convent school were the elderly teachers. Sadly, even the young men they occasionally saw on the streets did not come anywhere close to the picture of the handsome hero they had conjured up in their imaginative minds. None of them possessed any 'brooding good looks' either, whatever that cryptic phrase was supposed to mean. As for the Hindi movie heroes, most of them looked far too avuncular to stir up any romantic feelings in their adolescent hearts.

That was why the girls jumped with joy when their English teacher Ms Jennifer D'Souza gave them an assignment that involved sticking pictures of good-looking people in their notebook and giving a suitable caption to each, using a combination of an adverb and an adjective. The assignment gave Aditi a perfect excuse to get hold of the magazines that arrived from London every month. Those glossies were out of bounds for the girls, because Aditi's mother, who subscribed them to stay in touch with her life in London pre-divorce, considered their contents too adult for them. However, thanks to the English assignment, they now had her official permission to flip through the pages of those prohibited magazines.

It was in the dog-eared pages of one of those glossies that Aditi and Ellora saw a picture of Tom Cruise. As they gawked at the young actor, they jointly agreed that he was indeed very handsome.

"Now, what does one call someone as eye-poppingly and jaw-droppingly handsome as this man?" It was very unusual for a usually verbose Aditi to be at a loss for words. As she regarded the actor smiling at her from the pages of an old magazine, she pondered, "There's something about his crooked smile that makes him effortlessly cruise his way into your heart. Don't you think he's Heartbreakingly Handsome?"

Ellora, however, was too engrossed in trying to come up with a fitting caption for John McEnroe to respond. Sporting a red bandana, the sportsman looked as rakish and impudent as he was portrayed in the article accompanying the picture. He was not conventionally handsome, but there was something audaciously attractive about this Bad Boy of Tennis. Ellora wanted a word that accurately described the sportsman's smug arrogance. At first, she thought of the title 'Cockily Handsome,' and then after consulting her pocket thesaurus, she decided to change it to 'Haughtily Handsome.'

Thrilled at being able to coin a phrase without taking any help from Aditi, Ellora came up with yet another brilliant, if somewhat flawed expression for the next picture she found in a fashion magazine. The centre spread featured a bare-chested male model in a shiny green shirt. The brawny model stood with his hands on his hips. His silk shirt was deliberately left unbuttoned to show off his smooth and hairless chest that shone like polished pinewood. The man reminded Ellora of a pigeon with a puffed chest. His shimmering green shirt and his smug expression, on the other hand, reminded her of a strutting peacock.

A cocky peacock, if there ever was one! What if I call him Pea-cockily Handsome? Now that sounds like an interesting caption: Pea-cockily Handsome. Wow! What an apt description for this flashily dressed man with loads of attitude. Ellora was very pleased with herself to have hit upon so unusual a title; however, there lay the problem. The title was far too unusual. The word 'peacockily' sounded strange even to her own ears. Not sure if such a word existed, she looked it up in the dictionary and was very disappointed, when she could not trace it even in the thick Oxford Dictionary. Yet, the word, no matter how weird it sounded, could not have been more apt. It perfectly described the flamboyant model's cool cockiness. Besides, it was her very own word, her unique invention and she was not prepared to discard it just because the dictionary people were not ingenious enough to have invented it.

When Ellora showed Aditi her caption, she was duly impressed. "Pea-cockily Handsome! Wow! That's a gem of an expression indeed! So what if you can't find it in the dictionary! You're a genius Ellora," conceded Aditi, albeit a bit resentfully, for she would have much rather coined the phrase herself.

* * *

"Those were such happy, fun-filled days," muses Ellora nostalgically, as she absentmindedly watches the party crowd gathering at the poolside from her unhindered vantage point. Looking at those flashily dressed people, she is suddenly gripped with a strong desire to play her childhood game all over again.

"What better subject than these poolside people in their party apparel?" Unnoticed by the crowd, Ellora inspects her subjects, capturing the details of their faces, figures and fancy attire. Her eyes are automatically drawn to a short and chubby young woman in a gaudy orange *lehenga-choli* ensemble.

"She must be around twenty five," guesses Ellora, as she sizes up the woman who has captured her attention for all the wrong reasons. Her flaring *lehenga* is tight around her abdomen and hips, drawing attention to her tubby tummy and plump posterior, whereas her low-cut, sleeveless *choli* calls attention to her flabby arms and heavy bosom, considerable parts of which are popping out from the plunging neckline. The screaming orange of her outfit does nothing for her ruddy complexion and the cakey makeup does more damage than good.

The young woman enthusiastically waves at someone and as she does, her triceps hanging like limp saddlebags from her arms start jiggling uncontrollably. "Hey Jai, come and join us," she screams, waving her arms vigorously. The suspended saddlebags start waving at the man, as well, with double the vigour.

"Aditi would've probably called her A Blowzy Lady with a Lousy Dress Sense," says Ellora, as she witnesses the scene from far. Then, realizing that she has unconsciously hit upon a catchy phrase that perfectly described the voluptuous woman's atrocious dress sense, she exclaims, "Wow! Ellora Chatterjee! A Blowzy Lady with a Lousy Dress Sense. That's a perfect description for this hideously dressed young woman." She tries to shrug off her feeling of unease for being nasty to a total stranger. Nevertheless, now that she has successfully coined a caption that even a fastidious fusspot like Aditi would have applauded, Ellora is suddenly inspired to come up with some more. Her eyes are now drawn to Jai, the man whose attention had been sought moments ago so enthusiastically and with much jiggling from the woman in orange.

Ellora is not surprised that the young woman was so desperate to capture his attention. He is the same tall and handsome man whom she herself had noticed earlier.

"How would've Aditi described this guy?"

She scrutinizes the man, now talking to a group of enthralled youngsters hanging on to every word uttered by him.

"No, you can't call him Cockily Handsome. There's nothing remotely audacious or cocky about him. You can't call him Peacockily Handsome either, because he's very casually dressed and doesn't strut like a peacock, even though God knows, he has every reason to strut like one. What about Delectably and Delightfully Handsome? Indeed there's something very pleasant, unaffected and delightful about him."

Even as Ellora toys with the phrases that would do justice to his wholesome good looks, the man in question waves a hurried bye to his young friends and starts walking away from the noisy pool area to answer a phone call. Ellora is quite alarmed when she notices him stepping down from the elevated patio and walking towards the winding path that, if he continues walking on long enough, may lead him to her own sequestered nook. She is in two minds: should she stay put or should she abandon her private refuge to allow the man his privacy?

The zigzagging path has so far hidden her from view, but as the footsteps get closer, Ellora realizes that the two of them may come face-to-face any moment now. The prospect makes her quite nervous. She is aware that suddenly, for no apparent reason, her heartbeat seems to have picked up pace.

"Oh, he's Heart-poundingly Handsome," she tells herself in an attempt to make light of the impact the man seems to be having on her. She is completely baffled by her silly response to the man's impending approach; more so, because despite all her nervousness, she now wants to pull out lip-balm from her handbag and touch up her lips, which have by now turned very dry.

"What's wrong with you Ellora Chatterjee?" she admonishes herself, speaking aloud in a whisper that she alone can hear. "You've not reacted to any man in this manner for almost fifteen years now. Don't you think it's a bit late in the day for you to start going weak in the knees like a silly teenager with raging hormones for a man you've not even met?"

Even as Ellora sternly deals with her very nascent and very disconcerting reaction to a man she has so far seen only from a distance, the man in question starts walking away from her. He is still talking on the phone, but his voice becomes fainter and fainter, until Ellora can hear it no more. "Oh, I'm heart-broken," she sighs. But this time, she is earnestly self-mocking, ridiculing herself for reacting like a stupid teenager at the man's approach. Inwardly, she is relieved to note that it had taken her less than a minute to take charge of her feelings. After all, she has had years of practice.

With her heartbeat restored to its original rhythm and the cause of her temporary arrhythmia gone from the scene, Ellora decides to go back to taking pictures. Fortunately, the dragonflies are back. Some sit on the grass edging the pond, but most are hovering in the air in pairs. The brilliant orange of their bodies matches the orange goldfish that swim under the cover of the round leaves of the water lilies. "Time for action," she reminds herself and gets ready by discarding her fancy heels and tucking the pleats of her delicate sari inside her petticoat, so that she can walk around the pond without dirtying the edges of her borrowed sari. With sari firmly in place, she focuses her camera on her fidgety subjects, which surprisingly do not seem to mind her presence any longer. It is as if, they too are trying to make hay while the sun shines and while they are at it, they do not mind who captures them on camera and in what posture. She takes several pictures of the coupling dragonflies in quick succession, but just when she is about to take the last shot, she hears a male voice behind her.

"Are you the animal paparazzi or what?"

The voice startles her so much that she nearly drops her camera. She turns and is about to drop her camera again, when she discovers that the voice belongs to the same person whose approach had sent her heart racing a few minutes ago.

The man looks equally startled.

"I'm sorry. I didn't mean to startle you. Actually, I mistook you for someone else. I'm truly sorry for interrupting you so rudely," apologizes the man, looking very contrite indeed.

Ellora does not quite know what to say. She is not too happy about being caught sans her heels; more so because her sari is tucked high above the ground, exposing her naked feet and calves. As she quickly locates her discarded heels and promptly puts them on, discreetly pulling down the pleats of her sari to cover her exposed ankles, she is uncomfortably aware of the pair of eyes observing all her actions. She flushes with embarrassment that, of all people, this smart man should see her in her present dishevelled state. She makes a half-hearted attempt at smiling at him, not sure if she should be smiling at someone who, no matter how dapper and handsome he may be, is responsible for her utter discomfiture.

"Hi, I'm Jai." The man promptly introduces himself, realizing quickly that his sudden appearance on the scene followed by his uncalled-for comment has clearly startled the strikingly attractive woman who, for some odd reason, was running around barefoot, chasing pairs of dragonflies. Now that he can see how flustered she looks, he deeply regrets interrupting her so rudely.

"I didn't mean to startle you. I didn't mean to make that unwarranted comment either. It just slipped out. I'm really sorry." He sombrely repeats his apology.

"I think I gave you enough reason to warrant being called the animal-paparazzi," says Ellora, finding her voice for the first time.

In reply, the man flashes a dimpled smile that is quite disarming. The accompanying twinkle in his eyes, on the other hand, is rather disconcerting. Ellora decides to ignore the twinkle as well as the dimples by looking away.

"You look very familiar. Where have I seen you before?"

Ellora is surprised that the man is using such a done to death pickup line on her, but then she decides that this particular man is too suave and sought-after to have any need for resorting to such clichéd tactics. She, therefore, sees no harm in introducing herself.

"I don't think we've met before, but just in case it rings any bells, I'm Ellora. Ellora Chatterjee."

"Ellora! What a lovely and unusual name and yet it sounds so familiar. In fact it definitely rings a bell." The man narrows his eyes as if he is trying to solve an intriguing puzzle and then adds, "I've a distinct feeling that I've seen you before; but the question is: where? Now let me hazard a guess. Are you Aparna Ray's sister by any chance?"

""That's right. But how did you guess?"

"I must have seen your photographs in Aparna's house. We're neighbours, you see. In fact, your brother-in-law Rahul and I work for the same hospital."

"Oh! So he's the famous Dr Jai Sehgal," thinks Ellora. Why had it taken her so long to figure that out? His name should have rung a bell the moment he introduced himself. How many times had she heard her sister talk about her husband's handsome colleague? In fact, Jai's name had cropped up all the time during their conversations. And yet, she had failed to recognize his name.

Now that she knows who the man is, she is no longer awkward or awestruck in his presence. The man is extremely handsome, no doubt; more handsome from close quarters than he had appeared from a distance. But she can now appreciate his good looks without letting it affect her composure and more importantly, her heartbeat. Not only can she meet his gaze, but she can also casually take in his appearance like a passive observer.

She notes that Jai's face owes much of its charm to his dimpled chin that draws attention away from the long nose, which would otherwise dominate his face. His neatly combed brown hair reminds her of wind-swept paddy fields at dusk. His eyes, bright and intelligent, are a deep shade of brown, but appear a shade lighter as the last few rays of the sun are reflected in them.

Ellora is slightly amazed at her own capacity to be able to analyse the man's looks so coolly and with such precision. However, now that she can see how smart and neat he appears, she is once again conscious of her own scruffy appearance. Chasing pairs of dragonfly on a hot afternoon has left her sweaty and dishevelled. "I must be looking like a fried *puri* by now." However, as she frets over her oily forehead, all of a sudden just the thought of fried hot *puris* makes her feel very hungry.

The tempting sight of delicious kebabs being char-grilled

on the patio only works to fuel her already intense hunger pangs. She can smell their tantalizing aroma wafting faintly on the breeze.

"Looks like they're getting ready for the cake-cutting. I think we should join the party now," she suggests, but not very assertively. Hunger pangs notwithstanding, a part of her wants to linger just a little longer, so that she can continue chatting with the handsome man whose company she is beginning to enjoy very much. Or is that the reason a part of her wants to leave now? Possibly, for she is enjoying his company a bit too much for her own comfort. Besides, it is getting dark and she is acutely aware that the two of them are alone in a far corner of the garden. "What if someone spots us together?" She gets ready to leave, collecting her handbag and camera.

"Let's take a detour via the gazebo; it's a delightful walkway," suggests Jai.

They start walking side by side along the brick pathway that weaves through the beds of sweet smelling annuals and perennials.

"Your camera looks quite heavy. Let me carry it for you," offers Jai, as he observes Ellora struggling with her two bags as she tries to match his long strides in her high heels.

Ellora hesitates, but only for a moment before handing him her camera.

"I remember Aparna telling me that you've won many awards for photography," says Jai, as he inspects the camera that, even to his untrained eyes, looks quite advanced.

"That's so like my sister. She rarely misses an opportunity to publicize this fact to anyone who's willing to listen. But to tell you the truth, photography is just a hobby. I've not received any formal training. It just so happens that my research work requires me to go outdoors and study creatures in their natural habitats and having a good camera always helps."

"So is that the reason you were taking pictures of the

dragonflies?" asks Jai, the corner of his mouth slowly curling in a smile that he is earnestly trying to suppress.

Ellora is dumbstruck. For a few seconds, she does not know how to react and what to say. When she finally finds her voice, she ends up blurting out the first excuse that comes to her mind.

"Well, I was trying to photograph them for an article I'm writing on threatened aquatic insects." She concocts a clumsy lie with the ineptness of someone not used to lying. Inwardly, she is mortified. She was hoping against hope that the surgeon, despite the animal paparazzi comment he had made earlier, had somehow forgotten the excruciatingly embarrassing fact that he had caught her red-handed, clicking pictures of mating dragonflies. However, it seems, he not just remembers, but is also immensely amused by the fact. His eyes do not give away much, but there is a twitching around his mouth that looks suspiciously like an amused smirk.

He looks into her eyes and his lazy smirk is slowly replaced by an open and friendly smile.

"I'd no idea that these orange dragonflies were in danger of becoming extinct. Quite strange, considering that at this very moment I can see an army of them swarming around us."

It is evident that her spur-of-the-moment lie has been caught. What was she thinking when she came up with that ridiculous excuse?

"So are you saying that these dragonflies are no longer endangered?" he smilingly persists. This time there is no mistaking the glint in his eyes.

"Well." Ellora takes a deep breath before continuing. "Dr Sehgal, you've certainly put me on the back foot this time. Knocked me for six, so to speak. I confess, I'm stumped and don't know what to say. So let me come clean by admitting that I lied to you just now. You're absolutely right. These dragonflies are in no danger of extinction, not today, nor in the foreseeable future," she states with a forthrightness she did not know she possessed.

Ellora is acutely aware that Jai is looking at her with frank curiosity, eagerly waiting for her to continue.

"I normally don't go around chasing dragonflies, but there was a reason I wanted those pictures. Well, it's a long story. In fact, too long to be narrated in a hurry." She avoids looking at him.

"Sounds like an interesting story. Can't wait to hear it," says Jai, but does not persist when his companion chooses to remain silent. Relieved that the subject has been dropped for the time being, Ellora secretly hopes that she never has to recount the 'double-decker helicopter' episode to the man walking beside her.

They walk side by side without saying much, because there is so much to experience silently. The winding path unfolds hidden surprises at every turn. Life-size statues of deer, squirrels and frogs materialize all of a sudden, under bushes or tucked unobtrusively amid the lush foliage, looking very much a part of the enchanting landscape. They stop to admire a huge granite statue of a laughing Buddha that sits happily, surrounded by copious blooms of busy Lizzies, geraniums, petunias and carnations.

Even though the smell of grilled kebabs still floats faintly through the air, there is yet another enchanting and delightful scent of a different kind filling the air now. It is a heady floral fragrance, sweet, strong and slightly spicy. Ellora is not sure of its origin. It is an intriguing mixture of scents, probably created by a combination of the profusely blooming sweet alyssums, flowering tobaccos, honeysuckles and the night-blooming jasmines.

They stand silently in this corner for a few moments, breathing in the intoxicating perfume and taking in the entrancing beauty of the setting before resuming their walk. And then, out of the blue, he breaks the silence to ask, "You are a cricket fan, aren't you?"

Ellora literally stops in her track. The abruptness of the question does not quite justify the stunned look that momentarily clouds her face upon hearing the question.

"Now how did you guess that?" she asks, trying very hard to keep her tone as casual as possible.

"Well, because you used several cricketing terms like back-foot, stumped and knocked for six, a little while ago. These are phrases that only someone familiar with cricket would use. Not many people are likely to use these expressions in their day-to-day conversations," says Jai, quite oblivious to the turmoil he has just caused by bringing up the word 'cricket.' He, therefore, is also not aware of the huge surge of relief that Ellora is experiencing at this moment. The incipient frown that appeared between her shapely eyebrows upon hearing the question has now completely gone. She could not have been more relieved to know that Jai's query on cricket has nothing to do with her past. A past filled with some very painful memories, memories that are inseparably entwined with the game of cricket.

A visibly relaxed Ellora now smiles, as she answers his question.

"Yes Dr Sehgal, I love watching cricket. Like the millions of cricket crazy fans in India, I too have no compunction about spending an entire day sitting in front of TV and chewing on my nails while watching a nail-bitingly exciting match. But, to tell you the truth, I haven't watched much cricket since I've landed in America. Although I'm told cricket is quickly catching on in this country."

"Well, cricket is indeed getting quite popular here, but unfortunately, not enough to attract crowds, fans and sponsorships. At least, not as yet. It's way too long a game for people addicted to speedy sports like baseball and rugby. Not many Americans understand the game. Some even think you're talking about the insect when you mention cricket. Luckily, some of us simply can't do without cricket. In fact, we have our own cricket club where we play some serious cricket, though it's mainly played for fun. I play for our club whenever I manage to get time off from my busy hospital schedule. Our host Vicky Bhalla is one of our patrons."

"Wow. I never imagined anyone watched, let alone played cricket in this country. And to think you actually have cricket clubs here! What's the name of your club?" asks Ellora, not sure, if she ought to prolong the conversation on cricket.

"It's called Franconia Cricket Club. FCC in short. Our team has players from India as well as Pakistan."

"That's interesting. I'd love to watch your team play," says she, not knowing what spurred her to say something she probably should have refrained from saying. Her mother, for one, would certainly like her to stay away from people, places and events that have anything to do with cricket. The man walking beside her, however, is unaware of her conflicting thoughts and eagerly laps up her comment by promptly inviting her to their next match.

"Actually, you're lucky, because there's a match scheduled for next Sunday. We're going to play a T-20 match against the Tigers. Why don't you come to watch us play?"

"I'd love to, but I'm afraid I can't make it this time."

"Try to make it. A twenty-20 match against the Tigers is guaranteed to be full of nail-biting moments. Besides, your brother-in-law Rahul is batting for us this time. So that gives you plenty of reason to come."

"I'll surely try, now that........"

"So that's settled. You're coming next Sunday," Jai cuts in quickly, without letting her complete her sentence. Then, before she can protest, he adds assertively, "Please bring your camera. We always need good pictures of the players in action for our website. And........" he pauses enigmatically and then, flashing his dimples, he continues. "Just in case you get bored taking pictures of the players, you can switch to taking pictures of the animals that roam the trail bordering the ground. You'll find plenty of groundhogs, squirrels, birds, butterflies and, yes, even some threatened species like the orange dragonflies, mostly cavorting in pairs to ensure that they're no longer threatened. Let me assure you, there'll be no dearth of photo opportunities for you."

Ellora is not too perturbed by the loaded dig he made lightly. Nor does she mind the teasing smile accompanying it but this time, she decides to return the favour by doing a little teasing of her own. Her eyes glint with a hint of mischief, when she turns towards Jai and says, "Photo opportunities notwithstanding, I'll have to decline your invitation. But who knows? I may change my mind, subject to the fulfilment of a condition."

"And what, if I may ask, is your condition?"

"You'll have to stop mentioning dragonflies for the rest of this walk. Please stop referring to them, will you Dr Sehgal?" She requests in a voice that is at once pleading and commanding.

"Done. But I too have a request to make, since I'm in no position to impose conditions."

"And what, if I may ask, is your request?" she mimics his teasingly polite tone.

"Cut out the Dr Sehgal bit and call me Jai, will you?"

"It's a deal, Jai."

They both laugh heartily. As she watches him laugh, it strikes her once again what a distinguished looking man he is. "But he makes it so easy for you to forget that," reflects Ellora.

They are still laughing and talking when they reach the poolside patio together. By now, the place is teeming with guests. Ellora is uneasily aware that several pairs of eyes are watching them with great interest. Fortunately, the party is in full swing by now and most people are more interested in filling their glasses and enjoying the delicious kebabs than paying attention to who is arriving with whom. However, Ellora does not want to attract any more attention than their joint entry already has. She quietly takes her camera from Jai and then leaves his side rather abruptly, saying she has to go and find her sister, without giving him a chance to react.

****

Chapter 2

Vicky Bhalla, the chubby, cherubic and cheerful host has donned a white apron that reads "You May Kiss the Cook" and is juggling the lamb, chicken, and jumbo prawn skewers with the gusto and the dexterity of a professional chef.

The party that had started very early is expected to last until the wee hours of the morning. Now that most of the guests have arrived, it is time to cut the cake. A five-tiered cake is wheeled in.

Mr and Mrs Bhalla expertly cut it with the practiced ease of a couple who has been performing this annual ritual for the last twenty years. After feeding the cake to each other and posing for the mandatory pictures with their faces and fingers smeared with the rich, melting cream, Vicky goes on to make a speech.

He dramatically raises a toast to his wife Sweety and starts reading his prepared speech.

"Here's to my beautiful and homely wife Sweety, who, as you all will agree, is just as sweet as her name suggests. However, I've no hesitation in admitting to all my esteemed guests and my beloved friends that Sweety, for all her feminine sweetness, is my iron-shield, my punching bag, my Rock of Gibraltar."

As his guests clap enthusiastically, Vicky Bhalla pauses, waiting for them to finish. It is a long pause, during which he looks down, deep in thought. When he finally looks up and resumes his speech, his eyes are moist and his voice is muted.

"I had nothing, absolutely nothing, when I first arrived in this country."

He pauses once again to wipe the drops of perspiration that have appeared like a sudden crop of shiny pimples on his forehead. This time, when he speaks, his voice is no longer subdued. He now raises it to a theatrical pitch to state dramatically, "If I own several restaurants today, it's all because of my wife's sport. Whatever I've achieved today is all because of Sweety's sport." An emotional Vicky Bhalla now puts an affectionate arm around his wife, drawing her close to him.

Sweety blushes and smiles shyly, as her demonstrative husband hugs her tightly and plants a kiss on her forehead. He then points to "You May Kiss the Cook" written across his apron and demands a kiss from his wife. She bashfully obliges him by giving him a light peck on his cheek, which despite its lightness, leaves a deep magenta lipstick mark on his plump cheek.

Everybody claps and clicks pictures of the embracing couple, who kiss and hug some more for the benefit of the cameras. Meanwhile the hungry children greedily eye the cake and impatiently wait for the couple to finish their prolonged act, so that they get a chance to grab a piece.

Ellora cannot help smiling when she hears a woman standing next to her, loudly whisper to her husband, "How sweet of Vicky to attribute his success to his wife's sport! What sport does she play?" asks the woman in an audible whisper. Her husband whispers back, "I think he was referring to his wife's support, but it somehow came out as sport."

As they talk about their host, Vicky Bhalla himself, still beaming ear to ear, approaches the whispering couple and introduces them to Ellora.

"Allora, meet my esteemed neighbour Roger and his good lady Nancy. They have recently moved to our neighbourhood."

Ellora winces when she hears her host mispronounce her name, but she is too gracious to correct him in front of his 'esteemed guests.' Nancy, Ellora notes, is a thin woman with thin eyebrows. Severely tweezed into two thin arcs, her forever upwardly mobile eyebrows give Nancy a perpetually puzzled expression. Right now, she looks more puzzled than ever, because Vicky Bhalla's speech has left her completely baffled. She is still trying to figure out why the man kept calling his wife beautiful and homely in the same breath.

As if his curious choice of adjectives for his wife is not already perplexing enough, Vicky Bhalla adds to Nancy's confusion further when, upon being thanked for inviting them to his grand party, he responds by saying: "The playyar is mine."

"Why is he talking about some player all of a sudden? Could it be that Sweety does play some sport, after all?" Nancy's perplexed eyebrows shoot higher and higher with no immediate sign of descent until, after carefully listening to Vicky Bhalla for a while, she figures out on her own that their pot-bellied genial host, for some curious reasons, tends to pronounce 'pleasure' as 'playyar.' The intriguing puzzle solved, the thin arcs on Nancy's forehead temporarily rest in peace.

Ellora, who is completely engrossed in watching the fascinating ascent and descent of Nancy's yo-yo eyebrows, is suddenly brought back to earth when she is tapped on the shoulder by her sister Aparna.

"Where've you been? And what have you been up to, to look so down and out?" enquires Aparna in a whisper that is more like a hiss.

"Didi, are you sure you want to use the phrase down and out for my scruffy appearance? Don't you think I'm too well-dressed to be regarded as a destitute? I think the correct description for my present dishevelled state should be down-at-heel," corrects Ellora, her eyes twinkling teasingly.

"Whatever!" shrugs an exasperated Aparna, waving one of her jewelled hands in a gesture of utter impatience. An elegant and stylish woman, she has no patience with people who do not know how to take care of their appearance. Thankfully no one from her immediate friend circle seems to have noticed Ellora. They are all too busy filling their plates to notice how bedraggled her sister looks, with her sari all rumpled and hair all ruffled.

"How can you disappear for so long and then come back looking like this? And to think that I spent nearly two hours styling your hair and dressing you up for this party!"

"Come on, Di. Don't be so upset," cajoles Ellora.

Even though, Ellora calls her sister Didi most of the time, she sometimes contracts it further to Di, which usually seems to please Aparna. However, right now, Aparna is too piqued to be placated so easily.

"You're impossible, Ellora. Now do me a favour." She pauses to take out a small pouch from her handbag and then, orders her sister, "Go to the nearest washroom and wash all that grime and grease off your face. And while you're at it, make sure to make good use of as many bob pins as required to pin down that unruly mass of hair that has begun to look like an abandoned crow's nest."

Ellora accepts the proffered pouch without any protest or argument. She knows when not to argue with her sister. Besides, she herself is eager to wash her face and look more presentable.

"But why this sudden desire to look presentable?" The question surfaces in her mind like an uninvited guest turning up at the doorstep at a most inopportune moment, without so much as a knock. She decides to ignore the inconvenient question because it is certainly not a convenient time to even acknowledge it, let alone answer it. She has to hurry and make herself presentable enough for her elegant sister and her refined set of friends.

Ellora negotiates her way through the labyrinthine passageways to enter a guest bedroom. As she locks the bathroom door, she notes the poster of a cute toddler producing a well-aimed arc of sparkling urine straight into a toilet bowl. Below the picture, there is a printed message that reads:

> "If you sprinkle,
> When you tinkle,
> Please be sweet,
> And wipe the seat."

There is no dearth of tissues, toilet paper rolls and napkins to give anyone any excuse for not wiping the seat.

Ellora stands before the mirror to inspect her face and hair. "No, Didi was certainly exaggerating when she compared my hair to an abandoned crow's nest. True, there are unruly wisps of hair that have escaped from the clutches of the pins, but to call it a crow's nest and that too an abandoned one, is going a bit too far. But what else do you expect from someone who herself never allows a single strand of her hair to go out of place?"

Attributing her sister's criticism to her penchant for perfection makes Ellora feel better about her appearance at once. So much so, that she is now even willing to concede that the shine on her face is because of a happy glow and not because of the activity of overactive sebaceous glands. Nevertheless, she proceeds to follow her sister's instructions, because she does not want to annoy her any more than she has already done.

As she stands before the mirror in her sleeveless blouse and petticoat, Ellora avoids looking at the parts of her anatomy that she has learned over the years to take no notice of. She focuses her attention on her face and neck instead. Well, her forehead and the tip of her nose do look a bit shiny, she reluctantly concedes. She washes her face briskly with cold water so that the offending pores on her forehead and nose remain tightly closed for the rest of the evening. Now, all she has to do is to apply some make up, just enough to put a little colour back on her face, so that she can confidently stand up to her sister's critical scrutiny.

Ellora is about to drape her sari when she hears footsteps in the adjoining room. Shrill voices follow the sharp click clacks of high heels.

It becomes clear very soon that the two young women entering the room have done so with the sole purpose of venting their anger, for as soon as they enter, they start badmouthing their common foe, someone called Kim, in loud, highly agitated tones. One of them, a woman called Charu has a high-pitched voice that sets her apart from the other person called Alisha, whose voice is comparatively soft.

Standing behind the closed door, Ellora can hear every word spoken by them and is not happy about being forced into eavesdropping for the second time during the course of the same evening. She wants to get out as quickly as possible; but there's one hitch. She is standing in her petticoat and blouse. She tries to hurry, but tying a sheer chiffon sari is not something one can do in a hurry. She is still in the process of arranging the pleats, when she hears something that makes her pause and listen very carefully.

After having had their fill of dissecting Kim, whom they both seem to detest wholeheartedly, the two young women are now drooling over someone, whom they both seem to adore wholeheartedly. It comes as no surprise to Ellora that the object of their joint admiration is none other than Jai. This time, she has no compunction about shamelessly eavesdropping. She quickly tucks in the pleats of her sari and stands near the door, holding her breath to be able to hear the on-going dialogue more clearly. She eagerly waits to hear what the two young women have to say about Jai. That is why, she is least prepared for the unpleasant blow that is about to be delivered.

"If you stand behind a closed door and try to hear a private conversation not intended for your ears, you're most likely to hear something derogatory about yourself." This pearl of wisdom was given to her mother by her late father, when he had caught her standing near their son's bedroom, straining her ears to hear the heated argument that was taking place behind closed doors between their son and daughter-in-law.

"How right Baba was," ponders Ellora. However, like her mother, she is also in no mood to pay any heed to her late father's wise advice, as she unwisely continues to listen to a conversation that is certainly not intended for her ears.

The jarring high-pitched voice delivers the first blow.

"Jai left us on the pretext of answering a phone call. I saw him going towards the lily pond and you know what? After what seemed like ages, he suddenly re-emerged from the backyard but this time hand in hand with this woman flaunting her figure in a flimsy sari." The grating, grumpy tone is full of reproach.

"Oh how romantic! Adam and Eve emerging from the Garden of Eden to make an appearance together," gushes a girlish voice in an excited tone.

"Oh shut up Alisha. Don't start your mindless prattle," rebukes the husky voice.

Alisha, who seems quite used to her companion's rude ways, is too curious to let the rebuke stop her from asking, "I wonder who this Eve is. Do you know her?"

"You bet I do. But she's certainly no Eve. Her name is Ellora. She's Aparna Ray's sister. According to my sources, she's recently arrived from India on the pretext of doing some course, research, or some such, but my source also reveals that the real reason for her visit is to ensnare a well-heeled Bengali man."

"Was she wearing a blue chiffon sari? I saw a very pretty young woman getting down from Aparna Auntie's car. Could that have been her by any chance?"

"That's her but for heaven's sake, Alisha, don't refer to this middle-aged woman as a young woman. She must be nearing her forties."

"Really? You can't be serious Charu! She looks so young! Not a day older than twenty four or twenty five."

"I'm afraid you need glasses Alisha. I'll give you my optometrist's number."

"Thanks, but no thanks. My eyesight is perfect. The woman I saw certainly looked like someone in her twenties. And I must say she's a beauty."

"A sagging beauty."

"Charu, you do love shredding people to pieces, don't you?"

"You're so right Alisha. I do love shredding people to pieces and making mincemeat out of them. And so do you. So please spare me this holier-than-thou stance. Anyway, let's not change the subject. Coming back to our sagging beauty, do you have any idea where she disappeared suddenly after making that joint appearance with our handsome doctor?"

"I've no idea."

"Must have gone to find a new *bakra*. The cougar on the prowl, that desperate bitch!"

Ellora cannot take it any longer. She is livid with rage and indignation. She must confront the woman deriding her so maliciously for no apparent reason. She hurriedly drapes the rest of her sari. When she emerges from the anteroom, she has the air of a lioness coming out of her lair; a lioness with a mission all set to pounce upon the mean woman maligning her so maliciously, even though she has no idea how she is going to go about the pouncing business.

Facing the two women, whose jaws drop considerably the moment they set their eyes upon her, Ellora finally says in a tone that is far too calm to sound like an angry roar:

"The next time you bitch about someone so spitefully, please make sure that the person you're bitching about is not within hearing range of your high-decibel barks."

Ellora had not intended to make an offensive remark like that. Nevertheless, she is pleased with the impact her cutting comment has had on the two young women, both of who look completely shell-shocked, as they stare at her gawkily with their mouths open. One of them, a pretty girl of not more than twenty, looks absolutely mortified. Her face is now the same delicate shade of pink as her exquisitely embroidered *churidar-kameez*. The second woman, to Ellora's utter horror cum delight, is none other than the Blowzy Woman with a Lousy Dress Sense. She too is looking distinctly uncomfortable. Ellora stands there in grim silence, towering over the two short women, one petite and one dumpy and waits for them to say something. After a long and awkward pause, the two offending youngsters finally apologize, almost in unison.

Ellora does not wait to acknowledge their apology. With the swish of her chiffon, she glides out of the door without giving her offenders a second glance.

She is still smarting from the blistering personal attack, as she walks along the long, seemingly unending corridor. The spiteful lines are still ringing in her ears, causing a sharp, stinging sensation that is almost like a shooting physical pain. Accompanying the shooting pain is an equally agonizing sensation: a bottomless sinking feeling that is now gradually surfacing from somewhere deep inside her, engulfing her heart, numbing her brain and slowly replacing the torrid, maddening rage that overwhelmed her a few moments ago.

Ellora keeps walking away from the crowd. "I've walked down this path before," she thinks desolately, remembering how many times in the past people have wounded her ruthlessly with similar stinging, brutal verbal attacks. And written ones too.

****

Chapter 3

The tabloids called her a sexy siren. The wolf-whistlers called her a hot sizzling thing. The obsessive stalkers called her a shameless slut and an irate, thwarted lover called her a fucking whore. She was hounded, taunted, and vilified for falling in love and breaking rules.

The scandal, when it first broke in 1996, was not big enough to make national headlines, but was big enough to wreak havoc and shatter lives. Several lives.

The article itself had been quite brief, but the accompanying pictures spoke volumes.

It was not immediately clear who was behind the publication of those pictures. The motive, however, was very clear. Whoever had published that article along with the sensational tell-tale photographs, had done so with the sole intention of nipping the debutant batsman Rohinton Merchant's budding cricket career in the bud.

That the entire thing also ended up damaging the reputation of a small-town schoolgirl called Ellora Chatterjee was just an unfortunate coincidence; collateral damage. It could have been any other girl in her place and the contents of the article would still have been the same. Unfortunately, it was Ellora who had been caught on camera with the young cricketer, whose selection in the Indian Cricket Team had ruffled many high-flying feathers and had left quite a few angry and disgruntled aspirants with dashed hopes.

It did not matter that the article and the pictures were published in one of the lesser-known magazines better known for publishing unsubstantiated scoops and scandals. What mattered was that the pictures were there for everyone to see.

And they did speak volumes.

Even though the story first appeared in a relatively unknown tabloid with low circulation and lower credibility, it was soon picked up by several reputed newspapers and magazines that republished the pictures by blurring Ellora's face – pointless blurring that failed to prevent the resulting blot on her reputation – an ugly blot that would not fade away in the years to come.

And ugly memories that could not be blotted away even over a decade-and-a-half later.

Even now, as she walks down the long corridor, the crude jokes, the lewd propositions, the stinging remarks, the jeering catcalls and the leering laughter echo in her ears. She can hear all the vile names she had been called post scandal. Hateful, ugly names that don't stop resonating in her head even after so many years. They never would. Some memories are etched too deeply to be erased completely.

****

Chapter 4

Ellora walks in a daze for some time, not knowing where she is heading. She just walks, unmindful of her surroundings, staring blankly ahead at nothing in particular. And then, she comes to a sudden halt as a realization dawns upon her with a jolt.

Why are you so upset Ellora Chatterjee? she asks herself. *Is it because one of the women insinuated that you're a sagging beauty and a gold-digger who's here in America to catch a wealthy husband? Or is it because she called you a huntress on the prowl? A desperate cougar, waiting to prey upon younger men? But then, what's the big deal? Didn't you also confer upon her an insulting title a little while ago?*

Ellora knows that there is a difference between the kind of bitching she herself had indulged in and the kind of bitching the two young women had been engaged in. That spiteful woman, Charu, had literally been spewing venom.

It's kind of strange. She seemed to hate me with all her heart. Her tone was so full of bitterness. *But why should she hate me so much? We don't even know each other. Our paths have never crossed before.*

And then, it comes to her in a flash, even as she goes over the incident in her mind once again. *She is in love with Jai, this Charu. I feel sorry for her, now. Poor girl! So much in love with a good-looking man and with so little hope of any reciprocation from his side. I now understand why she hates me so much. She saw me with Jai and jumped to all kinds of conclusions about us. But dear Charu, put all your fears to rest. I've no interest in the likes of your dear Jai Sehgal. As you rightly said, I'm in America to find an educated and well-settled Bengali male, which I'll do in due course with some help from my family.*

Ellora smiles now. She is no longer angry or upset. Now that she recalls how 'jigglingly' Charu had sought Jai's attention near the pool, how fawningly she had been dancing attendance on him and how eagerly she had hung on to every word uttered by him, she is sure that her conclusion about her being in love with Jai is correct. *There's no other plausible explanation for her to abhor me so venomously and with such vehemence,* concludes Ellora. She derives a lot of peace from her conclusion. She even feels a little sorry for terrorizing the two young women (especially the pretty one in pink) a little while ago.

Now that her peace of mind has been restored, she is ready to face her sister and her cackling clutch of friends.

"There you are, at last," says Aparna when she catches sight of her sister. She looks at her approvingly, happy to see Ellora's glowing face, her eyes as big and bright as ever.

* * *

The poolside patio now resembles a banquet hall. Huge bouquets of stargazer lilies and roses preside over the round tables covered with crisp white linen. Each table is lavishly set with opulent silver cutlery, crystal glasses, fine-china and elaborately folded napkins. The buffet tables on the adjacent lawn have large serving bowls overflowing with rich curries, scrumptious biryanis, tantalizing tikkas and delectable desserts.

One side of the lawn has been set aside for the vegetarians. Here, a South Indian cook is deftly spreading ladleful of a runny white batter on an extremely hot cast iron griddle pan to churn out crispy brown paper *dosas*.

Nancy, who is a vegetarian by choice, watches the preparation of this extraordinary papery pancake with complete fascination, eagerly sniffing the unfamiliar and yet tempting flavour given off by the spicy preparation. She is spoiled for choice; she usually has very little choice of food in the parties thrown by her American friends. Most of the time, she has to make do with lettuce, mashed potato, French fries and beans. However, this party is something else and she has never experienced anything like it before. She is amused, amazed and appalled by the lavishness of this extravagant party. From overwhelming variety of foods, to overflowing wine, to overdressed men and women, to the overstated decoration, everything seems over-the-top and out of proportion. To her rational mind, it all seems a bit silly and ostentatious, but despite her reservations, Nancy is thoroughly enjoying herself.

* * *

Vicky and Sweety Bhalla are dancing to the tunes of traditional *Bhangra* numbers along with their entire clan and friends. After dancing energetically for some time, Vicky takes a temporary break to go around and personally make sure that all his guests are being properly looked after. He now stops by the table where Ellora, Aparna and Aparna's husband, Rahul, are eating. They are all by themselves, mainly because most of their friends have chosen to shake a leg on the dance floor before sitting down for dinner.

After making sure that their glasses and plates are full, Vicky Bhalla sits in an empty chair next to Rahul.

"What *Bhabhiji*?" He addresses Aparna, "Eating so early? No dance-vance? You should do some *bhangra-shangra* first to build up your appetite."

Vicky Bhalla now slowly moves his entire torso along with his chair so that he can face Ellora.

"And Allora, you too are eating so early? A young *Dilli-walli* like you should be on the dance floor, instead of sitting here with Rahul and Aparna," Vicky Bhalla affectionately scolds Ellora.

Aparna, forever the protective elder sister, comes to Ellora's rescue at once.

"No, Vicky, Ellora doesn't know many people in this gathering and she's usually a little shy around strangers. Besides, I'm to be blamed. I'm the one who insisted that the three of us should eat now, so that we can leave early. You see, Rahul's working tomorrow."

"*Oye*, no *work-shirk* on weekends Rahul," says Vicky Bhalla, making it sound like an order.

Ellora smiles, as she listens to the comment. *If Nancy were to hear Mr Bhalla now, she would be puzzled as to why our host is ordering Rahul-da not to shirk his work on weekends,* she reflects quietly, much to her own amusement.

"Tell your hospital to recruit more doctors," Vicky Bhalla commands authoritatively, as he gulps down his Patiala peg in one swig. He asks one of the uniformed waiters to bring him one more drink, tapping the table impatiently with his fingers until it arrives.

Once he is handed his glass of whisky, he takes another long sip before continuing, "Even Jai had to leave early and he also gave the same old excuse of work."

Ellora is considerably alarmed upon hearing Jai's name. She has not yet mentioned anything to her sister about her chance meeting with the surgeon in the backyard and she does not want Aparna to learn about it from a third party. She is somewhat disappointed to learn that Jai has already left the party and yet, at the same time, she is also relieved that he has left without seeing her. After listening to that ugly gossip full of insinuations, she wants to stay clear of all situations that would give people a chance to jump to any kind of wrong conclusions about the two of them.

Vicky Bhalla, in the meanwhile, takes another long sip from his glass. Now that he has paid the requisite attention to the ladies, it is time for him to shift his focus to Rahul, with whom he has some urgent matters to discuss. The forthcoming cricket match is playing heavily on his mind. As the patron of their cricket club, he wants to make sure that Rahul is not having second thoughts about opening the batting line-up for their team. Anxious to hold a serious man-to-man discussion with Rahul about the match, Vicky Bhalla now rotates his chair, so that he is face-to-face with Rahul and has his undivided attention. However, Rahul's attention is currently divided between tackling the luscious tandoori chicken on his plate and ogling the colourful chicks, doing a vigorous *bhangra* number on the stage. Therefore, he absentmindedly nods at his host, without letting his imposing presence interrupt either of the pleasurable activities that is keeping him preoccupied. Since his hitherto tame attempts to catch Rahul's attention have failed, Vicky Bhalla decides to employ a more physical attention-getting tactic by giving him a solid whack on his back.

"So Rahul, I hear you are going to bat in place of Deepak next week. Is it true?" says an ebullient, literally high-spirited Vicky Bhalla.

Still recovering from the impact of the staggering, but not entirely unexpected whack, Rahul discreetly pushes his chair backwards to move himself away from Vicky Bhalla's whacking range, before answering his question.

"Do I have a choice?" he pointedly asks before lowering his voice. He admits softly, "It's difficult to refuse someone like Jai who doesn't take no for an answer."

Ellora, who is suddenly all ears at the mention of Jai's name, couldn't agree more with her brother-in-law. Having had her recent brush with Jai's persuasive ways, she cannot help admitting to herself that it is indeed very difficult to say no to someone as charming and convincing as the smooth-talking surgeon. Nor can she help smiling, as she recalls how cunningly he had trapped her into saying yes to his invitation. However, even as their playful banter that took place in the backyard is replaying in her head, her sister plays spoilsport by derailing her happy train of thought.

"Do you hear that, Ellora? My husband is all set to bat

for FCC and he didn't even have the decency to inform me. How come I'm always the last to know about his adventurous plans?" complains Aparna, fixing her husband with a reproachful stare.

"He has not informed you yet, *Bhabhiji*? Rahul, you should have told Aparna Bhabhi. After all, she's your bitter half," jokes a sombre, but not entirely sober Vicky Bhalla with a straight face.

"Vicky, I was waiting for an opportune moment to let Aparna know, but then, you spilled the beans before I had a chance to tell her," explains Rahul with the easy-going smile of a husband who is quite used to doing a lot of explaining.

A shifty-eyed Vicky Bhalla avoids meeting Aparna's frosty gaze, as he tries to reason with her, "Well, *Bhabhiji,* you'll have to let your husband play for us this time. Both Jai and Rahul are indispensable for our team. These two batsmen are our best bet against those ferocious Tigers."

As she listens to Vicky Bhalla pleading his case, Ellora decides that no matter how hard-pressed she is for time, she will certainly make time to watch this match. She knows that her brother-in-law bats well, but she wants to know if Jai is indeed as good a batsman as he is made out to be. In any case, she has to come, she has already given her word to Jai. Or rather, she has been forced into giving her word to him.

"Why're you smiling? What's on your mind?" Aparna's sharp interrogation once again interrupts her happy thoughts, this time more rudely than before. Ellora tries to overcome her discomfiture by answering as honestly as she can, without disclosing all the details, of course.

"I was thinking of coming back next week to watch Rahul-da play. Sounds like, it's going to be an exciting match."

"Do you really mean it, Ellora? Oh, that will be so wonderful. I'll feel so much better about Rahul's batting, if you're with me." Resigned to the idea that she can do very little to stop her husband from playing his favourite game,

Aparna has visibly perked up at the idea of watching the match with her sister.

"Well, I'll definitely come, if that's going to pep you up. To tell you the truth, someone else has also invited me to the match and I've already said yes to his invitation

The moment the words are out of her mouth, Ellora realizes that she should not have sprung this unexpected surprise on her already perturbed sister in so sudden a manner. However, the arrow has already left the bow and it is too late to take it back. Now that she has started it, she might as well explain the whole thing to her sister.

"Now don't look so stunned, let me explain…." starts Ellora, but Aparna does not let her finish her sentence.

"Who's invited you for the match?" Aparna's tone is not sharp. Rather, it is soft, much too soft. Soft enough to be almost a whisper.

Ellora has not yet realized that her sister is anxious for their conversation to be conducted in whispers; therefore, she answers her question in a loud, excited voice, "You won't believe Didi! It's your neighbour Dr Jai Sehgal who asked me to …."

"Where did you meet Jai? Aparna quickly interjects in a barely audible whisper before ordering, "And for heaven's sake, speak softly."

It is clear to Ellora from Aparna's sharp tone that she is greatly disturbed by the news. She cannot help feeling a little irritated with her sister for making her feel guilty about a mere chance meeting with Jai in the garden. Why can't she talk about their meeting openly? Why does it have to be a hush-hush affair, only to be discussed in whispers?

Nevertheless, Ellora keeps her tone low while answering her sister, even though she can barely stop her irritation from creeping into her voice.

"I ran into him in the garden and you'll appreciate that when two guests attending the same party find themselves alone, it's not very unusual for them to strike up a conversation. In any case, Jai already knew all about me, because you've filled him in on me. It seems a whole lot of people attending this party know all about me. Many of them are even aware that I'm here in America to find a wealthy groom. Anyway, to cut this long story short, since Dr Sehgal is Rahul-da's colleague, I saw no harm in chatting with him while we were walking back together. Do you wish to know any more details about our meeting?" Ellora's tone is dripping with sarcasm.

"Why are you so cross with me Ellora? Anyway, forget it. Let's not discuss it now. We'll talk about it later, when we reach home."

Ellora wants to scream, "I'm thirty-three, for God's sake! I can chat with as many men as I want to without having to hide it from the world!" She wants to say all this and a whole lot more, and say it loud and clear and not in discreet whispers. But instead, she swallows her anger and eats her prawn curry and chicken *biryani* in silence.

Ellora is more irritated with herself than with her sister. Suddenly it strikes her that she, for the better part of her life, has been meekly answering questions posed by others, without ever having the guts to question why others needed answers to questions that concerned nobody else except herself.

By the time, a bearded and turbaned waiter in a crisp red and gold uniform serves them *kulfi-falooda*, Ellora's anger has considerably cooled down. The waning anger is slowly being replaced by a rising sense of remorse, particularly because Aparna, who has hardly spoken since their last exchange, is looking extremely sad. Ellora wants to apologize to her sister, but somehow, cannot bring herself to do it. While Rahul and Vicky Bhalla attack the delectable *kulfi-falooda* with the lusty gusto of men with a rapacious sweet tooth and continue to discuss their game plan for the match with equal fervour, the two sisters finish their dessert in complete silence.

* * *

The silence between the sisters continues during their drive back home.

Once in her room, Ellora is quick to remove her borrowed sari. Despite feeling sleepy, she carefully folds it and hangs it on a hanger, before proceeding to remove the dangling earrings weighing down her delicate earlobes.

"Ah! What a relief!" says she, as she slips into the comfort of her cotton nightgown. She is packing her things lying all over the bed, when she hears a knock on the door.

Ellora was expecting the knock. Whenever the two sisters have argued in the past, Aparna has always made it a point to resolve their differences at the first available opportunity.

"You're not too sleepy, are you?" Aparna asks before entering the room.

"No, I was just trying to finish my packing before going to bed."

"Would you like some hot chocolate or tea? I was going to make myself a cup of ginger tea."

"Sure. Ginger tea sounds good. I'll come down and join you in the kitchen. Just give me a few minutes to tidy this mess," says Ellora, pointing to the pile of clothes lying on the bed.

By the time Ellora comes down, tea is almost ready. Aparna is straining the steaming concoction into a large ceramic teapot.

"Let's go to the living room. We can sit comfortably on the sofa there," she says, as she hands the tea tray to her sister.

As they both stretch their legs on the low coffee table and sip the hot, tangy tea, Ellora observes her sister silently.

"She's going to turn fifty very soon, yet her face is so smooth and unlined," observes Ellora. Unlike her own oval face, Aparna has a round face like their mother's and her complexion is what an Indian matrimonial column would describe as 'very fair.' People often wonder why the sisters look so different from each other. Not many are aware that the two of them are actually cousins and not real sisters. Ellora lost both her parents at the age of seven, and ever since, her paternal uncle and aunt have become her parents and her cousins have become her siblings.

"Did you take a lot of pictures in the garden?"

Ellora was waiting for this. She knew that her sister would ask her this question sooner or later.

"Yeah, the garden was full of photo opportunities, just as you said it would be."

"Isn't it a marvellous garden? For all their flashy and rustic dehati tastes, the Bhallas have certainly done a wonderful job of landscaping the grounds surrounding their house. Did you see the lily pond?"

"Yes. In fact, I spent most of my time sitting there. It was so picturesque and tranquil out there and I could observe the party crowd from my secret refuge without being detected by anyone. I got some good shots of the water lilies and the dragonflies."

She hesitates but only for a split second, before adding, "Actually, that's where I met Dr Jai Sehgal. It was an awkward meeting. He caught me red-handed just as I was focusing my camera on the double-decker pairs of dragonflies, if you know what I mean."

"Really? That must have been awkward. You must've been so embarrassed."

"I was mortified! Didn't know where to look."

"I can imagine."

There is a silence, during which Aparna carefully weighs her words before broaching the delicate topic.

"I know you didn't like it when I discouraged you from discussing your meeting with Jai in front of others. I also know that you're peeved with me because you feel that I've announced to all my friends that we're looking for a suitable match for you. I think I owe you a whole lot of explanations."

Ellora opens her mouth to say something, but Aparna does not let her speak and continues with her explanation.

"Actually, I kept insisting that you speak softly because I didn't want anyone, least of all that big mouth Vicky Bhalla to get any fodder for gossip. Any woman seen in Jai's company provides fodder for gossip for the entire East Coast Indian community; no one is spared. You could be a pretty lass or a hideous old hag but if you're seen alone with Jai, you're a juicy topic for the gossiping tongues."

"I didn't know he's such a Casanova."

"No, you're getting me wrong. Jai's not exactly a Casanova, he's more of a ladies' man."

"What's the difference?"

"A Casanova actively seduces women; a ladies' man is someone who passively allows himself to be seduced by fawning females. Poor Jai. He's the hunted rather than the hunter. He doesn't actively seek women's company, they always seek him out. He may be at the hospital or in a social gathering but they always follow him around and flock around him like clucking hens eyeing a prized rooster. Well, Jai probably doesn't mind all the female attention that he invariably attracts but then, which man in his right mind would? "

"He sounds more like a lady killer to me."

"He's a lady killer all right; kills them with oodles of charm. His charm sure works like magic on most women, but unfortunately, it didn't work on the one woman who mattered to him most." Ellora waits, while her sister pauses enigmatically to gauge her reaction before continuing, "I don't think I told you about Jai's divorce."

If Ellora is shocked by this unsettling information sprung upon her all of a sudden, she is careful not to display any signs of it. Nevertheless, she certainly wants to know more.

"It's difficult to imagine a cheerful and affable person

like Dr Sehgal in a gloomy situation like divorce." Ellora is careful to use the formal Dr Sehgal instead of the informal Jai in front of her sister.

"Things are not always as they appear on the surface. Marriage is a complex and fragile institution. You don't always know how, when and why things begin to fall apart."

"I wonder what went wrong with Dr Sehgal's marriage."

"He's extremely tight-lipped about it, so none of us knows what actually went wrong. Of course, there're all sorts of speculations and theories. Some say his wife left him for another man."

"But he's so handsome, intelligent and witty. Why would any woman want to leave him for another man?"

"Unfortunately, all these ingredients are not enough to hold a marriage together. I'm very fond of Jai, but I'm sure he, too, must have been responsible in some ways for his failed marriage. It takes two hands to clap."

"You mean it takes two to tango?" poses Ellora smilingly. She is familiar with her sister's penchant for translating Bengali and Hindi idioms into English.

"Whatever. What I meant was, when a marriage fails, usually both husband and wife are jointly responsible."

"Possibly. But it does seem strange that his wife should walk out on him, considering many women would've given their right arms to be in her shoes," says Ellora wistfully.

Aparna inspects her sister's face for any tell-tale signs. Is her interest in Jai more than just casual? When she fails to detect anything conclusive, she asks her directly, "Tell me Ellora. Are you attracted to Jai?"

Ellora is taken aback. She had not expected her sister to ask her an invasive question like this so directly. She decides that a direct question deserves a direct answer.

"Well. I'll not lie about finding him very interesting. He's a very handsome man, no doubt and I enjoyed his company very much this afternoon. But that's as far as it goes. If you're presuming that my interest in him runs any deeper than this, then you're totally wrong. I haven't taken a serious interest in a man, any man, for a very long time now and Jai is no exception."

"I'm glad to hear that," says Aparna, before taking a sip from her cup.

"But just as a matter of academic interest, I would like to know why you're so GLAD to hear THAT. Considering, all of you pressurized me into coming to America to facilitate you in your husband-hunting mission, shouldn't you be glad that I'm helping you in this challenging quest by showing an interest, no matter how perfunctory an interest, in someone like Jai Sehgal? After all, he fulfils all the criteria stipulated by our late father. He's single, he's highly educated, he's extremely well-placed and he's a Hindu. He's even a surgeon to boot; a fact that would've made our father very happy, were he alive today. So tell me Didi and I repeat, this is strictly an academic question: what's wrong if I were to take a serious interest in someone like Dr Sehgal? "

Ellora patiently waits for her sister to answer her question, but Aparna takes an unusually long time to respond. When she finally speaks, she weighs her words carefully.

"Now that you've put me on the spot, I'm going to let you know something that I've deliberately kept from you, to avoid causing unnecessary hurt. When I met Jai two years ago, the first thing that crossed my mind was: Wow! He's the man for our Ellora. Rahul and I both agreed that his divorce notwithstanding, Jai would be an excellent match for someone like you. Before approaching him with the marriage proposal, we investigated his background thoroughly by making discreet enquiries and everyone, from his ex-colleagues to his close friends had only good things to say about him."

Aparna anxiously looks at her sister to gauge how she is taking this latest piece of unsettling information. Assured that

Ellora does not seem to be overtly perturbed, she continues.

"Unfortunately, things didn't work out the way we had hoped they would. Jai was quite honest when he admitted that with a painful divorce behind him, he was too disillusioned with the institution of marriage to have any desire left for having another go at it. We understood his qualms, but were hopeful that given enough time, he would start feeling differently about marriage. But two years have passed since then and he still continues to avoid the topic of marriage. We were not the only ones to have approached him with a marriage proposal. Every one of our acquaintances with a marriageable sister or daughter seems to have done so and has received the same standard reply."

"There I go, rejected by one more man. And a very desirable and suitable one at that. The list of men rejecting me gets longer and longer."

"Shut up, Ellora. You know, that's not true. Jai's refusal has got nothing to do with you. He's rejected at least twenty formal marriage proposals so far, not to mention the hundreds of hearts he keeps breaking regularly by rejecting all the informal advances. So please take heart and stop taking it so personally."

"I was just kidding, Dids. But tell me more about our Heartbreakingly Handsome doctor. Are you saying he's single-but-not-ready-to-mingle?"

"He's ready to mingle, but only when there're no strings attached. I don't keep tabs on his dating habits, but it's no secret that he's commitment shy."

The brief silence that follows is broken when a little cuckoo comes out of the clock and melodiously announces the time by cooing thrice.

"Gosh, it's three' o'clock in the morning. You'd better go to bed Didi, you look tired. I too must get some sleep. I've to start very early tomorrow."

****

Chapter 5

July 2011,
Mrs Morris's home in Edgewater, Maryland

"Here's a letter for you," informs Mrs Morris, handing Ellora a large envelope without looking up.

Ellora is relieved to note that her landlady is too immersed in sorting out her own pile of mail to start a conversation. Mrs Morris is less inclined to chitchat when she is going through her mail and Ellora is grateful for her silence. Right now, after a long day at work, she is not up to listening to Mrs Morris's long monologues.

The letter has come as a surprise to her, more so because it has been delivered to her home address.

Who could've sent me this letter? wonders Ellora, as she walks towards her room. She turns the envelope, but there is no sender address at the back. She hurriedly tears it open and is surprised to find a handwritten letter inside. She has no difficulty in recognizing her late father's characteristic handwriting. Accompanying the letter is a note from Aparna that reads:

Precious Ellora,

I'm sending you the last letter that Baba wrote to me a week before his death. Even though he took care to seal the envelope, he could never post it, probably because just after writing the letter, he had that massive heart attack from which he never woke up.

You'll need plenty of time and patience to decipher his

handwriting. His hands must have been shaking badly; nevertheless, he continued to write, because he had something important to say. It's only when you read his letter that you'll understand why I act the way I sometimes do. I've no other choice. I'm held hostage by a promise that I didn't even get a chance to make. I know I'm talking in riddles so just read the letter and you'll find some of your answers. We'll talk more about this, when you come home.

Can't wait to have you back with us again.

Lots and lots of love,

Didi

Ellora looks at her watch. There is still an hour to go before it is time for dinner. She sits down and opens her father's letter. It is clear to her at first glance that deciphering her father's spidery scrawl is going to require a great deal of effort as well as time.

"Let me give it a try, at least," she tells herself, as she focuses upon reading one word at a time, instead of struggling to read entire sentences. Once she gets used to reading the shakily scribbled words, they become more and more legible with each passing sentence. If only she had not paused a few times to wipe the tears that are flowing freely by now, it would have taken her lesser time to read the entire letter. She is sobbing so uncontrollably by the time she comes to the end of the letter, that she has to get up to wash her face. Thankfully, Mrs Morris is far away in the living room, watching a gem and jewellery show on television and is therefore, not able to hear her loud sobs.

Ellora comes back to her desk with a glass of water and starts reading her father's letter once again. This time, she notices the date on top. He had written the letter to her sister on the 16th May, 2006, just days before his death.

My dearest Aparna,

I am writing this letter to you in a state of distress. I have not been able to sleep for months. Night after night I lie awake, worrying about our Ellora. I do not know how long I am going to live, but before I die, I want to fulfil my last responsibility of getting her married to an intelligent and kind man - someone who will love and respect her despite her past. From my side, I am doing my best. I have even placed ads in the matrimonial columns of both The Times of India and The Hindustan Times. However, even though the response has been good, nothing has worked out so far mainly because of Ellora's obduracy. She is determined to reject all the men painstakingly chosen by me.

I know that someone as qualified and beautiful as Ellora is bound to find a good match in the long run, but then, time is running out. She is already twenty-eight and if she does not make up her mind soon, it may get more and more difficult for us to find the right man for her.

To tell you the truth, her entire focus nowadays is on her research and teaching. Marriage is the last thing on her mind.

I often ask myself, "Where did I go wrong? How could I break the oath that I took, while lighting the funeral pyre of my younger brother? An oath to nurture his daughter as my own. An oath to wipe away all her tears and to keep her always happy."

The more I introspect and search for answers, the more acutely I become aware of the fact that I have failed in the role of a protective father to my adopted daughter. When I look at her sad face, I cannot help comparing her to the happy child who used to visit us every summer with her parents. Do you remember the little girl who used to dance round and round in the entire veranda, looking absurdly cute in her flouncy frock? The girl who used to clap her hands and squeal in delight every time she spotted a bird or a stray puppy in the backyard?

Looking at that exuberant little girl who could have imagined that one day, fate would deal her so cruel a blow that she would forget how to laugh and smile? If there's one thing that haunts me more than the memory of the badly bruised bodies of my deceased brother and his wife, it is the memory of Ellora's traumatized and tearful face, as she sat next to her father and kept saying, "Baba, please wake up. I promise I'll be a good girl."

We brought home a very disturbed and insecure child; someone who would wake up in the middle of the night and howl for hours. Your mother and I took turns to hug and comfort her, while she screamed for her parents night after night. It was an emotionally and physically exhausting phase.

Given the tragic circumstance, we did our best to provide Ellora with a secure and loving home, but unfortunately, we failed her miserably when it mattered the most. I personally hold myself responsible for not being able to prevent the unfortunate incident that tore our lives apart. After the scandal broke, instead of being a strong and supportive father to my anguished daughter, I just went into a shell and refused to come out. It was a grave error of judgement on my part to have sent her away to a distant college. It was like disowning my adopted daughter and making her an orphan all over again.

I now want to atone for my past mistakes by finding her the right life partner, someone who will bring that exuberant smile back to her beautiful face. Unfortunately, I may not have time on my side. My latest cardiogram report is not very encouraging. This is the reason I am writing this letter to you. If something happens to me, I want you to take over my responsibility of finding a husband for Ellora. Promise me that you will fulfil the last wish of your dying father, Aparna.

I have so much more to say, but my hands are shaking and I must end now.

With all my love and blessings.

Yours,

Baba

****

Part II

Chapter 6

1985, Vijaypur, India

It all went back to the day Ellora's biological parents had died in a car accident.

Death is the ultimate breach of trust, the ultimate punishment that a parent can inflict on a child. For seven year old Ellora, who saw so little of either of her parents even when they were alive, it was also the ultimate form of rejection and she blamed herself more than she blamed her parents for rejecting her so totally and so irrevocably.

Her worst fears had come true. She had been forewarned that children who pester their parents invite punishment from God. And she had done her share of pestering, all right.

It all started when, after seeing a golden retriever puppy at a friend's house, Ellora began to pester her parents for a similar puppy as a birthday gift. Her parents yielded to her relentless demands by paying a late night visit to a remote farmhouse to fulfil her dream. Little did they know that the dream would turn out to be a never-ending nightmare for their only child! They were returning home with the furry gift for their daughter, when their car collided with a speeding truck, shattering windows, lives, plans and dreams in a matter of seconds, but leaving, by some quirk of fate, the puppy in the backseat totally unscathed. The birthday gift was intact, but the givers of the gift had bled to death by the time the rescue team arrived.

There was no puppy sleeping in a basket beside her when

Ellora woke up the next morning. The house seemed unusually quiet. She ran to her parents' bedroom and was heartbroken when she could not find them there. She went downstairs and was startled to see Sanjay Mama, her maternal uncle, talking to someone on the phone. His eyes were puffy and red. Even more shocking was the sight of Dida, her maternal grandmother, lying prostrate on the living-room divan.

In the years that followed, Ellora could not recall her own reaction at seeing her Dida, whom she loved very much, being carried away on a stretcher by total strangers in uniform. All she could remember was the haunting silence that filled the house following the departure of her grandmother and uncle – silence that was frequently pierced by the persistent and shrill ringing of the doorbell and the telephone. The house was soon full of people: friends, neighbours, colleagues, admirers, press and curious onlookers came in droves and gradually started filling the hall, kitchen, passages, garden and eventually the entire street. People she had never met before gave her a hug and said, "Poor thing."

When she could take it no longer, Ellora threw herself on the floor and began to howl so loudly and so heartbreakingly that everyone in the room started crying with her. She started coughing through her shrieks. Someone gave her cough syrup to drink.

When she woke up from her cough syrup induced sleep, she was happy to see her Jethu and Jethi, her paternal uncle and aunt, sitting next to her. She was still drowsy and wanted to go back to sleep. However, what she saw through her half-closed eyes made her sit up with a start. The bodies of her parents were lying side by side on the floor, covered up to their necks with white sheets. Her father, despite the bruises on his face, looked as if he was sleeping peacefully, but her mother's beautiful face had puffed up beyond recognition.

Ellora got up and ran towards them, but before she could throw herself upon their bodies, someone caught her. It was her Jethu, her father's elder brother. He gently lifted her and made her sit on his lap. She clung to him, feeling oddly secure for the first time since that morning. He looked exactly like her father and she derived comfort from his presence next to her. He held her and cried with her, the silent tears of a man who had to manfully hold back his own tears in order to remain strong for the child distraught with shock and pain.

For the little girl who was temporarily numb, when the tears came, they came in tumultuous torrents accompanied by uncontrollable sobs, hiccups and shrieks. She avoided looking at her mother's unrecognizably grotesque face, but her father looked serene and handsome even in death. She half expected him to smile at her and wink, as he sometimes did when he woke up from his nap and caught her bending over him and inspecting his sleeping face.

Why wasn't her father opening his eyes to smile at her? Had she done something naughty to annoy him? She stood up and went near her father, touching his face gently with her tiny hands.

"Baba, please wake up. I promise I'll be a good girl," said she, with tears rolling down her cheeks.

Unknown to everyone, a press photographer had captured the scene on his camera and that is how Ellora became the major focus of the entire tragedy. Her whispered plea to her father was reported widely in all the newspapers the next day and in the days, months and years to come.

Once the last rites were over, it was time to make important decisions. Ellora's grandmother was still in the hospital. She was partially paralyzed. Sanjay Sen, Ellora's maternal uncle was only twenty-three at the time of the tragedy; too young to bear the responsibility of an orphaned niece. Besides, he was training as a pilot and his erratic schedule ruled him out as a prospective guardian. In nutshell, the Chatterjees were the only relatives who could take the charge of the seven-year-old, even if it meant relocating her from a big city like

Delhi to a small town like Vijaypur.

Also hanging in balance was the fate of Babu Shona, the puppy that arrived home in a basket. The Chatterjees did not know what to do with the posthumous birthday gift from Ellora's parents. Your late-forties is not a time you are willing to embark upon something as demanding and challenging as keeping a dog, particularly if you now have the sudden responsibility of raising an orphaned niece. Of course, eventually the puppy accompanied them to Vijaypur, because doing otherwise had been unthinkable to start with.

****

Chapter 7

1985, Vijaypur

Despite its proximity to Delhi, Vijaypur could not have been more far-removed from the capital in terms of development. It was a small town all right.

When her parents were alive, the sleepy little town had been an exciting holiday destination for little Ellora. The palatial house of her Jethu and Jethi was an imposing double-storied bungalow with spacious, high-ceilinged rooms and pillared courtyards. High compound walls sequestered the house from the dusty, bustling by-lanes of the congested neighbourhood. Large Neem trees stood guard all around the house like helmeted sentinels, shielding the residents from prying eyes and unwanted noise from the outside world.

Ellora's favourite hideout during those happy, carefree vacations was the overgrown garden with its untamed thicket of trees, shrubs and creepers. She used to spend long hours in the garden playing with the gardener's daughter Kusum, who taught her how to make garland by stringing together the tiny white shiuli flowers. She loved inhaling the heavenly perfume that hung in the air in the early mornings, as she crouched under the flowering shrub to collect the fallen blossoms.

The best part of the day was in the afternoon, when unnoticed by anyone, Ellora would quietly slip into the garden, carrying her drawing-book and crayons with her. Her favourite spot in the garden was the raised concrete platform under the mango tree. She sat there and watched the purple sunbirds and butterflies flit from flower to flower.

The garden received its quota of bigger, noisier and nosier visitors. Ellora did not like the house-crows that created a cacophony of raucous caws and were often too cheeky for comfort. They harried the smaller birds, chased the squirrels and even tried to steal her crayons.

Also noisy, but not as nosy, were the rose-ringed parrots that came in flocks and raided the guava trees, leaving behind scores of half-eaten fruits on the branches. According to Kusum, these parrot pecked guavas tasted even better than the uneaten intact ones.

All by herself under the mango tree, Ellora spent the entire afternoon sketching the flying and fluttering creatures around her. She always cried when the vacations came to an end and it was time for them to leave Vijaypur.

* * *

Visiting Vijaypur after her parents' death, however, was an altogether different experience. As their car neared the main gate, Ellora's heart sank because she knew that this time around, she was entering the house not as a visitor, but as a permanent resident. She would not be returning to her own home in Delhi anytime soon. It was this realization that caused her to burst into tears. The loss of her parents led to several other concomitant losses. In one cruel sweep of fate, she had lost her home, school and friends, losses that filled her with gloom, fear, insecurity and rage.

Every evening, when the balcony adjoining the bedrooms was redolent with the fragrance of Rangoon Creeper, sorrow seeped into her little heart silently and soft-footedly without warning; sorrow filled with vast emptiness. Even with her child's logic, Ellora knew that the raw, poignant, palpable pain was something that was going to remain with her for the rest of her life. Unlike her Jethu, who spent hours inside the puja-room, trying to come to terms with the enormous tragedy, the seven year old girl had no such coping mechanism to thwart the intense pain that threatened to explode inside her.

She wanted to throw tantrums, huge tantrums. She wanted to throw things, throw up, cry, scream, break objects, kick, fall on the ground, even die. But she could not do any of those bad things because she wanted to be a good girl. Anguish expanded inside her chest like an ever-inflating balloon that had been forbidden to burst. All through the day, she walked around with that swelling, throbbing, bruising, suffocating balloon inside her chest. But, when it got dark and the hanging clusters of the Rangoon Creeper outside her window filled the room with its overwhelmingly sweet, melancholic scent, the child could barely hold the expanding balloon inside her little chest quiet any longer. So she would let it burst, with full force. Her screams could be heard as far as the nearby clinic, piercing through the high compound walls and the tall trees that cushioned the house from the outside noise. She cried loudly for hours, desperately hoping that her shrill cries would reach her parents and they would come running from heaven to pacify their distraught child.

In the years to come, whenever Ellora stood near the Rangoon Creeper that had wound its way around the balcony pillar to reach the rooftop, she associated its intense fragrance with the intensity of her melancholy following her parents' death.

****

Chapter 8

1985-1986, Vijaypur

In those dark days, a beam of golden sunshine came as a welcome relief, temporarily drawing everyone, particularly Ellora out of the well of darkness.

Babu Shona was programmed to please. And please he did with the exuberance of a spirit born to spill sunshine. Indeed, he was sunshine packaged as a puppy. The sight of him with his fluffy coat and floppy ears was enough to put a smile on your face, but Babu Shona wanted people around him to do more than just smile. He wanted everyone to laugh, rejoice and have fun. He pranced back and forth with excitement every time Sumitra Devi came out of the kitchen. Even strangers, appearing at the doorstep were greeted like long lost friends. But his clear favourite was Ellora. He worked himself into a complete tizzy as soon she came back from school. He was her shadow, sunshine turned into an ebullient, tail-wagging shadow.

It was obvious that Babu Shona was not a guard dog. He was a retriever and he took his job title quite seriously. He retrieved everything that was lost, misplaced, or out of sight. He furiously dug the soil in the garden in a compulsive bid to retrieve anything that might lie underneath. He was the retriever of buried treasures and lost articles. In the Chatterjee household that summer, he was also the retriever of buried joy and lost laughter. His lively presence in the house made it possible for those grieving for their dead to forget their grief and smile.

Ellora's parents could not have chosen a better parting gift for their daughter.

* * *

Things soon fell into a routine once the school session started.

Ellora's relationship with her new classmates was cordial at best. The girls shared jokes and secrets, but she was not a part of those exchanges. Her classmates were mean to her without meaning to be mean. They just did not know what to say to her or what to share with her. When you are young, being different can be a serious handicap and this new girl called Ellora Chatterjee was different all right. She was too tall, too intelligent and too well-liked by the teachers. Even her large brown eyes with flecks of green distinctly set her apart. Besides, she was an orphan and that made her extremely different.

The girls in her class were not the only ones to be perplexed by her somewhat outlandish appearance. As a matter of fact, her niece's green eyes and brown hair were a source of enigma as well as anxiety for Sumitra Devi, too. She had been raised to believe that beautiful girls were supposed to have large black eyes and long black hair.

"What a pity that the girl has inherited the wrong set of features from her parents," Sumitra Devi could not help thinking. "She has her mother's dusky complexion instead of her chiselled nose and her father's bulbous nose instead of his fair skin. And to top it, she has these curious green-brown eyes, which neither of her parents had."

"The girl will never have a delicate pink *dudhe-alta* complexion like her sister Aparna," Sumitra Devi conceded, *dudh* being milk and *alta* being a red vegetable dye used by women for colouring their feet. Ellora's was more of a milk and honey complexion, alas, with dollops of honey and just drops of milk. However, Sumitra Devi was determined to change the composition of her niece's complexion, so that it had oodles of milk and just drops of honey. And if possible, a pinch of *alta,* too.

Unlike her husband who worried about Ellora's future, she only concerned herself with the girl's current needs. The girl needed to be nourished with food, love and care and she had ample supply of all three. In her uncomplicated world, there were no complex long-term goals. She believed in tackling small, simple, attainable goals on a daily basis.

Every night when Sumitra Devi entered her niece's bedroom with a glass of milk, the sight of her doe-eyed niece in a short, frilly nightie filled her with a range of emotions. She felt a surge of love, compassion and sadness all at once for the orphaned girl who was now her charge and whose presence, despite the tragic circumstances of her arrival, had given a whole new meaning to her otherwise staid life. She had never felt so needed before, not even while raising her own daughter Aparna and her son Arnab.

"I'm your Maa," she would tell the howling child when, in the months following her parents' death, Ellora would wake up every single night and scream for hours for her mother. Even though the distraught child would cling to her for comfort and security, it was more than a year before she had actually started calling her Maa instead of Jethima. On her part, Sumitra Devi had never tried to force Ellora, even though it had hurt her slightly that the girl had not required much prompting to start calling her paternal uncle Baba instead of Jethu. But then, the rational person that she was, Sumitra Devi had comforted herself by attributing this to her husband's close resemblance to his younger brother. She could see why her niece had difficulty picturing her as her mother. Ellora's mother had been tall, slim, young, and beautiful, whereas she was short, stocky, middle-aged and plain; Sumitra Devi knew that it would be futile to try to replace the memory of the girl's mother. Therefore, instead of trying to achieve the impossible, she had focussed upon giving her unconditional love to the orphaned child.

In fact, she had been the one to have suggested to her husband that they should legally adopt their niece. It had bothered her very much that many of their friends and neighbours continued to regard them as Ellora's aunt and uncle.

Dr Akhilesh Chatterjee, who valued his wife's advice, had promptly contacted his lawyer. He fully agreed with his wife. The poor child had already gone through enough traumas without having to deal with any more insecurities and confusions.

However, despite the legal adoption, their orphaned niece had taken her own time to start calling them 'Baba' and 'Maa', the names by which she had addressed her own parents once. When she had finally called her uncle 'Baba', she had done so quite spontaneously and without any coaxing or coaching. Addressing Jethima as Maa, on the other hand, had not been as simple and spontaneous. It was easy to love her plump Jethima, but to call her Maa was somehow inconceivable. For all her motherly ways, Jethima was just Jethima; she could never replace her slim and beautiful mother. Nobody could.

Of course, eventually it had become impossible to hold herself back from that eternal fountain of love by holding on to the memory of her beautiful, but dead mother. Her dancer mother was not around when she needed a hug. Jethima was. And therefore, one day, without much ado, she had started calling her Maa.

From that day on, her uncle and aunt became her parents. Ellora never went back to calling them Jethu and Jethimaa.

****

Chapter 9

1985-1993, the early years soon after the tragedy,
Vijaypur

Sunday was the day assigned for eating mutton and Babu Shona became hyperactive on that day. He followed Sumitra Devi everywhere like an energetic lamb eager for his share of goat. A driven dog on overdrive, he barked at the slightest pretext and his high-decibel barks were invariably accompanied by high-speed wagging of tail.

Sunday was also the day assigned for beauty treatments. Sumitra Devi, in her quest to do something about Ellora's dusky skin and dull brown hair had taken upon herself to prepare homemade herbal pastes and shampoos. She mixed gram flour, turmeric and fresh cream to make a smooth paste, which she rubbed vigorously on Ellora's face, arms and legs. She then took Ellora to the bathroom and poured a pitch-black gooseberry concoction over her brown hair which was her tried and tested home remedy for converting dull brown hair into lustrous black.

When they all sat down for lunch and she ladled out generous portions of mutton curry in steel bowls, she would keep glancing in her husband's direction from out of the corner of her eye to see if he had noticed the perceptible changes in their daughter's appearance.

Visitors to the house noticed the transformation. This was in the mid-eighties, when television fever had not yet fully gripped the nation and popular mythological serials had not yet laid siege to homes, ruling everyday life and ruining social life. It was usual for friends like Bina Mashi and Shibu Mesho to drop in casually on Sunday afternoons. The couple was not related to the Chatterjees in any way, but they were good enough friends to be given the honorary title of Mashi (mother's sister) and Mesho (mother's sister's husband).

Bina Mashi would promptly compliment Ellora. "Just look at her glowing face. She's turning into a beauty." Compliment given, she would then drop her voice to a whisper to give Sumitra Devi some judicious advice.

"The girl is growing very fast. Sumitra, you need to be careful about how she dresses now. Look at her long legs. Those tiny shorts hardly cover her thighs. Take her to a good tailor and get some new frocks stitched for her, frocks that reach below her knees."

In fact, it was this penchant for imparting wisdom that had earned Bina-Mashi and her gang of friends the nickname of Binaca Geet Mala, after a popular countdown radio programme of the Hindi chartbusters. The nickname was given by none other than Aparna who, during her growing years in Vijaypur, had often been a victim of unsolicited advice given by many of these so-called friends of her mother. Actually, the epithet was collectively meant for four of Sumitra Devi's close friends: Bina, Kakoli, Geeta and Mala. It was a remarkable coincidence that their names could be acronymed to form the name of the popular radio countdown show. Just like the Binaca Geet Mala which broadcast the top hits every week, the four ladies lived up to their collective nickname by broadcasting the top gossip in town during their weekly visits.

"Here comes the Binaca Geet Mala to broadcast who is singing a romantic duet with whom," Aparna would tell her brother Arnab, who like herself, was often a favoured target of the gossiping gang.

"All India Radio is more like it. This is All India Radio giving you the latest Vijaypur news," Arnab would sarcastically add, mimicking the voice of a popular female newsreader.

"They are broadcasting stations all right, with their antennae powerful enough to capture the tiniest whiff of any budding romance, possible elopements or potential divorce," Aparna would conclude bitterly. The college-going brother and sister resented the fact that their gullible mother paid so much heed to the opinions and advice given by her gossipy friends.

Now that Sumitra Devi had an adopted daughter, her gang of advisors felt duty-bound to advise her all over again on how to raise a girl. Ellora was too young at the time to know the full ramification of living in a provincial small town, where everybody made it his or her business to mind everybody else's business. She was too young to know that if her skirts and sleeves got longer with each passing year, she had these well-meaning, advising aunts to thank for that.

****

Chapter 10

1993, Vijaypur

Despite the loving and secure environment of her new home, Ellora continued to miss her friends in Delhi and continued to feel like an outcast among her Vijaypur classmates. That is why Aditi Sharma's arrival was such a milestone in the fifteen year old orphaned girl's life.

However, befriending Aditi was not easy at first, for this new girl from London was brash, brazen and blunt and made no bones about it. She wore her brashness like a shield to field any unpleasant questions thrown her way.

"So Aditi, is your father also a dentist like your mother?"

"No."

"Then what does he do?"

"My father lives in London with his second wife. Do you still want to know what he does for a living?" she would ask scornfully.

Aditi Sharma did not put up with people who poked their unwanted and intrusive noses into her private affairs and promptly put such people in their rightful place. And when it came to putting her point across, she did not believe in mincing her words. She had a sizeable vocabulary for a fifteen year old, which she effectively used to cut people down to size, puncturing egos and inciting wars of words in which, needless to say, she invariably had the last one.

For Ellora, this bright, brainy and brash girl was a breath of fresh air, even though she made her slightly nervous. She did not know what was more unnerving about this cheeky newcomer: her extreme candour, her sheer poise or her utter disdain for what others thought of her. Whatever it was, she found herself drawn to Aditi like Newton's apple gravitating towards earth. Everything about Aditi fascinated Ellora, from her even white teeth to her sleek straight hair. The fact that she was a brilliant student as well, made it difficult for Ellora not to be in complete awe of her. The pull was strong and she could hardly stop herself from freefalling into an orbit that revolved around Aditi.

It was her dog-like devotion to Aditi that earned Ellora the nickname of Aditi's *chamchi*. Roughly translated, the word *chamchi* denoted a female spoon, a fawning item of cutlery. But Ellora had no compunction about being regarded as Aditi's *chamchi*. She admired her precocious friend's guts and her sharp intelligence. Aditi belonged to a world so vastly different from her own, that it was fascinating for Ellora just to be near her. She always invented ways to spend more and more time with her and that was why, when Aditi failed in Hindi (a language she had never studied before), she promptly offered to coach her after school hours.

What helped in cementing their budding friendship further was the fact that Aditi's mother was Sumitra Devi's dentist.

It was during one of Sumitra Devi's root canal sessions that Dr Amrita Sharma (who looked more like a dainty model than a drill-wielding dentist) suggested that their daughters study together after school hours. The dentist's chair is not the most comfortable place to vocalize your thoughts. However, the mandatory pause gave Sumitra Devi a chance to think over her dentist's suggestion carefully. And the more she thought over it, the more she liked the idea of Ellora and Aditi getting together after school. If truth be told, she was indeed concerned that her daughter was spending far too much time alone in the garden with their gardener's daughter, Kusum.

Yes, Ellora needs an intelligent and bright companion like Aditi instead of an uneducated, older girl like Kusum, decided Sumitra

Devi. As soon as she could open her mouth, she let her dentist know that she would be happy to have Aditi come over to their home to study with her daughter.

* * *

Aditi received a warm welcome in the Chatterjee household. Babu Shona greeted her with ebullient tail-wagging, sniffing her with a proprietary air as if to tell Ellora, "Any friend of yours is a friend of mine, too." Kusum was understandably more subdued in her welcome. She was quite eager, however, to show Ellora's new friend how to play a game called *gutta* with the help of five perfectly smooth round pebbles.

Babu Shona, who invariably followed the girls to the garden, was resentful of their growing camaraderie that excluded him. It was beyond his comprehension why the girls played such boring girlie games as *gutta* that did not require any running around or retrieving. Desperate for their attention, he pranced back and forth to get his supply of balls, rings and Frisbees, which he promptly placed in front of the girls, begging them with his soulful eyes to join the fun by playing his kind of exciting and manly games. The girls had no other choice except to give in to his comic pleas.

When they were not playing games, the four of them took strolls down the garden path, often stumbling upon hidden delights. The lone Calotropis bush that stood in a faraway corner was one such delight. Aditi was quite surprised to see the wild straggly shrub in the garden. "This shrub is called *Calotropis procera*," informed Aditi with unconcealed smugness.

This was another of Aditi's precocious flairs. She could effortlessly rattle off the scientific names of many plants. She owed this outstanding ability to her maternal grandfather Dr Manohar Kashyap, who was a retired botanist and had written many books on taxonomy.

"Yuck. It's a shabby shrub full of grubs," cried Ellora, wrinkling her nose upon spotting wriggling caterpillars on the silver-green leaves.

"Shut up, Ellora. Do you know that these caterpillars are potential butterflies?

If there was one thing Aditi enjoyed doing more than shocking people by making slighting remarks, it was to shock them by showing off her stupendous knowledge. And if there was one willing sucker eager to be shocked by Aditi's staggering capacity to rattle off facts and figures, it was, of course, Ellora. Sweet and docile, she was willing putty, ready to be moulded in Aditi's expert hands; an eager shadow, ready to follow in her brilliant friend's clever footsteps.

"What did you say the name of the shrub is?" asked Ellora.

"*Calotropis procera,*" informed a delighted Aditi. It always pleased her when her audience asked questions that she was able to answer.

"*Calotropis procera,*" repeated Ellora. "Seems like a long name for a plant."

"Most scientific names are long and complicated, my dear."

"Hmm. I'm sure this plant must have a shorter and simpler name, just as we, the *Homo sapiens,* have a simple name: human."

"It's called milkweed," answered Aditi and then, turning towards Kusum, she asked in her broken Hindi, "Do you know the Hindi name of this plant?"

"It's called *Aak.* Ellora's mother offers *Aak* flowers to Lord Shiva every Monday."

This was news to Ellora. She never lingered in the puja-room long enough to have noticed the Aak flowers offered by her mother to please and placate Lord Shiva every Monday.

* * *

The girls often sat on the raised concrete platform under the mango tree and chatted. They gossiped about their classmates and discussed their teachers. In the late afternoons, as the sunrays mellowed, the garden was resonant with birdcalls and redolent with sweet-smelling flowers.

"Let's take a walk," Aditi would suggest and the two of them would saunter along the paved pathway under the shade of trees.

"Your garden has character," Aditi, inhaling deeply, told her one day. Ellora did not quite get it. *How can a garden have character?* she thought to herself, but outwardly, she just gave an acknowledging smile.

"Oh! I feel so alive here! Look at these trees, shrubs and vines! They all look so mature and old, as if they have been standing here for thousands of years. They even have prehistoric, dinosaurian lizards lounging on their branches," she looked at her friend with a teasing smile, knowing how much her friend hated and feared the garden lizards.

Ellora was not sure if the overgrown and untamed backyard deserved such lavish praise. It was just a haphazard jumble of plants. They were exuberant plants that had been given free rein to shed leaves, drop flowers and spill berries onto the paths, or scramble up the walls in a wild, wilful, wily manner. There were too many tropical colours: blood red hibiscus, hot pink mirabilis, bright yellow tabebuia. It was a mishmash of strong, clashing colours. Even the fragrance was too robust.

"I prefer your garden. This garden is a hodgepodge of too many plants," said Ellora.

"If you like things to be humble and humdrum, my mother's garden is the place for you. But, I like things to be higgledy-piggledy. I love the hustle and bustle of this garden, where the hedges are hurly-burly, the borders are a hodgepodge of vibrant colours and the creepers run helter-skelter. My mother's manicured garden has a lot of Zen, but it lacks the zing of this garden."

For Ellora, listening to Aditi was like receiving a crash course in English vocabulary. As she listened to all the H-words spoken by Aditi, she was quickly filing away words like higgledy-piggledy, hodgepodge, helter-skelter, hurly-burly and hustle-and bustle in her memory to be used later in her conversations and English assignments.

* * *

Ellora liked things to be orderly and neat. She hated the hustle and bustle of her noisy neighbourhood. Though buffered from the disorderly outside world by a screen of tall trees, her home received its share of downtown din created by the throng of people who walked, talked and hawked outside those high boundary walls.

She preferred the peace and the harmony of Aditi's lake-facing neighbourhood and looked forward to visiting her friend's bungalow.

Aditi's dentist mother Dr Amrita Sharma obviously liked her garden to reflect her own dainty and understated personality. Pastel hues dominated the setting; no zingy zinnias, no merry gold marigolds and no boisterous bougainvillea were allowed in her serene garden.

Now that it was springtime, towering sweet peas, hollyhocks and delphiniums stood tall in the back borders, overshadowing shorter annuals like verbenas, cineraria and sweet alyssums. Collectively, they produced mounds of white, pink and purple blooms.

To Ellora, the whole setting seemed to her like a delightful watercolour painted in soft pastels. She started inventing excuses to spend more and more time in Aditi's house.

****

Chapter 11

1993-1994, Vijaypur

Sumitra Devi carefully trimmed the young pumpkin shoots, chopping the long vines into manageable lengths and discarding twigs that were either too hard or too tender to render any chewing pleasure. She made it a point to share these coveted vines with some of her Bengali friends. Once cooked in mustard oil along with a medley of seasonal vegetables, the green fuzzy shoots had the surprising potential to turn into something succulent and scrumptious.

Every morning, Sumitra Devi went to the backyard to survey which vegetables and fruits were ready for picking. She would instruct her gardener, who walked beside her during these inspection tours, which of the produce should be picked in large quantities for distribution purposes. Her fertile garden produced plenty. There were always surplus dolichos beans, lady's fingers, tomatoes, papayas and guavas to be shared generously with neighbours. Pumpkin flowers and shoots, however, were picked mainly for her friends Bina, Kakoli, Geeta and Mala. Today, all four of them were joining her for tea and that was why Sumitra Devi was sitting on the floor and chopping the edible shoots.

Even though there were maids to help her with various chores, Sumitra Devi insisted on chopping the day's vegetables herself on a *bonti*. Versatile and sharp, the foot-held, floor-mounted blade could chop, grate, skin, slice and dice in a matter of minutes, provided you had the knack, nimbleness and the nerve to handle that dicey tool.

Now, sitting on a low wooden stool in her kitchen, Sumitra

Devi divided the chopped pumpkin shoots into four equal piles and gently wrapped each portion in moist muslin cloth. Before leaving the kitchen, she instructed her part-time cook to fry the samosas. By the time her friends arrived, Sumitra Devi had changed into a starched, ironed and crisp handloom sari.

"Your samosas are superb as usual," complimented Geeta and then carped, "Mine never come out half as good as yours."

"It's her home-grown vegetables that add that special flavour to her samosas," offered Kakoli, biting into a hot samosa after dipping it in tamarind chutney.

"Kakoli is right. There's nothing like fresh herbs to spice up your recipe," said Sumitra Devi, her hands busily knitting a sweater for her granddaughter living in America.

"But Sumitra, why aren't you having any samosas?" asked Bina, who had temporarily kept her own knitting aside to enjoy the homemade samosas.

"I'm trying to control my weight," Sumitra Devi shyly confessed.

"Why should you start worrying about weight at your age? Women our age have earned the right to be plump. We don't need to compete with some of these younger women, who shamelessly prance around town wearing tight trousers and sleeveless blouses," stated Mala with the same relish with which she was devouring her chutney-drenched samosa.

"You're talking about our sexy dentist Dr Amrita Sharma, aren't you?" asked Bina, her eyes lighting up brightly. She quickly finished eating her samosa and cleared her throat before saying, "I think that woman should have been a movie actress instead of being a dentist. I'm told that some men go to her clinic not to show their cavities, but to ogle her curves. But can you really blame them? If you blatantly show off your curves in tight and skimpy clothes, what else can these poor men do except ogle them?"

They all laughed, except Sumitra Devi, who did not find Bina's comments particularly funny.

"I think we should keep in mind that Dr Amrita Sharma has spent all her life in big cities like Delhi and London before coming to this town and over there, wearing such modern clothes is no big deal. Even my Aparna started wearing pants and skirts after going to America," declared Sumitra Devi rather boldly.

"Well, once you get into those comfortable clothes, there's no getting out of them. Besides, as our Hindustani friends often say, '*Jaisa desh, vaisa bhesh*,'" said Bina, magnanimously exonerating her friend's daughter Aparna of any violation of the stringent Bengali dress code.

The last part of Bina's sentence was said in Hindi and, in a roundabout way, implied: 'When in America, do as the Americans do.' While referring to this popular Hindi adage, Bina had erroneously used the word Hindustani for people whose mother tongue was Hindi, not realizing that the word Hindustani actually denoted an Indian. For that matter, the other women in the room were also guilty of committing the same mistake during their conversations. Only Sumitra Devi knew the correct meaning of the word Hindustani and even she owed this knowledge to her son Arnab who, when he was a school-going teenager, used to flare up whenever his mother used the word Hindustani for Hindi-speaking people. He would promptly correct her by asking indignantly, "And what are you, Maa, a Pakistani?"

As she listened to her friends, Sumitra Devi could now understand why her grownup son and daughter, who now lived in America, often criticized her friends for being annoyingly gossipy and old-fashioned.

Sumitra Devi shuddered as she recalled how upset Aparna had become after attending one such morning tea sessions during her last trip to India. As soon her friends had left, her irate daughter had turned to her and said, "Maa, your friends haven't changed at all, have they? I'd rightly named them Binaca Geet Mala. I can't believe that even after so many years, they continue to sing the same old tune of, 'Who's

Going out With Whom!' Why do you invite these gossipy women for tea?"

Sumitra Devi had tried to pacify her incensed daughter by saying, "We don't always gossip. Our morning tea sessions are mainly an excuse for us to sit and chitchat about this and that, as we knit our sweaters."

"Chitchat about THIS shameless boy and THAT characterless girl, you mean," Aparna had sarcastically cut in and then continued the tirade by adding, "Maa, your friends are indeed busy women with busy hands and busier tongues. Busy doing chitchat-chitchat-chitchat, about this-that-this-that-this-that, busily knitting sweaters, embroidering tales and spinning yarns and indeed yards of yarns. Instead of spinning yarns about others, why don't they oil their own spinning wheels for a change? Frankly speaking, I don't understand why you even bother to associate with these gossiping ladies."

Despite being angry, Aparna was quite pleased with the way she had managed to interweave a comparison of the knitting ladies with spinning yarns and spinning yarns with spinning wheels.

Actually, Aparna was quite fond of peppering her sentences with idioms. The more idioms she used in her sentences, the merrier she felt. She had a mixed bag of English, Hindi and Bengali idioms, which she used liberally and interchangeably to enliven her chatter, natter and banter. Being trilingual had its advantages; she was never at a loss for idioms. If she could not think of a suitable idiom in English, she quickly outsourced it from her sizeable stock of Hindi and Bengali idioms. All she needed to do was to translate it verbatim into English. As far as she was concerned, a translated expression like, "Why don't they oil their own spinning wheels?" sounded infinitely more interesting than the regular, run-of-the-mill "Why don't they mind their own business?" If enlivening her language entailed borrowing idioms from Bengali, or even Hindi, she was all for it. No, Aparna, certainly did not believe in letting language come in the way of her freedom of idiomatic expression. Nor did she believe in keeping quiet when it came to speaking her mind.

Visiting Vijaypur was not always a nostalgic homecoming for Aparna. She had come a long way from the days when she was growing up in this town. Those days, she had not minded being surrounded by people who showered her with love but peppered those doting showers with heavy sprinklings of unsolicited advice.

Now that she was living in America where personal space was considered precious, almost sacrosanct and any encroachment of it was tantamount to transgression, Aparna's capacity for taking these sprinklings of well-meaning advice had reduced considerably.

However, if she had attended today's morning tea session, Aparna would have been much more favourably disposed towards her mother's gossiping gang of friends. In fact, she might even have revised her opinion about the Binaca Geet Mala broadcasting the same old tune of Who-Is-Going-Out-With-Whom; for the Mashis had decided to change their timeworn track by singing a refreshingly different tune, a tune dedicated to singing Aparna's praises. Their praises were sung so melodiously, that it was pure music to her mother's ears.

"Those who think the sari is going out of fashion should see our Aparna in one of her gorgeous cotton saris," said Geeta, who at fifty-one, was the youngest member of the gang of five.

Kakoli seconded Geeta's compliment by adding, "What a fine figure that girl has!"

"Aparna is no longer a girl Kakoli; she's now a mother of two," smiled a beaming Sumitra Devi, as she blatantly fished for more compliments for her dear girl.

Her bait was swallowed hook, line and sinker and as expected, a huge compliment surfaced instantaneously, like a trophy fish that had no other option except to surface, on the face of this crafty and nifty fishing.

Everybody nodded their heads in agreement when Mala put forth, "Nobody can tell that Aparna is a mother of two grown children. She looks even younger and prettier than before."

"For that matter, even our Ellora is showing signs of blossoming into a beauty like her elder sister."

Sumitra Devi was very pleased indeed. The morning had gone very well so far; her samosas were a big hit with her friends and now her day was made, because her friends were praising her dear daughters so generously. As she tilted her cup to sip the last few drops of tea and placed the empty cup back on the tray, her cup of joy was indeed overflowing

Bina, who was listening to this cloying exchange without giving any syrupy inputs of her own, decided to play spoilsport by drawing everybody's attention to some bitter home truths.

"Sumitra, do you think it's a good idea to let your daughter associate with this new girl, Aditi? You hardly know her family background," asked Bina.

"But we do know the family very well. Aditi is an incredibly intelligent girl and her mother Dr Amrita Sharma is my dentist."

It did not escape Sumitra Devi's attention that her friends were surreptitiously exchanging meaningful glances.

It was Kakoli, who finally broke the uncomfortable silence by saying, "But Sumitra, Aditi is from a broken home and we're all concerned about the kind of influence she may have on our Ellora."

At this point, Bina decided to disclose the most vital piece of information that she had been holding like a prized ace up her sleeve so far.

"It's not just a broken family; we're talking about a girl from a dysfunctional family. I believe Aditi's father, who lives in London, is a drunkard womanizer. Our pretty dentist had no other option except to divorce him and come back to India with her daughter."

There was a quick intake of breath from all quarters following this scandalous disclosure. Even Sumitra Devi caught her breath. They all knew that Bina, who had her sources, would never break breaking news like this unless she had verified it first.

When Sumitra Devi overcame her initial shock, her first reaction was that of compassion. "Poor Aditi," she sympathized. "Now I understand why she flares up when her classmates interrogate her about her father. But you've to hand it to Dr Amrita Sharma; she is doing a remarkable job of raising her daughter all by herself."

Sumitra Devi's friends could only gape at her in wonder. Bina was furious. What kind of a mother would take such dreadful news so calmly?

Later in the evening, as they all sat at the dining table with their respective husbands and chewed upon those utterly chewable pumpkin shoots like happy and contented cows, they simultaneously ruminated over their dear friend's potential troubles. If Sumitra did not watch out, this budding friendship could turn out to be her Pandora's Box.

* * *

Fortunately, things improved considerably in the next few years. The residents of Vijaypur no longer batted their eyelids when they saw Aditi and her mother walking in the streets, dressed in figure hugging jeans or short skirts. The newly arrived satellite channels had opened the Westside Window of their living rooms, broadening horizons, widening perspectives and expanding mind-sets. The dentist and her daughter were no longer regarded as ultra-modern aliens in anomalous clothes.

More importantly, even those who had been initially against the closeness of Ellora and Aditi stopped objecting to their spending long hours in each other's company. The naysayers no longer advised Sumitra Devi to say nay to their friendship; the Doubting Thomases no longer doubted the wisdom of letting Ellora associate with a girl from a broken family. Nowadays, the members of the Binaca Geet Mala opened their voluble mouths only to sing praises of the exemplary friendship between the two bright teenagers.

Aditi and Ellora had silenced everyone by continuing to get brilliant results year after year. The girls did not give any of Sumitra Devi's friends a chance to say, "I told you so," to her.

At least, not until much later.

****

Chapter 12

1994, Delhi

Although Ellora visited her ailing grandmother every summer, she did not really look forward to these annual trips. There was nothing much for her to do in Delhi except watching television or reading books. Bela-di, the elderly housekeeper was not very good company, even though the arthritic woman tried her best to impose her company upon the bored teenager. Whenever she could tear herself away from the engrossing TV serials that kept her glued to her seat all evening, Bela-di would start interrogating Ellora about her life in Vijaypur.

Ellora's maternal uncle Sanjay Sen, on the other hand, was great company. Whenever he was in town, he made sure to take his niece out for movies and dinners, but unfortunately, his visits were few and far between. A pilot with Lufthansa, his hectic flying schedule did not permit him to touch base with ground realities such as spending time with his invalid mother and orphaned niece, especially now that he had a girlfriend.

As much as Ellora loved her grandmother, she did not know what to say to her to fill the gloomy silence in the room once the part-time nurse left for the day. She had just turned sixteen that summer and like any other teenager, wanted to go out with friends and have fun; but instead, there she was, sitting quietly in a room with her paralyzed Dida for company. It was impossible to avoid those vacant eyes gazing at nothing in particular. It was difficult to ignore the tears streaming from the corners of those sad eyes.

What turned those depressing afternoons into something delightful and exciting, however, was Aditi's presence in Delhi.

"Give me your Delhi phone number and address," Aditi said in her usual demanding tone, as soon as she came to know that like her, Ellora also spent part of her summer vacations in Delhi. Their friendship was still budding and the idea that she could meet her friend even outside Vijaypur had simply not crossed Ellora's mind; but now that Aditi had suggested it, nothing could have been more welcome.

Suddenly the silent, gloomy afternoons were alive with activities and outings. However, the outings that the girls really looked forward to were their botanical excursions with Aditi's grandfather (Nana to the girls). Dr Manohar Kashyap often took them in his jeep to the outskirts of Delhi, where he often went in search of the rare trees that were once common in the city, but had now been pushed to the margins because of the ever expanding urban development.

That is how Ellora came to visit Balraj Ahuja's farmhouse in Mehrauli.

Balraj Ahuja was a landscape architect who lived on a huge South Delhi farmhouse surrounded by acres of farms, orchards and groves. He had met Aditi's grandfather at a botanical symposium and their chance meeting had led to an association that, in Aditi's words, was symbiotic.

"It's a mutually beneficial association. Whenever Balraj Uncle wants an expert opinion, he comes running to Nana, who knows trees like the back of his hands. Similarly, whenever Nana needs to study a rare tree, he comes straight to Balraj Uncle's farmhouse," Aditi informed her friend.

Ellora absorbed this information, as she took a sip of fresh pineapple juice. She was listening to her friend, but her eyes were all over the place, taking in the details of her fascinating surroundings.

Outside, Balraj Uncle and Nana sat on the covered porch, drinking something that looked very different from fresh pineapple juice. "It looks like beer; or is it wine?" wondered Ellora, without trying to confirm the accuracy of her uneducated guess for fear of appearing unsophisticated in front of her friend. Back home, her mother's friends often spoke of men in the habit of drinking alcohol in hushed tones.

Ellora must have stared at the drinking men longer than necessary, because her friend nudged her and said, "Now chillax. Don't look so scandalized, dude. Nana doesn't mind drinking an occasional beer or two to give company."

"I'm not scandalized," protested Ellora, mildly embarrassed at being caught staring at the drinking men with what must have been a shocked expression on her face.

"It's written all over your face Ellora. Your expressive eyes are like huge windows, giving full view of what's going on inside your head." Aditi liked teasing her sweet and naïve friend.

"Well, that's because I am dazed by everything around me. I've never seen a house so grand and grounds so vast."

"Isn't this place absolutely marvellous?" echoed Aditi excitedly. "Everything here is so magnificent. Even the trees outside are humongous and robust versions of their anaemic and dwarfish cousins lining the Delhi streets."

"It's a big house indeed, but there's hardly a soul around. Where's Balraj Uncle's family?"

"Balraj Uncle's wife died many years ago. He has a son called Roshan, who's studying at the School of Architecture and Planning."

Aditi paused to finish the rest of the pineapple juice in her glass in a quick gulp before continuing, "You must meet Roshan. He's such a funny, fun-loving clown who likes nothing better than poking fun at others."

"Hmmm," said Ellora, not too sure, if she was interested in meeting this poking clown.

Having finished their juice, the girls were ready for

something more solid and substantial; therefore, when the maid came back with a tray of steaming *idlis* and *paneer pakoras*, they could hardly wait to sink their teeth into those snacks.

Dipping her third *idli* into coconut chutney, Aditi, who had said very little while she ate, broke her silence by declaring, "Balraj Uncle carries a torch for my mother."

"What do you mean?" asked Ellora, clearly shocked by what she had just heard.

"You heard me. He's completely enamoured by her. If only my mother would stop acting so hoity-toity and hard-to-get, he would go down on his wobbly knees at the first available opportunity and propose to her with a diamond as big as one of those *Kadamb* puffballs you see on that tree." Aditi was pointing to a large leafy tree dotted with golden-yellow balls.

"Is that a *Kadamb* tree?" asked a very excited Ellora, for she had heard so much about the fabled tree, but was seeing it for the first time.

"Yes, the same old *Kadamb* tree that once grew on the banks of the river Yamuna and under the fragrant shade of which, Lord Krishna conducted his flirtatious romance with Radha and the *gopikas*."

The word romance immediately brought Ellora back to the unpleasant topic of another budding romance (albeit a one-sided one) between Balraj Uncle and Amrita Auntie that she desperately hoped would be somehow nipped in the bud.

"But why do you want your mother to marry someone like Balraj Uncle?" Ellora could not help asking, even though she knew it was the wrong question to ask.

"And what's wrong with my mother marrying Balraj Uncle?" retorted her friend angrily before adding, "He's wealthy and intelligent. He'll be a loyal and devoted husband to her. As a daughter who wants her long-suffering mother to be happy, I only hope that my mother starts taking her sincere suitor a little more seriously."

"I understand," muttered Ellora, even though she did not quite understand. To her adolescent mind, Balraj Uncle with his handlebar moustache and receding hairline seemed like a highly unsuitable match for someone as delicate and pretty as Amrita Auntie.

The whole idea is so absurd. No wonder, Amrita Auntie acts hoity-toity and hard-to-get. How can Aditi even think of making a match between such incongruously mismatched individuals? It'll be like Audrey Hepburn marrying Hercule Poirot.

Even as she looked outside and saw Balraj Uncle sipping his beer under the *Kadamb* tree, a ridiculous, but vivid picture flashed before her eyes, a picture in which, Hercule Poirot was getting down on his knees and proposing to Audrey Hepburn with a ring that, instead of diamond, contained a huge *Kadamb* flower. The entire vision was so ludicrous that Ellora could not help smiling.

"What's so funny?" asked her friend sharply.

"Nothing. I just remembered a question-answer joke that I read yesterday," invented Ellora quickly. She was a clumsy liar and was herself surprised at the swiftness with which she came up with that clever excuse. But she had no other choice; there was no way she could have told Aditi that the man she was contemplating as her potential stepfather reminded her of Hercule Poirot.

"So what's the joke?" Aditi persisted.

Ellora, who always filed good jokes in her memory, was once again quick to respond.

"What did Big Ben say to the Leaning Tower of Pisa?"

"Let's elope to Paris and get married on the Eiffel Tower?"

"Wrong. Think again," commanded Ellora.

"Now what can Big Ben possibly say to the Leaning Tower of Pisa? I'm sure it's got to do something with time and leaning."

"If you've the inclination, I've the time," Ellora quickly gave the answer before Aditi could guess it.

"Ha ha," laughed Aditi and Ellora joined her.

It had been so easy to laugh in Aditi's company those days, no matter how bossy, bad-tempered and brash her friend acted at times.

****

Chapter 13

1994, Balraj Uncle's farmhouse, Delhi

"Meeting Roshan for the first time is like shaking hands with a lightning rod; the shock of it can be slightly overwhelming," warned Aditi, soon after they hit the road.

Ellora, who was about to doze off, sat up from her supine slump to ask, "What do you mean?"

The girls were sitting in the back of the car to be able to chat freely. Nana had agreed to take them to his friend's farmhouse on two conditions: firstly, they would not laugh or talk too loudly during the drive and secondly, they would get ready by five in the morning.

"But that's an unearthly hour," Aditi had petulantly protested upon hearing the second condition. "Nana, why can't we start at a little more earthly hour, say by eight o' clock?" She had switched to the cajoling tone that she frequently used to sweet-talk her grandfather into submission. However, this time, the tone failed to work its desired magic. Dr Manohar Kashyap's tone was firm when he replied, "Because the night-blooming Kigelia flowers will be closed for the day if we reach late and I do need good pictures of the open flowers, preferably with the sunbirds sipping nectar."

The matter was settled and the girls woke up very early to be ready on time.

This was Ellora's second visit to Balraj Ahuja's farmhouse and she was highly excited at the prospect of going there once again. Only the prospect of meeting Roshan was making her slightly nervous.

Aditi did not help assuage Ellora's mounting nervousness when she expanded on her aforementioned warning by adding, "Roshan has a shocking sense of humour, which he combines with his thundering laughter to deliver high-voltage jolts to his unsuspecting victims. His jolts can come like a bolt from the blue, especially for people uninitiated in his brand of humour."

"Do you think he's going to be around when we arrive?" Ellora asked, trying her best to sound casual.

"Today being Sunday, he's quite likely to be home." predicted Aditi. She then made a feeble attempt at comforting her friend by saying, "But don't worry. Together, we can fix this lightning rod."

However, Ellora was all by herself when she found herself at the receiving end of the lightening rod himself. She was leafing through the pages of the latest issue of Stardust in total absorption, when she looked up and found this huge man standing near the door. The first thing that she noticed about the man was that he seemed to fill up a whole lot of space, making an otherwise spacious room suddenly appear very cramped.

"You must be Ellora," said the gigantic young man, taking a few long strides towards her before grabbing her hand and subjecting her to a bone-crunching handshake. Before a flabbergasted Ellora could react, he winked and said, "Pleased to meet you." The wink had not lasted for more than few seconds, but the handshake went on forever.

"Could this mountain of a man with a granite grip be Roshan?" wondered a stunned Ellora. Aditi had described him as a 'lightning rod' and she had pictured him to be a thin and wiry fellow, but there was nothing wiry or rod-like about this robust grizzly bear of a man, who was crushing her soft palm to a pulp. She got her answer when her eyes fell upon the solid silver bracelet dangling from the man's hairy wrist. It had his name engraved on it. "A tagged grizzly bear," Ellora

thought to herself, as she somehow managed to extricate her delicate fingers from his grip.

"You must be Roshan." She gave him one of her tiniest smiles.

"Wrong. I'm Cro-Magnon," he said it with a grin that turned his round eyes into narrow slits.

"I beg your pardon?" cried an incredulous Aditi, as she stepped in from outside.

"You heard me right, baby. My name is Cro-Magnon, the Handsome Hunk of a Caveman and I've come all the way from France to meet this beautiful Indian cave," said Roshan with a cocky smile, wrapping one of his arms tightly around Ellora's shoulder. Ellora, who was quick to disentangle herself from the grip of the solid, muscular arm, was beginning to look pale.

"Stop calling me baby and stop man-handling my friend," roared Aditi with feigned annoyance, as she threw a quick glance in Ellora's direction to see how she was taking it. Assured that her delicate friend had almost recovered from her first dose of a typical Roshanian buffoonery, she turned towards the offending buffoon to continue her mock tirade.

"So what did you say your name is? Oh yeah, Mr Cro-Magnon, the Handsome Hunk of a Caveman," said Aditi mockingly, as she put on an elaborate pretence of sizing him up critically by tapping his huge biceps that were literally bursting out of his t-shirt sleeves. She then took a step back, looked at him from top to bottom and raised one of her shapely eyebrows, saying, "The Handsome Hunk of a Caveman or the Incredible Hulk of Neanderthal Man? Or should we call him the Abominable Bulk of a Snowman? What say you Ellora?"

Not wanting to be left out of the naming game that was beginning to get interesting, Ellora quickly suggested, "What about The Big Foot with a Big Mouth, given his tendency to gravitate towards caves...."

"And putting his Big Foot where his Big Mouth is," Aditi completed Ellora's sentence. The two girls looked at each other and started giggling uncontrollably. Knowing that he stood no chance against the two quick-witted, giggly teenagers determined to beat him in his own leg pulling game, Roshan decided to throw in the towel by joining in their laughter.

"Okay, now tell me - have you had your breakfast?" asked he, suddenly deciding to act like a responsible host.

"How could we? We started at five. I'm ready for a hearty, high-calorie Punjabi breakfast," said Aditi, wondering what was on the menu.

"I've an idea. It's a pleasant breezy morning, so why don't we take a walk to the Amaltas grove in the backyard and break our fast under those golden chandeliers? As a matter fact, I've already instructed our cook Anand to prepare a picnic basket for us. Dad and Nana can also join us there. How does that sound?"

"Sounds like a brilliant idea," endorsed an enthusiastic Ellora.

"I don't think Nana and Balraj Uncle can join us, though. They have gone to the other end of the garden to have a look at the sausage trees," informed Aditi.

"Well, they can help themselves to a couple of sausages from the tree," said Roshan, his eyes turning into slits.

"Ve.....rrrry funny," said Aditi, pulling a face.

"But I guess neither of you would fancy eating massive tree sausages for breakfast, so let me go to the kitchen and check on the progress. Anand is making *aloo parathas*, omelette and *jalebis* for breakfast."

"*Aloo paratha*, omelette and *jalebis*! Sounds mouth-wateringly scrumptious," said Aditi, as soon as Roshan departed.

"Speaking of which makes me even more hungry," agreed Ellora.

As they impatiently waited for Roshan, the two of them tried to chitchat about things other than their overdue breakfast, but after a while, Aditi returned to the topic by saying, "I wonder how long it will take Anand to pack the picnic basket!"

"As long as it would take us to walk up to the Amaltas grove," said a grinning Roshan.

As the three of them started walking along the paved pathway zigzagging across the vast grounds at the back of the house, Aditi, in her usual blunt style, turned towards Roshan and asked, "How did your father manage to get so rich?"

"I'd say through sheer hard work. But, if you think my Dad is rich, you should see my friend Rohinton Merchant's home, which is three times bigger than ours. By the way, Rohinton plays first class cricket for Delhi and his property includes a sizeable cricket pitch with floodlights."

"Wow!" said the girls almost in unison.

"Rohinton is a brilliant batsman. Mark my words, he's going to make it to the Indian cricket team one day."

"Rohinton Merchant. I think I've read about him in the newspapers," said Aditi.

"Is he a cute-looking guy with a mop of curly hair, the one who recently hit a century against the Bengal team in the Ranji Trophy finals?" This was Ellora, who had suddenly turned uncharacteristically excited and chirpy at the mention of Rohinton Merchant's name.

"My my, sweet little Ellora, gushing over a cute-looking guy," intoned Roshan with an ear-to-ear grin. "I'd no idea Rohinton was so popular among schoolgirls. The bloke will be mighty thrilled when he gets to know about a beautiful girl calling him cute."

"You're not going to tell your friend anything. Promise me you won't!" pleaded a considerably alarmed Ellora.

"You stupid girl," said Aditi, "The more desperately you plead with him, the greater are the chances that he'll do exactly the opposite. Mark my words, before the day is over, this Rohinton guy will get to know that you find him cute, even though I doubt he'll take it as a compliment. Any man worth his testosterone is not going to be too thrilled about being regarded cute."

"I'm sure Rohinton won't mind," said Roshan with a wink before adding, "But I must admit Ellora, I'm pretty impressed by your knowledge of cricket. I'd no idea that people, especially girls your age, living in far off places like Vijaypur have even heard of the Ranji Trophy, let alone know the names of the players who play for it."

"Really?" asked Aditi, her tone sarcastic and her eyebrows arched.

"I swear," said Roshan, not quite catching Aditi's incredulous and angry tone. "Frankly speaking, looking at you, one can safely assume that you don't read any printed matter other than those silly filmy magazines , but I'm so glad to note that the two of you not only read newspapers, but even go beyond page three to read the sports page. If you know about an up-and-coming batsman like Rohinton, you're very much in the loop about cricket," said Roshan, nodding approvingly, as he graciously dished out what he thought was a compliment. He had no idea that at least one of the girls was highly offended by his patronizing comments.

"What an MCP you are Roshan Ahuja. Not just an MCP, but a stupid loathsome MMCP. You should be ashamed of yourself for holding such chauvinistic views." Aditi did not believe in mincing her words, not when she was angry. And right now, she was angry all right.

"What's MMCP?" asked Ellora, slightly baffled by the turn this conversation was taking.

"A man worse than an MCP, if ever there's one. To be more precise, an MMCP is a Metropolitan Male Chauvinistic Pig. He's a city-bred male with a patronizing attitude towards small town people in general and women in particular, because the pompous snob considers them to be genetically inferior and geographically disadvantaged and therefore less intelligent than his toffee-nosed self."

"And what's toffee-nosed, for heaven's sake?" asked an equally baffled Roshan.

"A snotty, stuck-up, snobbish, supercilious, MMCP like yourself, with your nose stuck so high up in the air, that the only way you can view small town girls like us is by looking down on us," said a fuming Aditi, her delicate nostrils flaring.

"But I was only trying to pay you a compliment, *yaar*. How does that make me toffee-nosed or stuck up? Or an MMCP?" protested a visibly shaken Roshan.

"You were paying us a compliment? I beg your pardon? Sir Roshan Ahuja, pray, tell us, just how were you bestowing this great honour upon two lesser mortals like us? By admiring the fact that we, two sixteen-year old schoolgirls from a small town, actually have the capacity and the propensity to go beyond the gossip columns to read something as masculine and metropolitan as the sports page? How condescending can you get?" asked an indignant Aditi, her face visibly red.

Roshan, whose face, on the other hand, was looking visibly pale, had the grace to apologize, once he understood what his fault was.

"If you put it like this, I do owe both of you an apology. I'm sorry Aditi for ignorantly acting like a pompous ass. I didn't see it from this standpoint; thanks for making me see it from your perspective."

"Considering that you sound quite earnest, your apology is graciously accepted but on the condition that you make our overdue breakfast materialize within the next five minutes. The rats in my stomach are turning riotous. And where's your Amaltas grove by the way?"

"There it is, right there," pointed a noticeably relieved Roshan, as they came to a point where the cluster of trees became visible.

"My goodness, what a spectacular flower show!" said Ellora, as her eyes fell upon the trees clothed in yellow blooms that hung in massive grape-like bunches from the branches.

Even Aditi let out a low whistle to express her delight.

There, standing in front of them were eight blossoming Cassia trees around an octagonal patio paved with fawn sandstones. Balraj Ahuja had obviously designed the area with entertaining in mind, for it was complete with an octagonal teak dining table and chairs.

A few feet away stood a thatched gazebo, shaded by a huge gulmohar tree. True to its English name, the tree flamboyantly set off the hut-shaped gazebo like a house on fire.

"Wow! Now that's what I call a Flowering Inferno, a tree on full blast to set the stage ablaze," declared Aditi, suddenly all perky and animated because she knew so much about the tree and here was her chance to stun her audience with some staggering details. "Do you know that this fiery Flamboyant Tree was named Poinciana regia after M. De Poinci, the 17th century governor of the French West Indies?" boasted Miss Know-All.

Aditi would have liked to enlighten her less enlightened audience some more on the tree, however, Roshan decided that it was time to shake Aditi out of her sleep-inducing lecture by delivering one of his minor jolts.

"Hey! Hang on Aditi. I thought you're starving, but looks like you had a heavy breakfast this morning."

"What do you mean?" asked Aditi, baffled as well as irritated for being interrupted so rudely just when she was on the verge of making a very interesting disclosure.

"Well, it's obvious that you already ate some heavy stuff, so we'll let you skip your breakfast. You can stand here the whole morning and admire the tree named after the 17th century governor, while Ellora and I go back to the Amaltas grove and eat our breakfast under some ordinary trees that don't have the good fortune of being named after some illustrious governor. What say you Ellora?" teased Roshan, his eyes twinkling brightly, even as one of them closed in the briefest of winks directed at her.

"Skip breakfast? Are you crazy? I'm going to do no such thing. And what's this nonsense about eating heavy stuff? I've only had a roadside cup of chai since this morning. Do you call that heavy?"

"You forgot to mention the thick Oxford English Dictionary and the heavy volume of Encyclopaedia Britannica that you chewed and gulped the first thing in the morning before starting your journey," said a grinning Roshan, letting his eyes do their disappearing act.

Aditi rolled her eyes, but said nothing.

"Or should I say masticated and swallowed instead of chewed and gulped?" Roshan continued his teasing.

"Masticated, swallowed, ingested, digested and regurgitated. And now I'm hungry all over again, so where's the picnic basket for heaven's sake? I'm ravenous," declared an impatient Aditi in a tone that was beginning to acquire an edge.

"Aditi doesn't get hungry like most of us do; she gets ravenous," laughed Roshan.

"Like a raven?" asked Ellora.

"Or a Ravan," suggested Roshan.

"With ten hungry mouths to feed, Roshan, we better grab our share of parathas and *jalebis* before this she-avatar of Ravan masticates and swallows them all," said a laughing Ellora. It was not very often that she got a chance to tease her domineering friend.

"Shut up you two," said Aditi with considerably less vehemence than her words seem to convey.

The three of them had reached the Amaltas grove and to the joint delight and relief of all three, Anand was standing there with the much awaited picnic basket.

****

Chapter 14

1996, Vijaypur

"My mother is getting married next month," Aditi announced to her classmates during the recess, stunning them all into a long silence.

The group of six girls, had assembled in the school canteen to drown their pre-exam jitters in cold drinks and comforting snacks, but with Aditi's dramatic declaration, the conversation no longer remained casual.

The silence lingered, punctuated by the sounds of munching and sipping.

Aditi waited for the girls to pass some catty comments now that she had deliberately let the cat out of the bag, but nobody displayed any signs of wanting to say anything. It was strange the way everyone had coolly absorbed the sensational news of her mother's forthcoming wedding without asking any probing questions. It was almost as if, she had thrown a heavy pebble into a pond and it had quietly sunk without creating any exciting ripples.

Finally, the prolonged silence was broken when someone asked, "And who's the lucky guy?"

"His name is Balraj Ahuja. He's a renowned landscape architect based in Delhi," informed a cheerful Aditi with hard-to-contain enthusiasm.

Now that the first ripple had hesitantly surfaced, it encouraged several other suppressed and submerged ripples to come out into the open. "Like the ripple effect," thought an amused Aditi, as she answered a deluge of questions posed by her friends. Despite bursting with curiosity to know every single detail of so extraordinary an event (it was not every day that one of them came to school and announced the news of her mother's forthcoming wedding), the girls took their time to start asking questions. Fortunately, today their temperamental classmate, infamous for her mercurial mood swings was not only in a good mood but was in a divulging mode as well; for she was smilingly answering all their questions without once snapping at them.

"Balraj Uncle has been pursuing her for over two years now. My mother, of course, gave him a hard time. She was not willing to consider remarriage after what she has gone through the first time around," disclosed Aditi. And then realizing that she had inadvertently dropped more pebbles than she had intended to and in the process, created more ripples than she had bargained for, she quickly changed the topic by saying, "The wedding will take place in Balraj Uncle's farmhouse in Delhi. The clientele of my stepfather-to-be include the crème de la crème of Delhi, including some famous designers, writers, cricketers and even film stars; so it will be a star-studded scintillating event glittering with Delhi's glitterati," Aditi smugly informed them before magnanimously adding, "You're all invited to the wedding."

Now that the girls knew how glittering and glamorous the wedding was going to be, they were all dying to attend it. However, they knew that their parents would never grant them permission to travel to Delhi to attend this outrageous event.

Even Ellora for that matter, despite being Aditi's best friend, was not sure if she would be allowed to attend the wedding. Nevertheless, she was determined to get her parents to say yes, no matter how challenging the task was going to be. In fact, if anyone was truly dying to attend the wedding, it was she and for good reason.

* * *

For someone whose first impulse had been to nip the budding

romance between Balraj Uncle and Amrita Auntie in the bud, Ellora could not have welcomed the news of their wedding with more enthusiasm.

It was not as if the idea of Balraj Uncle exchanging garlands and rings with delicate Amrita Auntie seemed any less incongruous to her now. As much as she liked the affable landscape architect, she still could not figure out how someone as dainty and exquisite as Amrita Auntie could have said yes to his preposterous proposal. But despite all her discomfort and bewilderment at such an inconceivable union, Ellora was all for the wedding; not only because Aditi wanted it, but also because she herself wanted it, for an entirely different set of reasons, of course.

* * *

Ever since returning from her last trip to Delhi almost a year ago, during which she had briefly met Rohinton Merchant for the first time. Ellora had done nothing except hope, wish and pray every single day that fate and the Gods would collectively collude to bring the two of them face-to-face one more time.

Even Aditi, who knew most of Ellora's innermost thoughts, was not let in on this well-guarded secret. Not that Ellora wanted to hide things from her best friend; but, she knew Aditi too well to risk telling her. She was sure that her friend would scoff at her for having feelings for Rohinton Merchant. She was very likely to dismiss them off as being the symptoms of puppy love. When it came to matters of the heart, Aditi was extremely level-headed. According to her, falling in love was akin to falling sick.

"Who wants to go around with a heart that beats abnormally and aches perpetually? There is nothing more ludicrous than a moonstruck swoony-loony-moony lover, mooning over his lost love by singing Achy Breaky Heart."

Such were Aditi's strong views on people falling in love and Ellora had no choice except to hide her irrational feelings from her rational friend. As a matter of fact, when she analysed her emotions pragmatically, she too was surprised at herself for harbouring such intense feelings for someone she had met only once and that too very briefly. And yet, she knew that those had been the most euphoric moments of her life. She wished to experience that elation all over again, no matter how silly and crazy her yearning might seem to others.

* * *

Ellora might have met Rohinton Merchant only once and that too almost a year ago, but she had known of the young cricketer for over two years now.

It all went back to the day when she had first chanced upon an article on him in one of the sports magazines. Titled 'A Rising Star on the Horizons of Indian Cricket,' the article went on to describe how the right-handed, stylish batsman from Delhi had played a "cracker of an inning" by scoring an unbeaten century that had helped his team to win the coveted Ranji Trophy. There had been a picture of Rohinton accompanying the article. The dapper young man in cricket whites stood with the bat carelessly slung over his shoulder. There was something about his boyish grin and his engaging face, framed by masses of curly hair that had reminded Ellora of her late father in his younger days.

Come to think of it, it was rather unusual for a young schoolgirl like Ellora to take such an obsessive interest in the game. Again, it all started, when her adoptive father found a cricket bat belonging to her late father during a spring-cleaning session.

"This is your father's bat," Dr Akhilesh Chatterjee told her, as he pulled out the old bat from a huge steel trunk overflowing with dusty mementos. The solid trunk had not been opened for decades because it stored disturbing memories that were better left undisturbed; memories tinged with the pungent odour of naphthalene balls that still clung to them tenaciously despite the mothballs having long since evaporated.

"May I keep it Baba?" she asked, just as Dr Akhilesh

Chatterjee was about to put the battered old bat back into the oversized trunk.

"Of course. Here, take these old school magazines also. They all belong to your father. You may even find his pictures in the sports section. You father used to be the captain of his school cricket team; his dream had been to play for India."

Back in her room, she flipped through the pages of those dog-eared, dusty magazines, until she found the picture she was looking for. It showed a group of young cricketers posing for the camera. Her father sat in the front row, looking extremely handsome in a navy blue blazer with embroidered school logo. His mop of curly hair made him appear very different from the image Ellora carried in her mind of her cardio-vascular surgeon father with his no-nonsense crew-cut.

She placed her father's bat on the mantelshelf in her study along with her own trophies and shields. Every time she looked at the bat, she wanted to know more about the young boy who had harboured an unfulfilled dream of playing cricket for his country.

And so began a quest to know more about her father. Ellora carefully went through every single page of the old school magazines in the hope of uncovering some new facts about him. She had so few memories of her father. Even when he was alive, she had hardly got to spend any time with him because of his round-the-clock hospital schedule. The discovery of the bat led to a frenzied search for more information on her father's cricket-playing days.

"Let's go to the town library," she would suggest to Aditi.

Aditi, of course, was always open to the idea of visiting the old library that housed thousands of rare books, gazettes and journals. Once inside the huge library, Ellora would head straight for the section devoted to sports and systematically go through the articles on cricket in the archived newspapers. Her painstaking research paid off and she eventually found one brief news item on her late father in a local newspaper called The Victory Times. The article described how Akshay Chatterjee, the captain of St. Paul's Boys School, Vijaypur, had made the highest score of 125 runs to clinch the victory for his team in the inter-school cricket tournament.

What started as an impassioned search to know more about her father, ended up becoming a favourite pastime. When Ellora was not in the town library, she was in her school library, going through the sports columns and pages featuring articles on cricket. That is how she came across articles featuring Rohinton Merchant, who like her father, had been the captain of his school cricket team before being selected to play for the Delhi cricket team. Every time she came across an article on Rohinton, she read it with great interest, but her interest in the promising all-rounder was just academic, at least to start with. It was only after she met him in person a year ago that her interest in the batsman no longer remained just casual.

****

Chapter 15

1995, Delhi

It had been a brief, chance meeting. Rohinton had informally dropped in during one of their early morning breakfasts under the Amaltas trees (which by then, was a standard annual affair).

"Hi everybody," he shouted from the bend.

Roshan, as soon as he saw his friend, stood from his chair with the alacrity of an agile, but corpulent Labrador and bulkily walked towards the new arrival to greet him with his usual effusiveness.

"Look who's here! My my, what a pleasant surprise!" said a beaming Roshan, as he enfolded his young friend in a tight bear hug.

"I'm leaving for London tomorrow, so I thought of coming and seeing you," said the cheerful young man and then, noticing the presence of the two girls he added, "but looks like you've company. Sorry to have barged in unannounced like this."

"You're welcome to join the party," said Aditi with a broad smile.

Ellora, however, was too dazed to say anything. She could not believe that she was actually face-to-face with the young cricketer about whom she had read so much. All these years, Rohinton Merchant had been only a picture or a description to her, seen or read on the pages of newspapers; she had to pinch herself to believe that the same young man had just walked out of those archived newspapers to materialize before her in the flesh. A lot of well-toned and muscular flesh too, for the young cricketer was dressed in a white T-shirt and a pair of shorts, that left considerable parts of his brawny legs and arms exposed. Standing there with his kitbag slung over his shoulder, he looked every bit like the fit athlete she had imagined him to be.

As he poured a glass of orange juice for his friend, Roshan enquired, "But how did you find your way to this place? Was someone at the gate?"

"Oh yeah, your Tiger-Lion was there. He told me where to find you," replied Rohinton, as he took a seat right opposite Ellora.

"Oh! Sher Singh," said Roshan with a delighted chuckle and then turning towards the girls, he said by way of explaining, "Tiger-Lion, as you must have figured out, is our gardener Sher Singh. Rohinton has picked up my habit of translating Hindi names into English." Then realizing that he had not properly introduced his friend to the gawking girls, he quickly added, "Oh! But let me introduce you first. Meet my friend Rohinton Merchant, the famous opener of the Delhi Cricket Team. And Rohinton, this is Aditi Sharma, my soon to be stepsister." Then, turning towards Ellora, he added, "And this beautiful girl, of course, needs no introduction. I'm sure you remember the name of your big fan, don't you?"

"Ellora?" asked Rohinton with frank delight.

"Absolutely right, the very same Ellora who thinks that, after Tom Cruise, you're the cutest thing on this earth," said Roshan, tongue-in-cheek, with a wicked wink directed at the furiously blushing girl.

A mortified Ellora was too tongue-tied to give a sharp tongue-lashing to Roshan whom, she wanted to strangulate at that moment. However, when she finally managed to find her voice, her tone was too soft to sound like an angry objection.

"Roshan, please shut up, will you?" she shyly protested, not sounding like someone who, moments ago, had been miffed enough to want to strangulate the stupid buffoon.

Surprised by her tone that was cloyingly coy (annoyingly so), Aditi fixed her friend with one of her 'what's-wrong-with-you Ellora?' gazes before commenting, "Sweet Ellora, when you want someone to shut up, you just say 'SHUT UP' instead of saying, 'Please Shut Up.'" While saying the last three words, she mimicked Ellora's shy and sweet tone almost to perfection.

Roshan and Rohinton exchanged amused glances, while Ellora avoided looking at anyone to hide her discomfiture. She intently inspected her polished toenails peeping out from her low-heeled sandals. But, she was feeling far too happy to sulk for too long and therefore, lifting her downcast eyes, she smiled and in doing so, found Rohinton's eyes resting on hers. His lingering gaze made her blush and she quickly looked away.

What's wrong with you Ms Ellora Chatterjee? Why are you acting like a moonstruck swoony-moony-loony lass pining for attention? Keep your emotions in check, she sternly told herself. Fortunately, Aditi was busy filling her plate and therefore, failed to notice this recent exchange of glances and the resultant change in the colour of Ellora's face.

"You know Ellora, Rohinton and I went to the same school," informed Roshan.

"Really?" Ellora was all ears.

"We both used to play for our school cricket team."

"Until you were expelled from the team," reminded Rohinton with a broad grin.

"This sounds interesting. Now Roshan, what exactly did you do to deserve such a harsh punishment?" asked Aditi, her eyes wide with anticipation.

"I rubbed our potbellied coach the wrong way by nicknaming him The Coach Potato. Goes without saying that he didn't like the nickname," said the joker with a poker face.

Everyone laughed. Ellora could not help noticing Rohinton's

eyes once again resting on her smiling face and it made her delirious with joy, but she forced herself to look away.

There was a bird hidden among the hanging clusters of yellow cassia blooms, rasping out a long series of staccato, snarling calls. They all looked up, but were unable to spot the noisy bird.

"So when is the wedding?" asked Rohinton, when the bird finally quietened down enough to allow conversation.

"Sometime in March end or early April, after the exams get over," informed Aditi.

"April is a good time. We can prepare the wedding stage under the silk cotton trees." This was Roshan, sounding very excited at the prospect of his father's wedding.

Ellora was not too sure if a wedding *mandap* under the trees abloom with gaudy red flowers was the right stage for someone as delicate as Amrita Auntie, whose preferred colour palette would never include a colour as robust as blood red.

Rohinton, in the meanwhile, looked at his watch and stood up, saying, "As much as I'm enjoying your company, I must leave now, for I've a net practice in an hour's time." He picked his kitbag up from the floor and started walking away. As he reached the bend, he stopped. Then, turning towards the group, he said, "It was lovely meeting all of you. I look forward to seeing you again. Hopefully, in April."

Ellora was aware that the last part of his speech was directed at her; Rohinton had been looking directly at her while saying it, as if he was talking to her alone.

As she watched him walk away, Ellora experienced a sinking feeling in her chest. It was a raw, unfamiliar kind of feeling. She had never felt so low and so high before.

****

Chapter 16

1995, Delhi/Vijaypur

"So, tell me, are you falling for Rohinton?" Aditi seldom bothered with preliminaries.

"What?" asked an incredulous Ellora, turning visibly red.

"Come on, Ellora, come off it. You're bowled over; clean bowled by the dashing batsman. It's written all over you face."

Ellora cringed. Unfortunately, coming clean was not an option, here. She knew her friend too well to risk it. Not now, at least, when the two of them were standing in front of a *golgappa* stall and hungrily waiting for the vendor to start serving them. She liked eating her *golgappas* in peace and was in no mood for a lecture which was sure to follow, if she were to admit to her fledgling feelings for Rohinton. Hence, just as the *golgappa* wallah handed them their plates and started punching holes in the crispy balls with his thumb, she too decided to punch a hole in Aditi's assumption by vehemently refuting it.

"Good heavens, Aditi, are you crazy? What made you jump to this ridiculous conclusion?"

"Well, as I said, it was written all over your face, the way you exchanged glances and blushed. Look at you, even now, just at the mere mention of his name, you're blushing furiously," said Aditi, as she gulped down a whole *golgappa*.

"I didn't know you were into face-reading these days," snapped Ellora in a rare show of defiance. The *golgappa* on her plate had leaked considerably in the few seconds it took her to retort and now she was left with just the round, crispy outer shell minus the tangy tamarind water.

"One doesn't have to be a face reader to be able to see what's there for everyone to see, so please don't try to deny your feelings for Rohinton," said Aditi, popping one more *golgappa* into her wide open mouth. The tart, tangy and minty tamarind-water seeped into her mouth to set it on fire, making her eyes and nose water simultaneously.

Still smarting from the after-effects of the fiery water, Aditi decided to tone her voice down to impart a word of wisdom to her naïve friend.

"If the love bug has not bitten you too deeply, then it's not yet too late to inoculate yourself against the risky germ. Do it promptly, for this particular bug is certainly injurious to your health."

"Stop sounding like the statutory health warning on cigarette packets, Aditi. And stop reading my face and drawing ridiculous conclusions, it's all humbug. I'm not bitten by any love bug."

This was a new Ellora, flippant, defiant and cool, almost callously so and Aditi was surprised to see this new avatar of her sweet and submissive friend.

"Deny it, if you wish to, but I must warn you that you're going to break a lot of hearts, yours included, if you don't keep your wayward heart in check now," cautioned the wise friend.

"Any specific reason for being so pessimistic, Ms Doom-Spelling Aditi Sharma?"

"Well, since you're refusing to see the writing on the wall, let me spell it out for you. Rohinton is a Zoroastrian and you're a Hindu and your respective religions prohibit an interfaith marriage. Can you imagine the reaction of your orthodox parents when they come to know of your serious interest in this young man?"

Ellora studiously avoided Aditi's unsettling gaze, as she ate her fourth *golgappa* in silence. Then, she shrugged her shoulders and said, "You're jumping to all kinds of wrong conclusions. I don't have any interest, neither serious nor non-serious in Rohinton Merchant. Period. Now shall we go back to eating our two remaining *golgappas* in peace?"

The conversation had taken place almost four months ago and since that afternoon, Rohinton Merchant's name never cropped up during their conversations, casually or otherwise. At least, not until the day Roshan called from Delhi to give them the good news; Rohinton had been selected for the Indian squad for their tour of Sri Lanka.

If Ellora was overjoyed to hear the news, she made sure to control her elation in front of her censorious friend. But much to her astonishment, it was Aditi who clapped her hands in excitement and said, "Just imagine, now we can watch him right here on our television screen."

* * *

When D-Day finally arrived and the two of them sat in front of the television in Aditi's living room, they could hardly contain their joy and thrill at seeing Rohinton on television.

"He's a treat to watch." Aditi was the first to break the pin-drop silence that followed as soon as Rohinton came out to bat.

"He looks so confident for someone who's playing his first One Day International," agreed Ellora.

They nervously chewed their nails, as they watched the aggressive Sri Lankan bowlers target their young friend with threatening attacks. It was only after Rohinton, (whom one of the commentators kept calling 'The Merchant of Delhi') seemed to have settled down and looked poised to hit a big score could the girls stop chewing their nails and breathe normally for the first time.

"Look at the way he's battering the bowling attack by hitting those dangerous balls for easy fours and sixes. I love the way he's swinging his bat like a swashbuckling superhero," said Aditi.

"You make him sound like a batsman turned into Batman and a bad-man-battering- Batman at that."

"Spoken like an inspired fan."

Ellora reflected upon the expression. Is that what she was, just an inspired fan of Rohinton Merchant

Suddenly, to the girls' utter consternation, there was some kind of tension on the field. The bowler said something provocative to Rohinton, before bowling a threatening bouncer that narrowly missed his helmet. Unruffled and cool, he swung his bat like a sword, before taking his position like a battle-hungry soldier in front of the line of attack. The next three balls were promptly thrashed away to three different corners of the ground past the boundary line.

"He's all fired up now. Look at the way he's wielding his bat like a sledge hammer to hammer the ball to all parts of the ground."

"That's what I call the right battitude! If you wish to throw an attitude on the field, throw it with your bat," said Ellora.

"Did you say BATTITUDE?"

"Yes."

"Is it a dictionary word?"

"I don't think so. But don't you think it captures Rohinton's current mood and actions quite accurately?"

"Absolutely," agreed Aditi and then decided that she too wanted to coin a new word to describe Rohinton's action on the field.

"And look how swiftly and smoothly he's taking those singles! Running like a panther with a purpose. Now that's what I call CATTITUDE!"

Ellora was happy that her friend, instead of trying to shove bitter pills down her throat, was back to being her cool and funny self.

****

Chapter 17

1996, Delhi

The post-Holi March in Delhi was a happening month. The crisp winter nip in the air had been replaced by a balmy buzz. Many trees were about to close shops by shedding all their leaves in preparation for the harsh summer, while others were replacing their already shed leaves with vibrantly coloured blossoms. It was as if, in a last ditch attempt to attract the birds, bees and butterflies, they had collectively decided to invest all their energies into decking up their bare branches.

Balraj Ahuja's farmhouse, too, was a decked up and lively place that particular March. Being a landscape architect who believed that landscaping was a living art and that his own yard was a live showroom for this art-in-action, he wanted to design his wedding stage in harmony with the trees, shrubs and climbers already growing in his garden. No truckloads of exotic floral extravaganza for him and his beautiful bride-to-be.

The silk cotton trees were still in bloom, but Balraj Ahuja was not in favour of tying the knot under those profusely blooming trees; the showy blooms were too robustly red for the delicate tastes of his dainty fiancé. Moreover, the bulky flowers of the silk cotton trees had already started falling on the ground with a thud. Of course, he wanted a shower of petals, but this hard-hitting, heavy shower of plump and fleshy flowers was not quite what he had in mind for his frail bride. Not just that, the trees attracted flocks of noisy birds like crows, mynahs and parrots, which not only belted out a cacophonous chorus, but also pelted down a highly unwelcome shower of bird-droppings from the branches. Once again, not the kind of shower Balraj Ahuja had in mind for his beautiful bride-to-be or his wedding guests.

After surveying all the other blossoming options in his garden, the landscaper decided that the rose-draped pergola in the front yard would be an ideal setting for the morning wedding. Festooned with cascading clusters of vigorously blooming pink and cream roses, the tall four-poster pergola set a striking stage for the simple Vedic ceremony. Everybody who attended the wedding that morning agreed that it was a stunning backdrop for the bride, who herself looked stunning in a pale pink *lehenga choli* embellished with pearls, sequins and Swarovski crystals.

She looks exquisite, thought Ellora, who had never seen Amrita Auntie dressed so elaborately in such traditional fineries. *Balraj Uncle, on the other hand, looks more like an ageing Mughal than his usual Hercule Poirot self,* decided she, as she looked at the balding bridegroom beaming in his gleaming cream *sherwani* like a Cheshire cat that had gulped more than its fair share of cream. "A Pleased as Punch Cheshire Tomcat with Handlebar Whiskers," she whispered to herself.

"Now stop it, you ungrateful girl," Ellora reprimanded herself, as she remembered just in time how generous her host had been towards her. Not only was she enjoying his lavish hospitality, but even the *lehenga-choli* she was wearing had been a gift from him.

It was an entirely unexpected (though not an entirely unwelcome) gift. She was taken by complete surprise when about a month ago, Aditi had first shown her the beautiful attire that Balraj Uncle had bought specially for her.

"Choose your colour," she had commanded, as she laid out two *lehenga-choli* sets before her.

"What for?" a surprised Ellora had asked.

"These are the designer clothes we're going to wear for the morning ceremony. My mother has decided that her two young bridesmaids should be dressed in soft lavender and apple-green to coordinate with her own *lehnga-choli*."

"But I can't take it! It looks way too expensive," said Ellora, even as she mentally weighed which one of the two colours would suit her better; both colours were somewhat pale for her not-so-pale complexion.

"Well, you don't have much choice, unless of course you don't want to be a bridesmaid," Aditi pronounced and then informed, "My mother's *lehnga-choli* is in a lovely shade of pink; it's called Audrey Hepburn Pink."

"Really? What an amazing coincidence!" muttered Ellora.

"Coincidence?" asked a puzzled Aditi.

Ellora hesitated for a few seconds and then decided to let out her secret.

"From the day I first saw Amrita Auntie, I thought she looked like Audrey Hepburn."

"Oh really? My mother will be very pleased to know this. She's a big Audrey Hepburn fan. In fact, Roman Holiday is one of her favourite movies."

* * *

Presently, as she threw pink rose petals at the couple sitting under the rose-pergola, Ellora could not help thinking all over again that while the bride in pink indeed looked like an Indian version of Audrey Hepburn, the groom unfortunately continued to look like Hercule Poirot even in his shimmering *sherwani*.

Amrita Auntie won't be too pleased if she comes to know what I think of her Prince in Shining Sherwani, who sadly is no Gregory Peck, thought Ellora. She then immediately reprimanded herself for harbouring such unkind thoughts for her generous and kind host.

Looking back, Ellora was happy that the choice to wear lavender had literally been thrust upon her. The colour suited her, conceded she, as she caught her reflection in a small mirror pasted to the vanity bag of a female guest. Even her hair was looking quite nice for a change. She was glad that Aditi had bullied her into getting it styled. .

The hairdresser had done nothing drastic to her hair and yet, it looked very different with the wavy, chestnut-brown tresses cascading softly down her shoulders to reach below her waist. Now that the last traces of the gooseberry-induced black tinge had been washed away, the newly emerged hair colour somehow seemed to have intensified the green flecks in her eyes. Even her skin did not look too bad, despite having more honey than ever. Probably the two deep pink roses that the stylist had pinned to one side of her hair were adding a little rose to her predominantly honey tone. She was seventeen going on eighteen that year and had never looked and felt more beautiful. And she was not the only one to think so.

"You're looking absolutely gorgeous."

Her heart skipped a beat when she heard that voice. For how many months had she waited to hear his voice? And yet, now that Rohinton was finally here, Ellora was afraid to turn around and face him. Nevertheless, she not only turned around, but she also quickly abandoned her duties as a bridesmaid on the wedding stage in order to greet him.

"Good to see you," she smiled shyly, even as she rather self-consciously tucked a wispy strand of hair behind her ear and ran the other hand through her flowing mane to make sure it was tidy. She had desperately hoped to see Rohinton at the wedding; and here he was at long last, after months of relentless praying and restless waiting. Was it a beautiful dream or was the person, whose thoughts had been sneakily creeping into her consciousness despite her best efforts to keep them at bay, actually standing in front of her?

"My goodness! What have you done to your hair?" asked he, sounding incredulous.

"Why? You don't like it?" asked she, very tentatively.

"I love it! I'd no idea that your hair was that long. But why have you been hiding the tumbling brown mass in a tight plait?"

"Because my mother likes me to wear my hair in a plait. It's only when I'm in Delhi that I occasionally let my hair down."

"In that case, you should visit Delhi more often sans your strict mother."

The suggestion did not sound as audacious and outrageous as it would have sounded had it been uttered by any other person; but as things currently stood, the person uttering the words could do no wrong in Ellora's eyes and therefore, nothing said by him sounded in any way amiss to the smitten teenager.

"When did you arrive?" she heard herself asking, her eyes furtively looking for Aditi who, she was glad to note, was sitting next to her mother, participating in a ritual. Everyone was engrossed in watching the fascinating rituals taking place under the floral canopy. The whole procedure would probably take only a few minutes, but Ellora was glad to have those few minutes alone with Rohinton without any distraction.

"I arrived just now, but now that I'm here, I'm planning to remain as long as you want me to," said he, fixing her with a gaze that once again made her heart skip a beat. And at the same time, she felt a surge of happiness in her lurching heart; happiness tinged with anxiety, because the moments were quickly ticking away.

"Will you be attending the reception this evening?" She hesitantly asked, even as she noted that Rohinton looked very handsome in the light blue silk *kurta-pajama* he was wearing.

"Well, I've another wedding invitation, but I've a good mind to skip the other one and party with my friends."

"Good idea," said Ellora, beaming with joy. Then, suddenly remembering that she had not yet congratulated Rohinton on his successful debut, she hurriedly added, "But before I forget, let me congratulate you for making such a brilliant debut."

"Did you watch all the matches?"

"Not all, but as many as I could. I couldn't watch the second one because I had my biology practical exam on the same day."

"That's probably the reason we lost by seven wickets, not to mention my own dismal performance on that unlucky day," he said a bit ruefully and then abruptly changed the topic. "But never mind. Let's talk about you instead. So, how are you? How did your board exams go?"

"I think I did fairly well in most subjects, except physics. That paper was very tough. I dread physics."

"I, on the other hand, dreaded bio in school," confessed Rohinton.

"But why? Bio is such an easy subject."

"I could never mug up all those complex Latin names, but I enjoyed the lab hours. Our biology teacher once gave us pond water sample for analysis. I remember seeing long green threads wriggling under the microscope. I'm forgetting their name...."

"Spirogyra?" suggested Ellora.

"Correct, spirogyra. Such fascinating bright green filaments! Just like the ones I'm seeing now."

"You're seeing spirogyras? How's that possible? There's no pond or pool around."

"But I can see two green pools teeming with spirogyras, said Rohinton, gazing into her eyes."

"Don't tell me you have telescopic and microscopic vision like Superman," laughed Ellora. "So tell me, where are these eutrophic pools teeming with spirogyras?"

She was purposely pretending not to have understood what Rohinton actually meant by 'two green pools.' She had read scores of romantic novels in which the beautiful heroine's eyes were described as 'clear blue pools.'

Indeed, the entire setting was so much like the descriptions in some of her favourite romantic novels with the lush, blooming garden, the rose pergola, her own lovely lavender dress and the fine-looking young man, who though not quite tall or dark, was still very handsome and suave. For the seventeen-year-old Ellora, who had secretly been infatuated with Rohinton for over two years now, it was like her ultimate romantic fantasy coming true, except for one disconcerting fact: there were too many unwanted people and intrusive elements in an otherwise perfect romantic setting. It bothered her slightly that even while he was talking to her, Rohinton's eyes were wandering everywhere. They were currently locked with the eyes of a slim and sensuous woman standing a few feet away, who in turn, was looking and smiling at him in a manner that seemed objectionable to Ellora.

Under the rose covered podium, the rituals were about to get over. Aditi and Roshan were waiting for the purohit's green signal to leave the stage. It was quite evident that Ellora's private moments with Rohinton were about to be over very soon. Therefore, despite feeling shy, she forced herself to look up and meet Rohinton's gaze rather boldly, knowing very well that her slightly flirtatious act was bound to elicit more exhilarating praise. She was already drunk on his compliments and the resultant delirium was kind of addictive.

"You mean to say nobody has ever told you that your eyes are like green pools?" asked he, gazing into her eyes with open admiration.

"Well, they're green pools, all right, but slightly muddy ones. Don't you think?"

This, of course, was Roshan. Only someone with his wacky sense of humour could ruin a perfectly romantic moment by making an utterly idiotic comment.

"When did you arrive?" This was Aditi, who purposely ignored the comments she just overheard.

"I came about ten minutes ago. Since you two were busy with the rituals, I decided to abduct your friend and have her exclusively to myself."

"So I notice," said Aditi rather dryly, not looking too pleased. Then turning to Ellora, she reprovingly added, "At least you could have informed me before taking off so suddenly with your abductor. You're one of the bridesmaids and were required to perform certain duties."

Roshan the clown gave an amused chuckle to humour his recently acquired step-sister. He then cleverly tried to change the topic by drawing Aditi's attention to their recent conversation.

"Rohinton says Ellora's eyes are like green pools and I say they're green pools alright, but slightly muddy ones. What's your verdict?"

"Highly muddy ones, considering you can hardly see the greens," came the curt reply.

"Aditi must be hungry. She's at her curt best when hungry," said Ellora, making an effort to smile at her snappy friend.

"I'm not being curt; I'm just being brutally honest. Your eyes have more browns than greens and therefore, I can't agree more with Roshan. If your eyes have to be regarded as green pools, the adjective muddy must qualify the phrase, so what if the word 'muddy' somewhat soils the phrase and spoils the praise?" said Aditi with her characteristic shrugging of the shoulders.

"Do you always bully your sweet and docile friend in this manner?" asked Rohinton, suddenly wanting to protect Ellora from Aditi's unwarranted attack. He then added, "If you ask me, the browns in her eyes only enhance their greenness."

"You must be eyeing those pools very carefully and exploring them very deeply to be able to unearth the handful of green algae hidden below heaps of brown mud," came the sharp retort.

"I think Ellora is right. You're hungry and therefore angry, so let's go and eat something before you cut all of us down to our respective sizes with your cutting curtness," said Rohinton with a smile.

No sooner had he finished speaking that a group of boys came running and surrounded Rohinton, jostling and nudging each other to claim their territories near the budding cricket star. A bevy of besotted young women also flocked around him, all vying for his attention. Soon, they were surrounded by several photographers, who hurriedly started clicking pictures of Rohinton with his young fans.

"He's clearly enjoying this," thought Ellora, as she quietly watched Rohinton signing autographs, posing for pictures and responding to the coquettish comments of his female fans with obvious delight and playful remarks.

"Don't worry, he won't be hounded so badly during the evening reception, where there will be many other stars to share the limelight with him. Many of the invitees are celebrities in their own right, so hopefully, the photographers and the autograph hunters will leave Rohinton alone," reassured Roshan with his routine wink.

****

Chapter 18

April, 1995, Delhi

Indeed, the evening reception held at a five-star hotel was a star-studded affair. Ellora and Aditi recognized an ageing film star and a couple of popular television stars. There were also some well-known designers, writers and politicians. All important enough to be sought after by dozens of photographers covering the event. Rohinton, too, was in demand, but as Roshan had rightly predicted, despite looking dapper and star-like in a black suit, he was not hounded as badly as he had been in the morning.

"It's a good thing, because now we can chat peacefully without being interrupted every now and then by intrusive fans," thought Ellora somewhat selfishly. She herself, on the other hand, was attracting more attention than she had bargained for.

"Are you the model who wore the showstopper sari for Nikita Beri's fashion show last week?" a very well-preserved and attractive middle-aged woman stopped her midway to ask. Ellora was too baffled by the unexpected question to give an answer right away and the woman, before she moved away, smilingly patted her back and said, "Never mind. But you do look like a show stopper in that gorgeous sari."

And to think that Ellora had not even been sure, if it would be the right kind of sari to wear for the evening party! Having seen the beautiful designer saris that Amrita Auntie and Aditi were going to wear, she had feared that her own Banarasi silk sari would be extremely old-fashioned for the reception.

This had been Ellora's main concern right from day one. What was she going to wear during the evening reception? Her limited stock of eveningwear consisted mainly of traditional silk saris and she knew that some of those garish saris would make her stick out like a vividly bandaged sore thumb among the trendily dressed crème de la crème of Delhi. That was why she had summoned Aditi to seek her opinion.

"What do you think of this one?" she had unfolded her most expensive sari before her friend. Spread on the bed, the intricately woven material had shimmered like the rippling waves of the ocean reflecting the last rays of the setting sun.

"Wow! That looks hot." Aditi had excitedly exclaimed.

"Do you really think so?" Ellora had asked, not quite sure if Aditi was serious or was just pulling her leg.

"To be frank, I don't like orange much, but this is such a beautiful shade; kind of sunset orange. And I simply love that rich gold border and those tiny gold flowers scattered all over. But show me the blouse you're planning to wear with this," Aditi had demanded.

"No, this won't do," Aditi had at once delivered her curt verdict upon seeing the matching blouse.

"Those long sleeves and that modest neckline will make you look like a behenji turned bahu from the congested alleys of Vijaypur. You need something bold and vibrant to liven up this old-fashioned sari."

"But I don't have any other blouse. What am I going to do?" Ellora had panicked. The prospect of going to her mother's favourite New Smart Tailors (who operated from a tiny hole-in-the-wall tailoring shop) always gave her panic-attacks. The elderly tailor, who was neither new nor smart, had a knack of turning even the trendiest materials into something dowdy and ill-fitting.

"You've a problem? Leave it to Diti!" Aditi had announced with a courteous bow before adding, "She's ready for anything. Anything short of assassinating your aunt. Diti will help you find a chic blouse for your not-so-chic Banarasi sari."

"Diti?"

"The A in my name, I should've added for your guidance, is silent."

"As in P G Wodehouse's Leave it to Psmith?"

"You're absolutely right and utterly bright, Miss Tube-light."

Tube-light was Aditi's favourite nickname for Ellora whenever she was slow on the uptake. But right now, Aditi was more focused on finding a solution to her friend's problem.

"You know what? Next Saturday, I'm off to Delhi with my Mom for trousseau shopping. I'll show your sari to Nikita, the designer who is designing Mom's bridal lehenga-choli. I'm sure she can design something trendy and hot to liven up this dated sari."

"Splendid," Ellora had said with a big, bright smile. "But only if you let me pay for the designer blouse."

"Ripping! I'll be toddling along, then. See you later. Toodle-oo," said Aditi, switching to Wodehousian slang, her current fad.

"Why are you in such a hurry to leave? Let's go to the garden with Babu Shona."

Babu Shona, who had cocked his head quizzically the moment his name had been mentioned, enthusiastically supported the proposal by placing one podgy and persuasive paw in Aditi's lap. Despite being almost ten, he had not lost his puppy-like playfulness.

* * *

True to her promise, Aditi came back from Delhi with what she considered to be the perfect blouse for Ellora's sari. And that was why she was furious when her friend told her in no uncertain terms that she wouldn't be caught dead in that skimpy thing.

"Why the hell not?" Aditi had demanded to know, making

no attempt to conceal her mounting anger.

"Don't you see? It has straps in place of sleeves and is almost backless. Have you ever seen me wearing something so daring and immodest?"

"Immodest my foot. You're not going to roam around the bazaars of Vijaypur wearing this *choli*, so don't give me all this nonsense."

Of course, all that bullying and brainwashing by her best friend had worked, for here she was, wearing a skimpy, deep purple blouse embellished with heavy *zari* embroidery. There was no doubt that the ultra-modern contrasting blouse had breathed completely new life into her old Banarasi. Ellora could see why the designer blouse made from less than a yard of material had carried a price-tag that was more than the price of her six yard sari.

* * *

"You're like dusk draped in sunset." Aditi paid her this unusual compliment, when Ellora finished draping the sari.

"Did you just call me dusk? Is this orange sari making me appear duskier?" asked a considerably alarmed Ellora.

"Come on, Ellora. What's wrong with being dusky? It's better than being blandly wheatish any day. But if the word dusk bothers you, let me rephrase my praise," saying this Aditi took a few steps back and inspected her friend from head to toe from her new vantage point.

"Wow! What a transformation! Those luminous shoulders and that burnished bronzed back of yours are meant to be displayed in blouses sans sleeves and backs. You remind me of an antique copper statue in an ancient temple; a copper statue draped in gold."

"Thank you," said Ellora. She once again inspected herself in the full-length mirror. Everything about her was aglow with radiance, from her honey-brown skin, to her expertly piled up hair, to her brown-green eyes. She was pleased that someone as critical as Aditi thought she looked like a temple statue. Her dancer mother was also often compared to the statues of ancient temples. But then, was Aditi really paying her a compliment, or was she referring to her tanned skin by calling her a copper statue?

"Trust Aditi to pay ambiguous compliments," thought Ellora, as she finished scrutinizing herself in the mirror.

Some other compliments she received that evening were quite unambiguous, though. Total strangers stopped her to tell her how gorgeous she was looking. Even Roshan, who hardly ever paid attention to what his female friends were wearing, noticed her sari and came up with a flattering quip.

"You look like a lush rainforest on fire," he grinningly told her.

"Stop making me sound like a slash-and-burn agricultural field," Ellora smilingly protested.

"You certainly seem all set to set the world on fire." This was Rohinton who, to Ellora's utter delight, was looking at her with open admiration.

"Well, the fire won't last for long, if this lush rainforest is worth her torrential downpour," Aditi was quick to comment, tongue in cheek.

"My dear step-sis, you just poured some very cold water and dampened a very hot compliment," said Roshan, with his habitual wink.

The party was well under way with many of the celebrity guests making their token appearance to greet the newly-wed couple. Amrita Auntie looked stunning in a burgundy and gold creation, but Balraj Uncle, instead of looking like her handsome consort, looked more like her personal body-guard in a shiny black suit that, according to Aditi, was an Armani. "The Balding Mughal in a Shimmering Sherwani is back to being Hercule Poirot in Shiny Armani," thought Ellora.

"A penny for your thoughts," teased Rohinton, interrupting

her flow of thought.

"I was admiring Amrita Auntie. Isn't she a vision in that beautiful sari?" she asked quickly, in an attempt to cover up her wicked thoughts.

"Is she? Well, I didn't notice her or anyone else, because I've my eyes fixed only on one lovely vision in this entire gathering."

With that explicit and uninhibited statement, Rohinton had made his intentions very clear. He was not going to beat around the bush. Aware that he only had a couple of minutes to say what he wanted to say to her, he came to the point without further ado. "I want to meet you alone." There was an urgency in his tone, as if, meeting Ellora alone was a matter of life and death to him.

"How's that possible?" she whispered, very much mindful of the fact that their private conversation was not really private.

"Let's make it possible. Let's meet tomorrow morning. I'll see you outside the house at six. All you've to do is get up early and take a walk to the main gate. I'll be waiting for you there."

"Impossible. What if Aditi gets up? What am I going to tell her?"

"Tell her the truth. She's just your friend and not your local guardian. You don't need her consent to go out with a friend. You're eighteen for God's sake." He sounded impatient.

"Seventeen. I'm not yet eighteen," corrected Ellora.

"Okay seventeen. So what? You're going to legally be an adult very soon, so you might as well start behaving like one. Either we meet tomorrow, or we wait for another year to pass before seeing each other again, so decide now."

"You're asking me to choose between the devil and the deep blue sea," said Ellora, her tone slightly coquettish.

"Choose this known devil and you won't regret your choice," said Rohinton with a teasing smile.

"Let me think about it," said Ellora, not quite happy about acting so hard-to-get.

"What do you have to think about?" Aditi, who had just joined them had overheard only the last sentence.

"I want Ellora to accompany me to my net practice tomorrow. I'm going on a long tour and am not too sure when I'm going to meet her again. That's why I want to spend some time with her," said Rohinton. He then paused for a moment before adding, "Alone." He certainly was in no mood for beating around the bush.

"Do you want to go?" Aditi looked at Ellora with an expression that was difficult to gauge, but was quite unsettling nevertheless. What was it about Aditi's tone that disturbed her? Was it disapproval or was it resentment? How could her best friend act so censorious at a time when she herself was feeling delirious with joy?

It was almost as if Aditi could read her friend's mind, because instead of waiting for her to respond, she abruptly turned towards Rohinton and said rather sharply, "Take her to your net practice by all means. She's all yours."

The tense moment came to an end when Roshan returned with two pleasantly plump young women, both with beaming smiles and adoring glances reserved exclusively for Rohinton.

"Rohinton, meet my friends Anthology and Good-line. They are dying to meet you," introduced Roshan.

"Ro--sha--an," protested one of them petulantly, pouting her plump lips for good measure.

"Well, Kavita and Surekha, if you insist upon the original names," said Roshan, shrugging his massive shoulders.

"If you're bent on distorting my name, at least do it accurately. The English translation of my name is Poem and not Anthology," said the pouting young woman as she pouted some more.

"But Kavita, don't you think you look more like a

voluminous collection of poems rather than a thin little solitary poem?"

"Enough Roshan," reprimanded his step-sister in a tone that warned him not to go too far with his jokes about people's names. However, the other young woman called Surekha did not quite mind Roshan's brand of humour. She egged him on by saying, "But then Roshan, I'm also not exactly like a line, no matter how good a line my parents thought I'd grow up to be, when they named me Surekha."

"Well, Surekha, I'm afraid, Euclid certainly didn't have you in mind when he defined a line as length without breadth."

"Roshan, now you're indeed crossing the line," warned Aditi in mock anger.

"It's okay, dear. Being with Roshan has its merits and demerits," said Surekha with a sweet smile and then added, "I didn't get your name......"

"It's Aditi."

"Aditi. That's a beautiful name. Good that your mother didn't give you a name that your brand-new stepbrother can distort."

"She's Boundless, but believes in binding others with her stringent terms and conditions," came the translation promptly with enlightening footnotes.

Ellora was too immersed in her own world to pay much attention to this friendly banter, although she heard enough of it to feel relieved that her own name had been kept out of the discussion. She did not want to be called a cave when she was feeling like a bubbly brook; a boundless, bouncy, bubbly, brook, all set to flow freely. However, she forcibly steered her wandering mind back to the on-going conversation.

Kavita, the voluminous Anthology, was talking to Rohinton. It was obvious that the young woman was desperate to have his attention. She was looking at him in a way that seemed objectionably flirtatious to Ellora. Thankfully, Rohinton had eyes only for her. Every now and then, even as he pretended to listen to Kavita's playful prattle, he glanced in her direction and smiled. It was during one such moment that Ellora made up her mind not to keep him waiting at the gate the next morning.

****

Chapter 19

April, 1996, Delhi

Ellora woke up quite early and got ready very quietly, taking great care not to wake Aditi. She was therefore, taken aback when her friend half opened her eyes just before she was about to step out to say, "Be good," before going back to sleep.

Outside, the world seemed up-and-about despite the early hour. The newspaper had already been delivered, a cleaner was briskly sweeping the front driveway, two gardeners were tending the flowerbeds and the gate-keeper was sitting on a chair near the gate, absentmindedly puffing on a smouldering biri. Several early birds were chirping and hopping from branch to branch in search of fat, juicy worms.

Ellora did not have to walk up to the gate. Rohinton was waiting for her on the covered porch overlooking the front lawn. He got up to greet her, looking sleepy but happy. He was wearing a navy-blue polo shirt with a pair of blue jeans that, Ellora noticed, made his athletic legs appear longer and leaner.

"I'll go and get my car. I'd to park it in the backyard last night because there was no place in front."

"I'll come with you," said Ellora, conscious that one of the gardeners had stopped watering the plants and was watching them with frank curiosity.

The two of them started walking down the concrete path adjoining the compound wall.

"Didn't you go home last night?" asked Ellora, trying to match Rohinton's long strides.

"By the time we dropped some of Roshan's friends to their faraway homes, it was already past three, so I crashed here for the night with Roshan snoring next to me."

"Did you manage to get some sleep?" asked Ellora, still struggling to keep pace with her athletic companion. She desperately wished that she had had the good sense of getting into something more comfortable than the high-heeled sandals she was wearing this morning.

"No, I couldn't sleep at all. But it was the thought of meeting you in the morning rather than Roshan's snoring that kept me awake," said Rohinton, looking deep into Ellora's eyes. Something about his looks and smile told Ellora what might come next, so she quickly tried to divert his attention by asking, "How far is your car parked from here?"

"We're almost there, but if you're not comfortable walking in those high heels, we can take a shorter route," saying this, he led her to a gravel path that cut diagonally across the yard to reach the back entrance.

There were trees all around, shading the paths, shedding leaves and shuddering gently every time a light breeze blew past them.

"So, when are we going to your net practice?"

"Net practice?" Rohinton looked so amused that Ellora wondered if it was a silly question to ask. Seeing her confused and hurt expression, he quickly added, "There's no net practice today. I just made that up on the spur of the moment last night. I've a better place in mind; we'll go to a quiet little cafe that serves excellent coffee."

"Sounds good." Ellora said it quite cheerfully to hide her disappointment. She had been looking forward to accompanying him to his net practice and being introduced to some of the famous cricketers playing for Delhi. And in her heart of hearts, she had also nurtured another secret hope; that on their way back from practice, Rohinton would take her home to meet his parents. However, now that she knew they were going to a quiet little coffee-shop, she quite looked forward to it. There were so many things she wanted to know about Rohinton and so many things she wished to share with him; it was probably not a bad idea to go to a place where they could sit and chat peacefully without having to whisper to each other.

The morning breeze was cool and fragrant. Ellora inhaled the scented air and tried to identify the source of the elusive floral scent coming from somewhere deeper in the garden.

"Are you looking for something?" asked Rohinton, watching her puzzled and wide-eyed expression with delighted amusement.

"I'm trying to find the source of this delicious whiff; it's so intriguingly familiar. I'm sure I know its origin, but just can't put my finger on it."

"Do you want to follow the trail and trace the source?" asked Rohinton, slightly amused by his lovely companion's inquisitiveness about something as intangible and vague as a familiar fragrance.

"Why not? Let's try."

They started walking towards the deeper, more secluded parts of the garden. Ellora stopped when she found three bauhinia trees bearing lilac flowers.

"Ah! Now I know why the scent seemed so familiar. We've so many of these bauhinia trees in the municipal garden in Vijaypur. I should've known," said she, closing her eyes in an attempt to inhale the heady perfume. Dressed in a denim skirt and a frilly white blouse, she looked very different from the sensuous seductress of last night; there was no trace of any make up on her face and yet it was aglow with the dewy freshness of youth.

"You look like a schoolgirl in a skirt-blouse," said Rohinton, not quite sure how to pay the enchanting, childlike woman an appropriate compliment.

"But I AM a schoolgirl. My board examination result is not out yet," said she with a sweet smile, even as her eyes darted across the branches, following the movements of a purple sunbird flitting from flower to flower in search of nectar. Then, as the foraging sunbird flew away, her wandering mind was brought back to what Rohinton was saying.

"What I meant was, you look very different today. I've never seen you in a skirt and blouse before."

"I wear them quite often when I'm in Delhi. They're part of my Delhi wardrobe," informed Ellora with a broad smile.

"Delhi wardrobe? And what's that?"

"It's a term Aditi has coined for the set of clothes that I wear exclusively in Delhi. In Vijaypur, I avoid wearing short skirts and sleeveless dresses. It's a small town and people talk if you expose your legs or arms. But here I'm free to wear what I want. My uncle who lives in Frankfurt always brings suitcases full of clothes for me and that's how I've a collection that makes up my Delhi wardrobe."

"I see," said a puzzled Rohinton, not quite able to see the logic of having two different sets of clothes for two different cities. Essentially a Delhi boy from a westernized family, it was beyond his comprehension why one couldn't wear short skirts in a small town.

"What's wrong with wearing short skirts?" he asked, covertly glancing at Ellora's fitted denim skirt to see if it was really short. He found nothing wrong with its length. In fact, he quite liked the fact that it stopped short of her knees and exposed her legs. Not many girls known to him personally had such long and shapely legs.

Ellora saw him staring at her legs and blushed. He saw her blushing and smiled tenderly, gently putting an arm around her shoulders.

In the years to come, the memory of what happened next and how one thing led to another was quite blurred and blotted out, but the memory of what eventually followed was something that could not be blurred, blotted out, erased or wished away in a hurry.

Emboldened by the fact that Ellora did not object to his placing his arm around her shoulder, Rohinton went one step further. He pulled her closer to him, wrapping his arms around her waist. She looked at him, quite alarmed but not quite surprised. He did not give her a chance to resist or say anything by kissing her on the lips without further ado. At first, it was just a gentle brushing of lips, but soon it turned deep and probing, his tongue making darting forays into her mouth. She stood still, not sure how to stop Rohinton from kissing her in that strange, intrusive manner. Nothing she had read, seen, or discussed had prepared her for this kind of deep, rough, and wet kiss. Wasn't she supposed to like it? Wasn't she supposed to moan with pleasure? Wasn't she supposed to melt into his arms? Then why was she so desperate to get out of them?

Unaware and unconcerned about her lack of response and her passive resistance, Rohinton continued kissing her, even as he led her to a nearby garden bench and made her sit on it. He sat down beside her, his one hand caressing her back and the other gliding down her shoulder and throat to reach her neckline. He ran his fingers over the lacy edge of her blouse for some time before bending down to start kissing her throat.

"You are so delicious, Ellora. You feel so good. I want to feel and touch every bit of you," saying this, he kissed her collarbone, licking the hollow above and caressing the soft contours below it. She gasped, startled that a man's touch could do this to her. She knew that she could not let him continue, yet a part of her wanted him to continue. However, when Rohinton started unbuttoning her blouse and his fingers started making illicit forays into the parts of her body where nobody had ever touched her before, she knew she had to stop him.

The moments did not last too long, but they changed her life forever. She was not able to live them down, not for a very long time at least.

And to think that it was just a kiss! Or was it just a kiss? Rohinton certainly had more things in mind than just a few passionate kisses. However, whichever way one looked at it, the fact remained that it was Ellora's first kiss. And in the years to come, her only kiss.

Years later, when the pain associated with the memories of that kiss had lost its poignancy and Ellora could bring herself to recollect and relive some of those moments, she could finally recall the incident, at least in part, without being overwhelmed by a sense of unbearable anguish and shame. At long last, she was able to analyse her own reactions at being kissed so suddenly by someone she had secretly admired for years. She could recall how stunned, confused and overwhelmed she had been by the unexpectedness of that kiss. She could also recall that her first impulse had been to push Rohinton away. And yet, instead of doing that, she had passively submitted, letting him kiss her, at first tentatively and gently and then very passionately and deeply, without offering much resistance. It was only when he had proceeded to unbutton her blouse and began caressing her breasts that she forcibly pushed him away.

"Why hadn't she pushed him away right away? Why had she waited until his kisses grew too passionate, too invasive and too smothering for comfort?" These were some of the disturbing questions that had haunted her for years. There were also unanswered questions that were unanswerable and were therefore promptly bottled up the moment they popped into her head. Questions such as: had the kiss really been all that unexpected and unwelcome? Hadn't she often lain awake at night, dreaming about being kissed by Rohinton? Hadn't she secretly hoped to be kissed by him, when they took that path leading to a secluded part of the garden?

The years might have blunted the poignancy of the pain, but they had not reversed the guilty verdict given by all those who were entitled to judge her and also by those not entitled to do so. She had been guilty of harbouring passion that good girls from good family were not supposed to have, at least not until they were respectably married.

Yet, one thing she was able to do without suffering from any pangs of guilt or shame was to acknowledge the fact that the kiss itself had been rather disappointing and had, in no way, fulfilled any of the expectations that she had from her first kiss. These expectations had been built up over years of reading novels in which the heroine (more often than not, a stunningly beautiful demure damsel) invariably found herself in the ever so strong arms of the ruggedly handsome hero.

And that was why she had waited with bated breath like a fool for all her unrealistic expectations to come true. She had waited for the world to come to a standstill, for the ground under her feet to start trembling, for a streak of fire to run through her body, for lightning to strike, for sparks to fly and for the air to crackle with their heated chemistry. She had waited for any celestial or earthly signs that would signify that the two of them were born to love each other. Unfortunately or fortunately, nothing earth-shaking took place, except her heart beating too fast and her limbs turning too wobbly to support her.

There was nothing magical, blissful, or breath-taking about the kiss itself. If anything it was smothering and even slightly nauseating. It was too wet, too fleshy, too physical and too carnal an act to uplift it into something soulful, celestial and blissful. In fact, the act reminded her of the intrusive probing of the delicate bauhinia petals by the purple sunbird; the same tiny bird that, just a few minutes ago, had been flitting from branch to branch in search of nectar.

Were her expectations too high or was Rohinton a clumsy kisser? Or had she been rushed into a very passionate and a very demanding kiss a bit too soon? Had Rohinton ruined the moment by touching her body in ways that made her feel violated and cheap?

Ellora had no way of knowing because there were no more kisses to compare it to. For all intents and purposes, her first kiss remained her only kiss in the years to come.

****

Chapter 20

May, 1996, Delhi

The pictures were published nearly a month after their kissing and cuddling had been caught on camera. Altogether, there were five published photographs, all of them high-resolution, obviously taken by a professional photographer.

Captioned 'Playing the Field Instead of Practicing his Fielding', one of the photographs showed Rohinton grinning broadly, as he stood between Aditi and Ellora, one of his arms wrapped around Aditi's waist, the other resting possessively around Ellora's bare shoulder.

The second picture had also been taken during the evening reception. Titled 'Clean-bowled by the Bold Maiden,' it showed Rohinton gazing at Ellora with undisguised admiration and Ellora gazing back with equal ardour and adoration in her eyes. There was no physical contact between the two and yet it seemed like an intensely intimate moment. The camera had captured it all: their nascent attraction, their budding feelings, their sizzling chemistry and the scintillating desire in their eyes aglow with feverish anticipation and raw passion.

There was only one word to describe Ellora in that picture: sexy. From her piled up mass of brown hair, to her daringly uncovered back, to her exposed collarbones and luminous shoulders, to her large, liquid eyes, everything about her was radiant, lush, sensuous and alluring.

In the third picture, Ellora and Rohinton were seen walking side-by-side in a path shaded by trees. Despite having been clicked from a considerable distance, the shot had captured every detail of their happy faces with the help of a powerful telephoto lens.

The fourth and fifth pictures were undoubtedly the most telling and incriminating of all. Captioned, 'The Lovebirds caught Red-handed', the pictures, though quite grainy and indistinct, had clearly caught a young man and a young woman in the act of passionate kissing and touching. It was not difficult to guess (particularly after seeing the second photograph) who the young man and the young woman in the pictures were.

Had it not been for the Indian cricket team's disappointing defeat in the triangular One Day International in Sharjah, the article would have died a natural death, without anyone being the wiser. Nobody would have come to know about Rohinton Merchant's secret rendezvous in a backyard with a girl called Ellora Chatterjee. However, the Indian team's defeat meant that the fans back home needed culprits to point their accusatory fingers at. And young Rohinton, not yet an established player in the team, proved to be a convenient scapegoat.

While most newspapers cited Rohinton Merchant's sloppy fielding and his lacklustre batting as two of the main reasons for India's humiliating defeat at the hands of arch rival Pakistan and for losing in the crucial finals against South Africa, it was a magazine called Scoops from Delhi's Belly that published a sensational, no-holds-barred inside story, painting the young batsman as a flamboyant Casanova with a colourful personal life. Written with the sole purpose of maligning Rohinton Merchant and questioning his selection in the Indian team, it described him as a skirt-chaser more serious about chasing women and playing the field rather than playing serious cricket for his country. There were accompanying pictures to illustrate the point, pictures taken just days before the start of the Pepsi Cup tournament, pictures that spoke more eloquently than the proverbial thousand words.

The year was 1996. The world had yet to become a cyber-village where news and rumours sprouted wings at the click of a button to reach far and wide. Nevertheless, this was no ordinary news item. This particular story had all the ingredients that make stories travel fast and reach far-and-wide; ingredients such as youth, glamour, cricket and the whiff of a brewing scandal. In a country where cricket is a national obsession, the story about a newsworthy young cricketer neglecting the game to play around with a beautiful, sensuous teenage girl was bound to make news. Everyone wanted to know more about the private life of this young cricketer who, despite making a brilliant debut, had failed to live up to their expectations. They all wanted to know why the promising young batsman had failed so miserably to deliver on his promise and that too at a time when it had really mattered.

Needless to say, any published item that explained Rohinton's poor performance during this cricket tournament could not have gone unnoticed for long. Not when the item was accompanied by such sensational and telling pictures.

Even though the story first appeared in Scoops from Delhi's Belly (a relatively unknown tabloid with low circulation and lower credibility), it was soon picked up by several reputed newspapers and magazines that republished the pictures and blurred Ellora's face. It was pointless blurring that failed to prevent the resulting blot on her reputation. A blot that would not fade away in the years to come.

****

Chapter 21

Bad news, they say, travels fast but in this case, the news travelled at its own leisurely pace before reaching its destination.

Roshan saw the article and the accompanying pictures as soon as they were printed, but decided to keep quiet, fervently hoping that the entire unpleasant thing would blow over without anyone getting any whiff of the brewing stink. He blamed himself for the entire mess; he had been the one to invite a freelance photographer (a friend's friend) to stay at their farmhouse during the four-day wedding celebrations. He had wanted him to take candid shots of the wedding guests, particularly his friends. Little had he known that the photographer would click candid pictures of some very private moments between two of his friends and sell those scandalous pictures to a second-rate magazine.

Unfortunately, the stink did not blow over, nor did it remain contained. No sooner did some reputable dailies and periodicals get a whiff of it than they printed a watered down version of the story along with photoshopped versions of the shocking photographs. They, of course, had a name to maintain and therefore, took precautions to protect the reputation of the girl by obscuring her face behind a grid of squares.

To some extent, they did succeed in hiding the face of the strikingly beautiful teenager seen with Rohinton Merchant in the pictures. Thanks to the digital manipulation, Ellora's pixelated face was not recognizable. For many, she remained an anonymous mystery girl responsible for distracting a very promising cricketer from delivering on a very crucial promise of bringing home coveted cups.

It was not until much later that the archived news item (which had died a natural death) was resurrected and the larger-than-life posters of the original photographs splashed all around the town.

****

Chapter 22

July 1996, Vijaypur

Who could have imagined that things would turn so nasty and vindictive? It must be admitted though, that things had never quite been pleasant from the beginning.

Joining Vijaypur Government College had been Hobson's choice for Ellora. Unlike Aditi, who was all set to join a private college in Delhi, she had no other option except to join the only science college in town.

Getting admission in two different cities implied that the best friends would no longer be together, but neither Ellora nor Aditi was overtly upset over this temporary separation. It was just a matter of a few weeks and then, both of them would be joining the All India Medical Institute in Delhi. Such was their confidence in their pre-medical entrance exam results that neither of them had any misgivings about not getting admission in the prestigious institute.

However, when it came to going to her new co-educational college without the reassuring presence of Aditi by her side, Ellora was a bundle of nerves. All her confidence would evaporate the moment she stepped inside the gates of Vijaypur Government College. Nothing in her sheltered school-life had prepared her for the kind of uncouth male students she would have to encounter there; the louts who greeted her approach with wolf-whistles, catcalls and suggestive comments or broke into some cheap Hindi song, proclaiming their undying love for her.

It was not that Ellora had never been teased before. She had received her share of undesirable male attention, particularly on the streets of Delhi, where they had often been followed around by depraved young men, making lewd passes and singing vulgar songs but then, such incidents had always taken place when she was with Aditi who knew how to handle those pathetic roadside Romeos. Her hands-on-the-hips confrontational posture along with a thundering "Kya hai?" was intimidating enough to induce those lazy loafers into backing off, but not before they had fired some more crude remarks as a parting shot. After all, they had to save face in front of the curious bystanders, who invariably gathered around them at such times to watch the whole drama with gaping mouths and unconcealed glee.

Unlike her firebrand friend, Ellora could never bring herself to challenge her tormenters in college. She did not possess Aditi's hot-tempered, reckless, devil-may-care confrontational attitude towards those who dared to overstep their boundaries and step on her toes. In fact, Ellora was just the opposite. Faint-hearted and meek, she woke up every morning with a sinking heart because she dreaded the prospect of coming face-to-face with her persecutors in the campus.

It was strange the way they invariably materialized as soon as she entered the main gate. It was as if they had been lying in wait for her. They greeted her arrival with loud claps and whistles. One of them, a tall, burly, moustachioed guy called Ginger, who was much older than most other students, invariably threw himself on the ground and melodramatically prostrated himself at her feet, forcing her to step back and walk as far away as she could get.

Unfortunately, there was no walking away from those louts. They followed her around everywhere, singing a popular song from the late seventies.

"Dil ke tukde tukde karke, muskurake chal diye." You break my heart into pieces and are walking away with a smile on your lips. It was the burly guy, the leader of the pack, who

led the chorus. Walking a few steps behind her, he sang the lines with great gusto, pausing briefly after each line to emit a deep sigh like a heartbroken lover.

Of course, there was no smile on Ellora's lips those days. In fact, her face was constantly wrought with fear, shame and mortification at being humiliated so publicly in broad daylight in front of so many students.

When they were not singing *"Dil ke tukde tukde kar ke..."* they belted out *"Tu cheez badi hai mast mast,"* that translated to: you're an intoxicating, sexy thing. It was another chartbuster that was more contemporary, more crass and more mortifying to Ellora's sensibilities. She had a strong urge to turn around and slap all those who were calling her an object of desire. But far from slapping her tormenters, she could not even bring herself to lodge a complaint against them with the college authorities.

If truth be told, Ellora blamed herself rather than her tormentors for her current plight. If those boys had singled her out for harassment, it had to be her own fault. There must have been some reason (reasons she could not figure out or fathom) for those hounding predators to have picked her as their pet prey. She must have done something to have caught their fancy. It was all her fault; she had brought it upon herself.

"It's all her fault. She's brought it upon herself." How many times had Ellora heard her mother's friends using this age-old refrain for all the young girls unfortunate enough to be teased by ruffians in the streets? It was for this very reason that she could not bring herself to tell her parents about the humiliating torture she was going through. How could she tell her mother about it, knowing how much it was going to embarrass her in front of her friends?

There was no one else to reach out to for advice or moral support. Ellora had never felt so helpless and so friendless before. The new girls in college maintained a safe distance from her. Even her school friends had started avoiding her. They did not wish to complicate their lives by associating with someone who had captured the attention of Ginger and his cronies. The guys were notorious; they all came to college to have fun and their main idea of having fun was to harass new students, particularly girls. Unfortunately, this year, they had singled out Ellora as their chosen target. Everyone felt sorry for her, but then, hadn't she brought it upon herself?

Ever since she had come back from the wedding in Delhi, something about Ellora had changed; her hair was no longer in tight plaits and her eyes were inexplicably larger and brighter than ever. Even her clothes were smarter, shorter and tighter, making her stand out among the new batch of students. How could anyone not spot this girl who looked so eye-catchingly different from the rest of them? "No, Ellora had certainly brought it upon herself," they all sombrely opined.

It was an unspoken rule in Vijaypur Government College that the newcomers had to walk with their eyes downcast. They were also supposed to dress in clothes that did not invite attention. Those who defied these unstated orders were inviting trouble and inviting Ginger's attention was trouble all right.

Already in his late-twenties, Ginger was in no hurry to leave college and join the family business of printing books, banners and brochures. He hated being inside those noisy, suffocating units. He would much rather be in the vast, open college grounds swarming with chicks he could ogle.

However, after spending nearly six years in Vijaypur Government College, Ginger was getting slightly tired of ogling and whistling at those boring, homely chicks. Thankfully, this year, things had improved, and how! There was this new girl in college, who not only inspired him to let out a long, low, appreciative whistle, but also compelled him to burst into silly love songs. Where had this girl been hiding all these years? Why hadn't he spotted her before?

Ellora was Ginger's chosen target; his new game bird to be

hunted for sport. When he was not openly declaring his love for her by singing film songs, he was stalking her quietly in the long corridors of the science department. He seemed to know Ellora's timetable by heart, for no sooner would her class be over, would she find him standing near the door, waiting for her to emerge. Her so-called friends would leave her side as soon as they saw him, making it easier for Ginger to follow her everywhere. When alone, he did not sing cheap songs, he preferred reciting Urdu couplets.

The fact that Ellora steadfastly ignored his overtures and refused to make any eye contact with him was not enough to deter him from his purposeful pursuit. However, after a few weeks of persistent chasing, he was beginning to get slightly tired of Ellora's frosty indifference. It irked him no end that she looked right through him as if he did not exist. Her cold unresponsiveness was beginning to try his patience.

One day, he accosted her in a deserted passageway. She was walking towards the chemistry lab located at the other end of a long corridor, when he suddenly appeared before her and blocked her way.

"Why do you treat me as if I'm invisible to you?" he asked in a tone that was pleading as well as demanding.

Ellora was petrified, but she tried to keep her composure by refusing to meet her persecutor's penetrating gaze.

Exasperated, Ginger grabbed her by the arm and demanded, "Why are you torturing me like this, my darling? Don't you realize how much pain you're causing me by acting as if I don't exist? Can't you see that I'm head over heels in love with you? " He was beginning to look like an aggrieved dog whose master had been ignoring him.

There was pin-drop silence following this shocking declaration. A horrified Ellora, her arm in the steely grip of her obsessive admirer, helplessly looked around her for help, but there was no one except the two of them in that long, dark passage. Not that she had expected anyone to come to her rescue, considering how everyone (even her so-called friends) tended to look away when Ginger stalked her regularly in the corridors and made those inappropriate passes at her.

"Look at me. Don't avoid my gaze." This was more of a command than a plea, but Ellora refused to comply, her eyes focussed firmly on the cement floor.

"I said lift your eyes and look at me," Ginger repeated his command, this time in a voice thundering and menacing enough for Ellora to comply.

"My my! What beautiful eyes, like two green pools. I want to drown in these deep pools." He promptly recited a cheap Urdu couplet in praise of her eyes.

Ellora was mad with rage. The reference to 'green pools' for her eyes took her back to another day, when Rohinton had used a similar expression. How dare this repugnant ruffian taint the cherished memory of that beautiful morning with his trashy praise?

Suddenly, standing in that dark and gloomy passageway, she was desperate for the sunny days she had left behind; the days when she, Aditi, Rohinton and Roshan had made a jolly foursome. How things had changed since then! The incongruity of her current plight hit her hard. She despised the lecherous lout leering at her gleefully and touching every part of her body with his dirty eyes. She felt tainted. She wanted to vomit. She wanted to spit on that loathsome grinning face. She tried to free her arm from Ginger's grip, but his fingers dug deeper into her flesh. She looked at him in anger, her eyes blazing with unconcealed contempt and brimming with unshed tears; tears she was forcibly holding back.

"You're angry. Thank God for that. At least I've managed to evoke some emotions in you. So what if it is only anger? Anger, as they say, is the first step towards falling in love." Saying this, he let go of Ellora's arm and instead took hold of her face, cupping it with both his palms. Then, lifting her chin with one finger, he cheekily asked, "Ellora, my darling, are you falling in love with me? Now come on! Don't be shy. Answer me, my love. Say that you love me, my precious, my sweet little angel, my shy little sweetheart."

The endearments did it. They made Ellora incensed enough to forget her fear. Shaking with rage and white with indignation, she used all her might to push away the hands defiling her face.

"You're pathetic! You're sick and you make me sick. I wouldn't look at someone like you even if you were the last man on this earth." She spat out the words furiously and with a shudder, as if the very thought of having to respond to someone so repugnant was unbearable. Then, without giving her stunned intimidator any chance to recover, she pushed him away with a force she had not known she possessed and started running, the click-clack of her heels echoing in the long corridor.

Ellora went home and made the call she had been thinking of making for some time now. She couldn't take it anymore. Things had gone beyond her endurance and she needed to talk about her harrying ordeal with someone who would understand her situation without being judgemental. Her first impulse was to tell her mother, but after giving it careful thought, she decided against it. Her mother would be mortified and she might even stop her from going to college. No, telling her mother was out of question.

Instead, she chose to make a long-distance call to Delhi. The phone rang a number of times before Rohinton finally answered it. Without giving her a chance to speak, he told her brusquely that he was busy and would call her later. Three excruciating days went by, but he never called. Finally, Ellora phoned Aditi and told her everything from start to finish.

* * *

It was easy to be prudent in hindsight. It was easy to conclude many years later that calling Aditi that afternoon had been a grave mistake. Everyone said so. They all pointed out that things would not have got so out of hand, if Aditi and her stepbrother had not come running to Vijaypur after receiving her phone call.

Once Ellora had made the phone call, things started moving too quickly for her to comprehend what was happening. Of course, once the whole nasty chain of events was over, there was plenty of time to try and comprehend the entire incomprehensible situation. Plenty of time to try to interpret and analyse the nightmare that refused to go away. Plenty of time to blame, regret, grieve and shed tears.

What had she been thinking when she made that long-distance call to Delhi? How could she have imagined that her impulsive, fiery and fiercely loyal friend would listen to her uncontrollable sobs on the phone and would do nothing about it?

In the years to come, try as she might, Ellora could never reconstruct the exact chain of events that had eventually led to the humiliating scandal; the scandal that changed her life forever.

The details were all gone. Only a few sketchy images remained. The first such hazy image was that of Aditi and Roshan waiting for her near the parking lot outside campus.

"Let's go to the principal's office and lodge an official complaint against that rogue. Let's teach that bastard a lesson he's not likely to forget in a hurry," said Aditi without any preliminaries.

Had the idea of teaching Ginger a lesson seemed outrageous to her at that moment? Had she opposed her friend's plan of making an official complaint against her tormenter, or had she been happy to go along with it? Ellora had no memory of how she had reacted when Aditi had made that suggestion. All she could recollect was another hazy image of the three of them walking together towards the college gate, with Aditi and Roshan guarding her from either side.

Ginger's gang started clapping and heckling her as soon

as they spotted the three of them. As always, they were sitting on the boundary wall, waiting for Ellora. If they were surprised to see her new companions protectively flanking her on either side, they displayed no signs of it. They climbed down from the boundary wall and started walking behind the three friends in a semicircle, singing songs and whistling. She could not recall the songs or the comments but they were lewder than ever, just as the whistles and the catcalls were louder than ever.

After a few minutes, Aditi decided that she had had enough and it was time to confront those scoundrels and give them a piece of her mind. She turned around and walked up to the group with Roshan following close behind her. She went straight to Ginger, whom she could recognize from Ellora's description. As she spoke to him, her words were drowned by the hooting and booing from his sidekicks. Aditi angrily ordered them to shut up in a voice loud enough to be heard above their catcalls. There was a moment's silence and then they all started jeering at her. Someone mocked her British accent, someone blew a kiss at her, saying she was welcome to shut him up by kissing him on the mouth and someone else called her a fucking bitch. Then one of them said something obscene; something really obscene, with lewd gestures and loud guffaws. Roshan, who by now could barely control his rage, walked up to the fellow and slapped him hard. A fistfight ensued.

Again, the pictures were quite hazy and her own role in the entire nasty fracas even hazier. However, the picture of Roshan lying on the ground was something Ellora could not easily erase from her memory. She could never forget the frightful sight of her humungous friend falling down on the ground with a loud thud. She could never forget how huge and muscular Roshan looked, even as he lay prostrate, writhing helplessly in pain, his white polo shirt stained red and his mouth oozing blood.

The college principal was informed, an ambulance arrived,

Aditi's mother and stepfather arrived from Delhi within hours of Roshan being rushed to a private hospital and a police complaint was lodged within the next twenty-four hours.

The local newspapers published the news the following day. They did not mention the names of the two girls involved in the fight, but everyone in town knew who they were. They also knew about the active role one of the girls had played in starting the scuffle; a violent scuffle that had landed one of the boys (the girl's stepbrother) in the hospital and the rest in jail.

Ellora's parents looked bewildered, aggrieved and shaken for days following the incident. They could not believe that instead of approaching them for help, their daughter had sent for her immature and impulsive friend, who instead of solving the problem, had made a complete mess of it. Privately, they were furious with Aditi and her step-brother; nevertheless, once they overcame their initial shock and outrage, they extended all the help and support they could provide to the troubled family.

Dr Akhilesh Chatterjee regularly visited the hospital where Roshan was admitted to make sure he was receiving proper treatment and care. He accompanied Aditi's stepfather, Balraj Ahuja, to the police station to ensure that Ginger and six of his partners in crime were promptly arrested. The two of them also made the rounds of the Vijaypur Government College to ensure that the principal took disciplinary action against all the seven boys involved.

Those were dark days. However, little did anyone know at that time that darker days were looming ahead.

****

Chapter 23

It happened one week after Aditi and her family had left for Delhi with Roshan still bruised and bandaged. The posters and pamphlets sprung up overnight. They were all over town, pasted on the boundary walls, STD booths and shop windows, hanging from electric poles, lampposts and treetops.

The phone started ringing from early morning. Everyone wanted to be the first giver of bad news, everyone wanted to get to the bottom of it, everyone wanted to tut-tut and express their shock, everyone wanted to cluck-cluck and commiserate with the hapless Chatterjees.

Dr Akhilesh Chatterjee and Sumitra Devi had already seen the shocking posters; they had been stuck all around their compound wall. Bhanwar Lal had been the first one to have spotted them. He had meticulously ripped them off the walls, making sure that not even a scrap of those disgraceful posters tainted his master's whitewashed walls. It was a good thing that the loyal gardener did not know how to read; otherwise, his distress at witnessing something so shameful would have increased considerably.

Dr Akhilesh Chatterjee could hardly speak and Sumitra Devi could hardly stop sobbing. They were both in a state of shock. How could their daughter betray their trust like this?

Could that brazen and sensuous girl in those huge life-sized posters really be their sweet, innocent child? She looked almost unrecognizable, but alas, the girl in the posters was their daughter all right. Why was she wearing that vulgar, skimpy blouse that exposed her entire back and shoulders? Why was she looking at that young cricketer in that seductive manner? And who was that shameless girl in the other poster titled "*Awara* Ellora"? Could the girl who was being kissed by that cricketer be really their daughter? Why was her blouse unbuttoned? Why was his hand inside her blouse? How could she have allowed him to touch her body like that? No, they had given Ellora the right upbringing, brought her up with the right values; their daughter would never do something so disgraceful to destroy the family reputation. It was a reputation built over generations, a reputation that now lay tarnished on the floor, a reputation that was in shreds like those torn posters.

One look at those posters and Ellora broke down, tears coming in torrents. She sat in her parents' bedroom and sobbed. The only time she had sobbed like that was when both her parents had died. In a way, this was another day of mourning, another sad day of death. Something died inside her parents. Something died inside Ellora.

****

Chapter 24

The scandal refused to die down. The newspapers and magazines picked up where the posters had left off and together, they made sure that the entire country was talking about an eighteen year old girl's indiscretion. An indiscretion that had destroyed the country's chances of winning a prestigious cup, an indiscretion that ended the prestigious career of a promising cricketer, an indiscretion that had cost the family of the girl in question its prestige.

It was a heavy price to pay for a few moments of recklessness.

It was an unfortunate coincidence that the posters surfaced just days before Rohinton Merchant was dropped from the Indian cricket team, bringing a premature end to his promising career. His dismissal from the team made national headlines. He had once been an emerging star who had ignited mass hysteria among cricket-crazy fans. Unfortunately, today, the once loved batsman only elicited strong hatred or pity. "He deserves to be dismissed," they all expertly opined, as they eagerly devoured every word of the sensational news along with their biscuits with their morning cup of tea. "That's what happens to all those playboy cricketers who play around with pretty fans instead of playing serious cricket."

Not many in the country knew at that time that the pretty fan seen in the pictures had been a schoolgirl from a small town. Radiantly beautiful, the teenager had lit up the dull pages of the newspapers and magazines. And so had the dashing young cricketer. Jointly, they had made a scintillating couple. It was too pulsating a story to kill or stifle. Those who still had compunctions about revealing the girl's identity, printed the pictures while blurring her face out, the way they had done before. However, most other national dailies and periodicals did not take the trouble of pixelating Ellora's face this time. They were not going to deface the sensational story by masking the stunning face behind it. They were not going to hide the identity of the sizzling lass responsible for causing the billowing career of a fiery young cricketer to go up in flames.

* * *

When the phone was not ringing, the doorbell was. Friends and well-wishers came over without invitation or appointment. They came to see how the poor couple and their errant daughter were coping with this latest crisis. They came to support, commiserate, hold hands, offer advice and suggest damage control strategies.

And of course, they came to say, "I told you so."

The Mashis and the Kakis hugged Ellora and howled as if she was suffering from a terminal illness.

And to think that they should have been hugging and congratulating her, instead of offering their tearful sympathies! They should all have been celebrating the news that had come that morning in the newspapers (which had carried good news for a change). Ellora's pre-medical test result was out and she had stood third: two places behind Aditi, who had topped the all India merit list.

Ellora saw the news as her escape route to freedom. She was now free to join the medical institute in Delhi. She was free to leave behind a town that had given her nothing but pain, disgrace and humiliation in recent times. She was free to move on with her life at long last.

Or was she?

"You can't let Ellora go to Delhi after all that has taken place. You can't let her be in the company of that Aditi. The girl is trouble with a capital T. How many times we tried telling you this, but you wouldn't listen to your friends," lamented Kakoli.

"Now that our worst fears have come true, we must make sure that Ellora does not join the medical college in Delhi," said Bina. Everyone nodded their heads synchronously, looking like elderly *Tanjore* dolls with roly-poly bobble-heads briskly bobbing.

Ellora was livid, as the snatches of this conversation reached her ears through her partially open window. She wanted to go downstairs and gag all of them, especially Kakoli Mashi, who for some odd reasons, was suddenly cackling like a duckling that has been severely spanked. The woman's high-octave, staccato cries grated on her nerves. Even Babu Shona was in considerable distress, for he had started whining miserably. Poor thing, he had to be locked up inside a room because of the dog-hating women. His unhappy barks made Ellora very sad. She was furious with the women responsible for her and Babu Shona's solitary confinement.

As she brooded and simmered standing near the window, Ellora noted that suddenly everyone was quiet. She carefully drew aside the curtain and looked at the women sitting in the hall below. They all sat in a circle with frowns, furrowing their foreheads.

"They all look like grieving hens attending a condolence meeting," thought she, miserably.

Indeed, they were like sad and sombre hens. A brood of fat brooding hens, all sitting and discussing how best to bury the embryonic aspirations of a foolish fledgling that was trying to fly too high and had crashed-landed in the process. They now had the noble mission of making sure that the faltering fledgling never found its wings again. They had to ensure that the wilful, naughty fledgling never tried to fly high ever again.

When they were not spouting gems of wisdom, they were tut-tutting or cluck-clucking, at times individually, but more often than not, in synchronized chorus. Someone would let out a loud tut-tut or cluck-cluck and everyone else would follow suit, as if they were waiting for a cue to start a fresh round of cluck-cluck-tut-tut.

* * *

Notwithstanding all the words of wisdom and warning from their well-wishers, Ellora's parents debated every night in the privacy of their bedroom about what course of action they could take under the difficult circumstances. Should they listen to their friends and stop their daughter from joining the medical college in Delhi? Would that be the right thing to do, given the fact that getting admission in the coveted institute was the opportunity of a lifetime? Not many students aspiring to become doctors were handed such a golden opportunity. It was indeed a matter of great pride and prestige for Dr Akhilesh Chatterjee that his daughter had stood third in the all India merit list and had been accepted by one of the most prestigious medical colleges in the country.

"Akshay would have been so proud of his brainy daughter, had he been alive to witness her brilliant success today," Dr Akhilesh Chatterjee had said to his wife, when he first saw the all-India pre-medical test result in the newspaper.

"It's good thing that your brother is not alive today to have witnessed all the disgrace and shame his daughter has brought upon the family," Sumitra Devi had reminded bitterly. She was astonished that her husband, who had not spoken much ever since the scandal broke, was finally breaking his silence only to praise their wayward daughter. She herself could not look at Ellora's passport size photograph in the newspapers without being reminded of the disgraceful life-size posters that had been displayed all over town not too long ago.

How could her husband be happy about the news, knowing what it entailed?

They both argued night after night. Sumitra Devi was totally against sending Ellora to Delhi. It was not as if AIIMS was the only available option for their daughter, She had excelled in the state entrance exam, too and could get admission in any one of the three regional medical colleges to which she had applied. In fact, Sumitra Devi was all for sending Ellora to the nearby Kishanpur Medical College.

"How can we send our daughter to some second-rate college, when she has procured admission in the topmost medical institute in the country?"

"How can you even think of sending Ellora to Delhi, after all that has taken place? Do you want your daughter to start seeing that Parsi boy all over again? Isn't the disgrace she has already brought upon the family enough? Do you want bigger scandals?" Sumitra Devi wanted to know.

"I think your fears are slightly exaggerated. I don't think our daughter will have anything to do with that boy ever again. She has learnt her lesson - she realizes that she has made a huge mistake for which she has already paid a heavy price."

"We all have," interjected Sumitra Devi quickly, just in case her husband had forgotten that the two of them had paid a heavier price for their daughter's brazen deeds. The entire town was abuzz with ugly gossip involving her. Even her own household had not been untouched by the scandal. In fact, she had had to fire one of the drivers when she overheard him making some very cheap remarks about Ellora. The maids had also gossiped about those posters and had to be scolded into shutting up. But how many people shooting off their mouths could she fire? How many wagging tongues could she silence?

"Look Sumitra, we can't go on blaming and punishing the girl for the rest of her life. Have you taken a good look at her face lately? Don't you see how sad and miserable she looks these days? She hardly talks or smiles. She's genuinely repentant. Every time I look at her, I see remorse in her sad eyes. Do you want to make her more miserable by refusing to let her go to Delhi? As parents, we have the authority.

We can stop her from joining AIIMS, but then we'll blame ourselves for the rest of our lives for depriving our daughter of a coveted opportunity, which not everyone in the country is brilliant enough to get."

"In short, you don't want to clip her wings. You want to give your wayward daughter the freedom to fly away to Delhi, so that she can mix freely with that playboy cricketer so more of her scandalous posters are splashed all over the country."

"Your fears are exaggerated." Akhilesh Chatterjee told his wife.

"But they are not unfounded," insisted his wife.

"I'm confident that our Ellora won't see that boy again - not if I ask her not to. She'll never disobey me. She's my good girl," said Akhilesh Chatterjee before falling into a fitful sleep.

****

Chapter 25

It was clear as soon as the discussion began that Sumitra Devi's fears about her wilful daughter were neither unfounded nor exaggerated. Rather, Dr Akhilesh Chatterjee's confidence in his good girl's willingness to obey his orders was completely misplaced. His good girl was no longer keen to defend her coveted title by acting like one.

Not see Rohinton Merchant ever again? What was her father talking about? How could he make such an unfair demand of her? No. Sorry. She was going to make no such promise.

"I love Rohinton, don't you understand? I love him," she had tearfully appealed.

"What did you say?" roared Sumitra Devi. "Love him? Don't you have any shame left? How can you make such appalling declarations in front of your father?" Sumitra Devi was boiling with rage. She could not believe that her daughter, this chit of a girl, was actually challenging her father's authority in this brazenly insolent manner.

The irate mother continued her tirade by adding, "It's all my fault. I should've listened to my friends and stopped you from associating with that precocious girl Aditi, who introduced you to those indecent adult novels at an age when all other girls from your class were reading innocent fairy tales. You love that Parsi boy? Ha! Do you even know the meaning of love? Letting a man who's not even your fiancé kiss you and touch you all over in broad daylight is a brazen act of sin and not love. Eighteen year old girls are not supposed to indulge in such disgraceful and immoral behaviour in the name of love."

Ellora looked at her mother, her eyes blazing with barely concealed hatred and defiance. She wanted to ask her mother, "When you conceived your first child at the age of seventeen, what was it Maa? Was it an act of love, or was it a brazen sin? How is my love for Rohinton any different from what you felt for Baba, when you first fell in love with him after marriage?"

However, she was too timid to ask any of those defiant questions. She was too drained and defeated to argue with her mother. Instead, she just buried her face in her arms and broke into loud sobs, shoulders heaving, hiccups choking her throat, tears streaming down her cheeks to leave watermarks on the polished mahogany table. Despite being almost incoherent because of the accompanying sobs, her words were coherent enough to leave her anguished parents speechless for a while.

"Why did my parents have to die? Why did they leave me alone in this world like this? Had they been alive today, my parents would've never stopped me from seeing Rohinton. They would've never scolded me for loving him. They would've been happy for me. They would've respected my decision. They would've made an attempt to meet Rohinton and get to know him, instead of asking their daughter to stop seeing the boy she loves with all her heart. My parents would've never made me feel guilty for falling in love."

There it was. The bottled up bitterness was sobbingly spilled out. Days, months and years of cumulative pain, frustrations, resentment, grumbling, whining, trauma, agonies, aches and hurt were all laid bare on the table (along with her tears) for her adoptive parents to see.

Sumitra Devi started crying. Dr Akhilesh Chatterjee got up from his chair and stood behind his sobbing daughter, stroking her head, giving her water to drink, wiping her tears with his clean handkerchief, imploring her to stop crying, his own voice heavy with his unshed tears.

* * *

Were my tears spontaneous and unbidden or did I tactically shed those well-timed tears to quash the opposition? Did I really miss my dead parents, or did I strategically bring up their names to make my adoptive parents feel guilty? Did I use the worst kind of emotional blackmail on them to get my way?

Those were some of the disturbing questions (among many others) that haunted Ellora, whenever she looked back upon those dark days several years later. She had no one-word 'Yes' or 'No' answers to some of those uncomfortable questions. Her only argument in her self-defence was that she had been too young, too traumatized, too much in love and too much in need of love and understanding to have any compunction about using tears as weapons of manipulation.

Whatever the teenage girl's motive had been, the tears and sobs had had their desired effect on her distraught parents. Intentionally or unintentionally, she had got them to lay down their arms by using weapons that were more powerful than their joint resistance.

"Does this boy Rohinton Merchant also love you?" Her father's calm tone was soothing and reassuring. Ellora was glad that the discussion, that a few minutes ago, was going nowhere had finally taken the right turn.

"Of course, he does," she had confidently replied.

"Is he seriously committed to you?"

"What do you mean?" She was genuinely taken aback by that unexpected question – she had not considered her relationship with Rohinton in terms of commitment.

"I mean, does he have any intentions of marrying you?"

"Of course, he does," she automatically repeated her previous answer, feeling like a parrot that had been taught to utter only those four words. She, of course, was lying through her teeth. Their budding relationship had not yet blossomed to a stage where they had had a chance to discuss serious stuffs like marriage or commitment.

"And what about his religion?"

"What about it?"

"Are you aware that he's a Parsi?"

"What's wrong with being a Parsi? You're making it sound like it's some kind of disease," Ellora could hardly stop herself from retorting sharply.

"I wish it were a disease. Treating a chronic disease is easier than fighting the age-old malady of prejudice that is handed down from generation to generation. Do you know the full implications of inter-faith marriage? Do you know the kind of opposition and criticism that will come your way? The kind of adjustments and sacrifices you will be required to make?"

"I'm ready to make any sacrifice for Rohinton. I love him," she had fervently declared, aware of how wan and defeated her mother was looking all of a sudden.

"If this is how strongly you feel about this boy, then I will not try to stop you from seeing him. However, in view of all that has been published in the newspapers about the two of you, your mother and I want to make sure that there are no more scandals involving our daughter. We want to make sure that Rohinton Merchant is committed to you. If he's as serious about you as you claim he is, then he shouldn't have any objections about making your relationship respectable by formalizing it, so that the scandalmongers have nothing scandalous to report."

"What do you mean?" Ellora was stumped. Had her father just lobbed a googly at her to throw her off balance? Even as the possibility crossed her mind, she was irritated with herself. What the hell was wrong with her? Why couldn't she stop herself from using these silly cricketing phrases even in a serious situation like this?

Looking at his daughter's stunned and flustered face, Dr Akhilesh Chatterjee quickly added, "Marriage, of course, is out of question right now. Both of you are too young for that. Besides, you both have a long way to go before you take such a major step. You especially, are going to be too busy studying and training to become a doctor to even think about marriage for the next several years. However, I'm aware that it's not going to prevent you from seeing Rohinton Merchant regularly once you're living in Delhi. And this is what is making your mother and me extremely uneasy. We're worried about you. We don't want some unprincipled publication to print malicious gossip about our daughter all over again."

"We're back to the square one, aren't we? After all the discussion we've had, we come back to the same conclusion. That I should stop seeing Rohinton."

"No, that's not what I'm suggesting," said her father quickly before his tearful daughter started sobbing and saying hurtful things to them again.

"What I'm suggesting is that if the two of you wish to continue seeing each other, you must obtain the consent and the blessings of Rohinton's parents. Also, there should be some kind of formal engagement to assure us that Rohinton is serious about you and that his parents have no objections to your relationship."

"Engagement? But I'm too young to get engaged," protested a flabbergasted Ellora.

"If you're not too young to fall in love with a man who you claim reciprocates your feelings, then you're not too young to get engaged either. An engagement will give your relationship the respectability that it currently lacks. It will give both of you the freedom to meet each other in public places without any unscrupulous photographer surreptitiously hiding behind a tree and clicking your pictures without your knowledge. It will discourage unprincipled editors from printing your pictures in their newspapers and labelling you as one of Rohinton Merchant's frivolous love interests. Once you're formally accepted by his family, they will have to respectfully refer to you as Rohinton Merchant's fiancée."

Dr Akhilesh Chatterjee waited for his argument to sink in and when he saw that his words were having their desired effect on his daughter, he made his next suggestion.

"In fact, your mother and I would like to meet Rohinton and his parents without further delay. Do you think Rohinton would be open to the idea of meeting us?"

"I don't know. I'll have to call Rohinton and find out."

There it was. She had inadvertently let her parents know that she was in touch with Rohinton by phone. However, her parents did not seem to have noticed anything strange or objectionable in her statement.

"In that case, talk to him as soon as you can," said her father. Then, he kissed her lightly on the forehead, saying, "Your own father may be gone, but so long as this father of yours is alive, he will not watch you shed tears and do nothing about it."

****

Chapter 26

Ultimately, the decision of not joining the medical institute in Delhi was Ellora's and her parents could do nothing to make her change her mind.

How could she go there, after learning all the things she had learnt in the last few days?

She should have seen it coming. She should have picked up the warning signals. She should have wondered why Rohinton was not calling her or returning her calls ever since the scandal broke.

Not that Rohinton had called her frequently even before those horrible pictures had been published. Their telephonic communications had been few and far between, given all the hurdles they had had to cross before they could be connected. Ellora had not enjoyed those hush-hush conversations; she was always so jittery. What if her parents had suddenly woken up and caught her red-handed in the act of talking to him at such an unearthly hour?

Ironically, now that she had her parents' permission to call him, Rohinton was not answering her calls. And to think that not very long ago, he had been the one who had insisted upon calling her at all odd hours, despite her strong reluctance and resistance!

If truth be told, Ellora needed more time to sort out her feelings after that rather intimate and invasive kiss that had not only made her very uncomfortable, but had also left her cold. But Rohinton, who was obviously a better talker than a kisser, cleared away all her post-kiss queasiness and qualms by seducing her all over again on the phone. He did not call too often, but when he did, he spoke nonstop till the wee hours of the morning.

And then, all of a sudden his phone calls stopped. Just like that. He did not pick up her calls either. Where was he when she needed him the most?

After the tearful scene with her parents, the frustrating cycle of making calls that were never answered started all over again. When Rohinton finally picked up the phone, he did not sound too thrilled. Of course, he said all the right things. He told Ellora that he was happy to hear her voice. He even remembered to congratulate her on her brilliant performance in her pre-medical test. And yet, something was seriously amiss. He was talking to her, as if he was playing a mandatory over. Why did he sound so distracted and ill at ease? Why did she get a feeling that he was in a hurry to end their conversation and get on with whatever he was doing before she called? Was there someone else in the room with him overhearing their conversation?

Ellora had a strong hunch that their conversation was about to come to an abrupt end and therefore she quickly came to the point.

"Listen, I've news for you. My parents want to meet your parents."

"What for?" Was that edge in his voice surprise or irritation?

"What do you mean by, 'What for?'" she asked, mimicking his sharp tone.

"Well, Ellora, this is just not the right time for any kind of parent-to-parent meeting, if you know what I mean."

"No, I don't know what you mean. Would you kindly elaborate?" She could not help being sarcastic.

"Look Ellora, I'll be honest with you. It's not a good time. In fact, things are pretty tense at the moment. My parents have taken the news of our friendship very badly. They were in a state of shock when they saw all those pictures in the newspapers. They still are. How can you even suggest meeting my parents at a time like this? Don't you understand what my family is going through? Don't you understand what I'm going through, especially after being dropped from the Indian team without any rhyme or reason?"

"Rohinton, how can you say that? My heart cries when I think of how unfairly you've been treated and how unreasonably you've been let go from the team. It's just not fair." Ellora meant every word she said.

"Just imagine! Being dumped so unceremoniously on such flimsy grounds! But mark my words, I'm not going to sit back and mope. I'm going to work very hard to win back my place in the team, even if I've to spend all my waking hours practicing my shots. They can't write me off just like that. I'm going to improve my batting so much that they'll have no other option except to take me back. Look Ellora, at present my main goal is to regain my place in the team. I don't have time for anything else. Please forgive me, but you'll appreciate that I do need to work very hard without any distractions or disturbances."

Her long silence was taken as her mute acceptance of his explanation, for before she could interrupt his speech, Rohinton had quickly wished her luck and then disconnected.

Just like that. Without even asking her once, what she herself had been going through ever since they had literally hanged her in public by hanging those life-size posters from every wall, pole and tree of the town.

Instead of sounding gentle and reassuring, Rohinton had sounded piqued and reproachful. Where was the besotted admirer who never tired of calling her every sweet name in his lexicon? She used to be his honeydew, his sweetheart, his sweet pea; she used to be his darling, his dearest, his precious Ellora. And now, all of a sudden, she had been downgraded to being just Ellora, no endearing prefixes, no loving suffixes; just plain Ellora, the silly reason responsible for his senseless sacking.

What had he been trying to convey when he had said that he needed to work very hard towards his goal without any distractions or disturbances? Had he been implying that she was a kind of distraction he could do without?

It took Ellora some time to absorb the full implications of their entire conversation. It was a good thing that both her parents had been away when this happened At least, she did not have to face any uncomfortable interrogation from them. She was free to lock herself in her room and cry.

After nearly one hour of crying, Ellora calmed down enough to be able to rewind and replay the entire conversation in her mind. The more she analysed Rohinton's words, the nearer she got to the bitter truth. She could see the ugly, self-centred side of her boyfriend, now that she was no longer looking at him through rose-tinted glasses.

Their entire conversation had revolved around him. It was all about him; about his misfortunes, his disappointments, his frustrations, his struggles, his victimization, his hurts and his uncalled-for dismissal from the Indian team. When he had not been talking about his shattered dreams and his crumbling cricket career, Rohinton talked about his distressed and disappointed parents. Where did she fit amid all this if at all she fitted somewhere? Did she have a place, any place, in his grand scheme of things? Did she figure somewhere, anywhere, in his ambitious plans for future?

More importantly, had she just been royally dumped without so much as a 'it-was-nice-meeting-you'? Did he just discard her from his life as unceremoniously as he himself had been discarded by the Indian selectors?

"No," Ellora told herself through her sobs. Her Rohinton could not be so heartless and cold. She probably caught him at the wrong time in one of his rare foul moods. It was quite understandable that he should be grumpy and brusque, given the sorry state of his cricketing affairs. She was confident that he would call her as soon as he realized how much he had hurt her with his callous comments.

For the next couple of days, Ellora could do very little except hover around the living room phone, anxiously waiting for it to ring. At last, when she could not take it anymore, she decided to call Rohinton again. She called not once, not twice, but at least a hundred times. Until her fingers ached from dialling his number. Until her ears ached from listening to the monotonous tone of the unanswered rings. Until her heart ached from the awful hurt of not being loved by the heartless jerk, whom she still loved with all her heart.

She was so used to her calls not being answered that when Aditi picked up the phone after the first ring, Ellora did not immediately know what to say to her friend. Aditi, of course, sounded happy to hear her voice. She was all concern for her friend. She understood what Ellora was going through. However, when the topic turned to her recent conversation with Rohinton, the understanding tone suddenly turned accusatory and disapproving. Aditi was using almost the same words and exactly the same tone that Rohinton had used; she was accusing her of not being considerate enough to understand what the poor fellow was going through.

"What a daft idea! Ellora, how could you even think that Rohinton would jump at the stupid suggestion of introducing his parents to yours? Don't you realize that his parents are orthodox Parsis who'll never willingly accept the news of their only son seeing a Hindu girl? Can't you imagine how upset and shocked his poor parents must have been after seeing those tell-tale pictures in the newspapers?"

The line of accusation was so similar that Ellora started wondering if Rohinton had discussed their recent conversation with Aditi.

"Have you been talking to Rohinton?" Ellora could not help asking.

"What do you mean?" Aditi sounded very offended by the question, but after a brief pause, she decided to answer it. "I've met Rohinton only once since coming to Delhi. He has no time for fooling around with friends. He's dead serious about getting back his place in the Indian team. And if you ask me, you should also leave him alone, instead of nagging him with your unreasonable demands."

When she was done with giving Ellora a piece of her mind, Aditi switched to giving her friend a conclusive and unequivocal piece of advice. "I think you should give up on Rohinton. It's time for you to face the fact that your relationship is not likely to evolve into anything more than just friendship. In fact, given all the bad publicity Rohinton has received because of being captured on camera with you, he may not even be very open to the idea of going out with you again."

Judging from the long silence that followed her harsh words, Aditi probably knew that she had gone a bit too far and had probably put things a bit too candidly. She tried to undo the damage by saying something that sounded less foreboding, "But who knows? Things may change for the better."

When even her uplifting words failed to generate any response from Ellora, Aditi decided that she would go back to thrusting the bitter pills down her friend's throat; sugar coating was not quite her cup of tea, anyway.

"But if you listen to my sincere suggestion, don't hold on to any fragile hopes. You'll only be prolonging your agony by pinning your hopes on someone who's no longer pining for you. As your friend, I can only ask you not to waste your precious tears on a helmeted batsman whose field of vision doesn't extend beyond his cricket field. Don't cry over him Ellora, he's not worth it. No man on this earth is."

It was not until later, much later, that the rumours of the betrayal by her best friend reached Ellora's ears. She came to know from more than one source that Aditi and Rohinton had often been spotted together in restaurants and discotheques. Once it was confirmed that the rumours were not just rumours and that Rohinton was indeed spending a lot of time with Aditi instead of practicing his shots, Ellora made the decision of not joining the medical college in Delhi. Nobody, not even her father, could make her change her mind. Her decision was irrevocable.

****

Chapter 27

"A girl's reputation follows her wherever she goes," her mother had tried to caution her once. She was wrong. "A girl's reputation precedes her wherever she goes," thought Ellora bitterly.

Hers surely did.

Everyone in her new college already seemed to know about her scandalous past, which was not surprising, considering it was not too long ago that her pictures were splashed in all the major newspapers and magazines.

As far as Ellora was concerned, the campus atmosphere of Kishanpur Medical College was no better than her previous college. Decent girls from decent families maintained a decent distance from her and the handful of girls who were friendly, had motives other than friendship. They came and sat next to her only to quiz her about Rohionton Merchant. They were incredibly curious about the handsome batsman who they continued to adore despite his dismissal from the Indian team. They wanted to know the entire inside story with all its spicy scoops and all the juicy details. Ellora, of course, ignored these girls. However, she was in no position to ignore the other questions that came her way, especially the ones asked by her seniors, who had decided to zero in on her as their special target for ragging that year.

Despite being banned by the college administration, ragging was rampant on campus. The senior students forced the juniors to come in small groups to isolated spots, where they subjected the newcomers to all kinds of humiliation and torture: some were given bawdy songs to sing, some were asked to perform raunchy item numbers, while others were asked to enact crude scenes from Hindi movies.

Ellora, however, was always singled out for special ragging sessions. She was invariably taken to a dark lecture hall, where she was asked to stand on the dais and enact an imaginary romantic scene with an imaginary boyfriend called Rohinton. While she silently stood on the podium, adamantly refusing to meet any of the mocking eyes, some of the senior boys would invariably join her on stage and volunteer to enact Rohinton's part with her. They mercilessly taunted her for ignoring their rude overtures and crude comments.

"She thinks she's too good for the likes of ordinary men like us. She only fancies famous batsmen," saying this, they would all burst out laughing.

When the ragging stopped, the teasing began. Surprisingly, this time around it was not a student, but a professor who began to show an unhealthy interest in her. Dr Gupta, who taught them anatomy, was nicknamed 'The Toad.' It was an apt name for the short, pot-bellied man with a pointed head that rested on his rotund torso with no discernible neck in between. His protruding eyes were like that of his namesake amphibian; they moved in all directions, but more often than not, they rested on pretty faces and Ellora's was one of the favoured faces that year. The toad covertly watched her from the corners of his toady eyes, while he paced up and down the podium, dictating notes. He paid her extra attention during the lab hours. Dissecting cadavers made Ellora queasy. She had dissected animals before, but this was her first exposure to dead human bodies. Her face would go white and her hands would start shaking, as she cut through the preserved flesh reeking of formaldehyde. Dr Gupta would invariably come to assist her. He would stand so close to her that she could breathe the scented hair oil he generously applied on his wavy hair to keep it smoothly undulating. He would hold her shaking hands and show her where to find the artery she had been looking for. He never let a chance to touch her physically or tease her verbally pass him by.

One day, while correcting her lab report, the Toad remarked on the arrows she had drawn neatly to label the parts of the heart.

"Don't draw arrows my dear, they pierce through my fragile heart and break it into pieces," said he in a voice loud enough for the whole class to hear. Everyone laughed, except Ellora, who clenched her fists to control her indignation.

* * *

Things did not improve with time, in fact, they only got worse. The posters resurfaced and so did Ginger after staying underground for some time following his release from prison. It was not difficult to guess who was behind the huge posters pasted on the walls outside the campus.

Ellora saw the amused smirks and the rude stares. As she walked through the corridors, the male students watched her eyes popping and jaws hanging, trying to discover similarities with the seductive siren on those posters. They were quite disappointed though. The timid girl who walked to her classes with her eyes downcast was nothing like the hot poster-girl oozing oomph and sex appeal. What a pity! Draped in a fiery orange sari and a skimpy blouse that covered very little of her long slim back and shapely shoulders, the sensuous poster-girl was the type of sumptuous beauty whose life-size pictures they would have liked to hang on their bedroom walls. It was quite another matter that some prim and proper girls from the same college, mainly the decent girls from decent families, were so outraged by those posters that they wanted to hang the poster-girl herself from their bedroom ceilings.

* * *

The drive from Vijaypur to Kishanpur usually took about two hours and Ellora utilized that time to revise her class-notes. That was why she failed to spot Ginger when he first started following their car. When the chauffer complained about a man on a motorbike coming dangerously close to the car, Ellora quickly looked out of the window. Despite the helmet covering his face, it was not difficult to recognize her stalker. Ginger at once took off his helmet and gave her an elaborate salute accompanied by a broad grin. Ellora went pale with shock and fear. It was like seeing a ghost. How had he got out of prison so soon? She turned around and instructed the chauffer to drive faster. Ginger honked from behind them and sped past other vehicles to come alongside them and waved at her from a closer range. Despite her heart pounding violently in her chest, she tried to ignore his mocking smile, pretending to read her notes.

The next morning, Ellora found her father waiting for her in the car.

"The driver told me what happened yesterday. I'll accompany you to your college. Let me see how that scoundrel dares to harass you again," he calmly told her.

When Ginger's motorcycle emerged from one of the street corners and started following their car soon after they left home, Dr Akhilesh Chatterjee asked the chauffer to pull over. As expected, Ginger too stopped his motorbike, took off his helmet and waited behind them with an amused grin on his face. He got off his bike as soon as he saw Ellora's father walking towards him.

Ellora nervously watched them from the car window. Her father looked frail and vulnerable in front of the burly man, who looked even more intimidating in his bright red T-shirt. Ellora knew from the way beads of perspiration had appeared on her father's knitted brow that he was seething with suppressed rage. She could not hear him, but could make out from the way his hands moved that he was warning Ginger of dire consequences, if he did not stop stalking his daughter. Ginger, on the other hand, was listening to him with the condescending air of a grownup hugely amused by a stupid child talking utter rubbish. He hardly interrupted her father's nonstop flow of words, but his impudent smile said it all. At one point, he threw back his head and started laughing uproariously, as if whatever the elderly doctor had just said was incredibly funny.

When her father finally returned to the car, Ellora noticed how pale and exhausted he looked all of a sudden. She felt miserable and guilty. In her selfish involvement in her own miseries, she had completely overlooked how unhappy she had made her ageing father.

They both silently watched the grinning offender, as he went back to his motorcycle and kick-started the engine. He waited on his motorbike for their car to start and then started following them, as if nothing had happened, as if it was the most natural thing in the world to do.

For the next three days, her father accompanied her from the house to college and from college to the house, while Ginger followed their car unobtrusively on his motorbike, taking great care to maintain a respectable distance between the two vehicles. On the fourth day, Dr Akhilesh Chatterjee sent the security guard of his clinic with Ellora, while he himself went to the police station to lodge a complaint.

The sub-inspector refused to register the case, saying he could not file a written complaint for a crime that had yet to be committed. Instead, he decided to give well-meaning advice to the distraught father; it was strictly verbal advice, nothing official about it. Just brotherly advice from one father to another.

"We're living in a dangerous world, Doctor Sahib. Yesterday, a student threw acid on his girlfriend for ignoring his overtures. If you ask me, the fault mainly lies with the parents, who unfortunately are too lenient and indulgent nowadays. They don't discipline their sons and daughters even when they cross the limits of decency. If I were you, I would try to keep my daughter under control and make sure that she dresses modestly, so that she does not catch the attention of those lecherous and dangerous men roaming the streets and corridors. Boys will be boys. Young men are like hungry predators who will charge whenever they see tempting female flesh."

"I'd come here to lodge a complaint against a dangerous lout who has been stalking my daughter. When I need an advice, I'll go to a lawyer," the doctor told the sub-inspector before getting up to depart.

After coming home from the police station, Dr Akhilesh Chatterjee went straight to his study, where he sat down and wrote several letters to various officials before collapsing on his chair with chest pain. It was his first heart attack.

When her father came home after being discharged from the hospital, Ellora was by his bedside most of the time. The roles had reversed.

"Have you sent a leave application to your dean?" Dr Akhilesh Chatterjee asked Ellora.

"I'm not going back to that college. I've decided to drop out." She dropped the bombshell with great trepidation, not at all sure if she was doing the right thing. She scrutinized her father's expressions to see how he was taking it and when she found him looking quite unperturbed by the news, she continued, "But don't worry Baba. I'll reappear for the All India Premedical Test next year. I promise you that I'll top the merit list this time and will join whichever medical college you want me to join."

"But you'll waste an entire academic year," reminded her father, even though he himself had been thinking along those same lines and was glad that his daughter had the wisdom and the courage to make this bold decision.

"I'm not going to sit idle. I'll study all the medical text books in advance. I'm going to top all my exams from now on. I'm going to be the topmost cardiologist in the country, that's a promise Baba. I'm going to be your good girl. I'll never give you any reasons to feel ashamed of your daughter."

"Who said I'm ashamed of you?" asked her father, tears streaming down from his eyes and wetting the pillow beneath his head.

"You're too good a father to say that, but I know that I've given you enough reasons to be ashamed of me. But Baba, today I promise you that I'll make you very proud of me. But you also promise me that you'll never fall sick again. I need you Baba. Promise me that you'll not leave me the way my own parents did."

****

Chapter 28

They all regarded it as a grave mistake. They all thought she had missed an important boat that would have taken her to her dream destination. But Ellora never looked back or regretted her decision of dropping out of Kishanpur Medical College. Nor did she regret her decision of not joining any other medical college the following year or in the years that followed, even though it meant breaking the promise she had made to her father of becoming the topmost cardiologist in the country.

Although she broke her promise, she did not break her father's heart. In fact, it all happened with her father's wholehearted approval and consent.

Dr Maya Bose's visit to their home to see her ailing father was the milestone event that changed the course of Ellora's career. The widow of a close family friend, Dr Bose was the principal of an elite girls' college in a hill station called Nand Nagar. She was the one to have persuaded the Chatterjee couple that Ellora must get away from the unwholesome and unsafe environment of Vijaypur.

"Why don't you send her to my college, instead of letting her waste an entire academic year? The management of Gargi College always welcomes outstanding students like Ellora."

For the Chatterjees, this was the best piece of news they had heard in a long time. Both of them were seriously concerned that Ellora was spending all her time cooped up in her room without ever stepping out of the house. They would have done anything to get their daughter out of her gloomy shell, even if it meant sending her away to a remote town

Ellora, on the other hand, agreed to accompany Dr Maya Bose to Nand Nagar only to please her parents.

Fortunately, all her cumulative phobias for colleges were at once laid to rest the moment she stepped inside the campus of her new college It was nothing like any of the educational institutions she had attended so far. There were miles and miles of greenery all around, rain-fed brooks gurgled down the hills surrounding the campus, which itself reverberated with the happy notes of hundreds of bird species that lived in the trees and bushes standing all around.

The all-girls residential college had acres of grounds for playing every type of outdoor and indoor games including cricket and polo. The college conducted regular classes for professional photography, filmmaking, pottery, art, music and dance. The students were a friendly lot. There were so many activities to keep their minds and bodies gainfully occupied that no one had the time for idle gossip. Even if some students knew about Ellora's involvement with a famous cricketer, they were not interested in making a big deal about it.

For the first time in several months, Ellora felt happy when she woke up in the mornings. She looked forward to going to her classes instead of dreading the prospect. With each passing day, she found herself growing more and more fond of her new surroundings. So much so, that when the time came for sitting for her premedical exams, she informed her parents that she did not want to pursue medicine. She dreaded the prospect of dealing with the smells of dead bodies and illnesses. She would much rather deal with living things that blossomed, bore fruits and were fragrant. She wanted to study subjects like botany and environmental biology.

Dr Akhilesh Chatterjee was happy for Ellora. He did not let the thought that none of his three children would follow into his healer's footstep disturb his natural state of equanimity. Sumitra Devi, on the other hand, was secretly disappointed. She had wanted Ellora to be a doctor like her husband and her late-brother-in-law. She was also concerned about what her friends would say when she gave them this latest piece of bad news.

****

PART III

Chapter 29

July 2011,
Springfield, Virginia

"His wild oats have finally come home to roost," comments Aparna with a degree of relish, as she eagerly devours the newspaper article along with her oats porridge.

Ellora knows without being told, that the oats her sister is referring to have nothing to do with the one she is having for breakfast. She knows the story only too well; the newspapers are full of it and so are all the news channels. Everything you read and everyone you meet has something to say about the two-timing governor who fathered a secret lovechild with his former housekeeper.

"It's crazy! Just imagine, being a sixty-plus married man and behaving in this wild manner by sowing his wild oats here, there and everywhere like some promiscuous youth on a testosterone overdrive," says Aparna, as she quickly runs her eyes over all the juicy details of the article.

"Well, it seems, he didn't have to venture too far from his home to sow those wild oats, since he could sow them in his very own backyard," says Ellora.

"A very yielding and fertile backyard, indeed. But what really disgusts me is the fact that even as he sowed his wild ones in the backyard, he continued sowing his legitimate ones in the front yard and that too side by side," says Aparna with a shudder. Despite living America for several years, she has yet to discard her Indian sensibilities in matters such as this.

"And that too, without the front yard knowing what the hardworking gardener was up to in the backyard," quips Ellora with an amused smile. Being with her elder sister always loosens her up enough to make such utterly silly observations.

"What a shame! Why do seemingly clever men possess such stupid libidos, libidos reckless enough to wreck their marriages? If I were the wronged wife, I would cut the root of such libido at the source, so that there are no more oats, either wild or valid ones, to be merrily scattered here, there or anywhere."

Aparna would have continued to castigate and castrate the bearers of all such marriage-wrecking libidos, had she not remembered just in time that she should get ready, if she wanted to accomplish all the things she has set out to do this morning. Topping her to-do list is driving down to the Maine Avenue fish market in DC.

"Listen, we're driving down to the Southwest Waterfront to buy seafood. Rahul wants me to carry crab-cakes and fish cutlets for tomorrow's match. We must start now if we want to reach the place before it gets too crowded," informs Aparna, as she quickly gulps down the remaining tea from her cup.

"Now?" asks Ellora, slightly staggered by the pace with which things have been happening ever since she arrived the night before.

"Yes now, as soon as you finish your omelette. But listen, you don't have to come with me if you're not up to visiting a fish market first thing in the morning," says Aparna, as she gets up and starts clearing the table.

"I'll come with you, just give me a minute."

In less than ten minutes, the sisters are on their way to the Southwest Waterfront.

"Let me warn you, seafood smells can be a bit overwhelming. If I'm not mistaken, you have a delicate constitution when it comes to strong smells," says Aparna as soon as they hit the road.

"Didi, let me remind you in case you've forgotten that I've not only dissected smelly rats and cockroaches in college, but have also handled human cadavers during my short stint as a medical student."

Ellora at once regrets broaching a topic that has many painful associations and is thankful that her sister is too engrossed in listening to the instructions given by the recorded female voice in her car's GPS to make any comment.

When the taped instructions stop, Ellora, cleverly changes the subject, by asking, "Has Rahul-da always been fond of Bengali food?"

"Actually, the older he grows, the more Bengali he acts. With each passing year, his deep-seated Bengali DNA is coming more-and-more to the fore. Thanks to his resurfacing Bengali taste buds, I've to hunt around for herring and carp all over the town."

Aparna pauses briefly to focus upon changing her lane before stating, "But I shouldn't carp too much. After all, marriage is all about accepting your husband the way he is, warts, farts and all."

"Didi! STOPPIT, you're disgusting," cries a horrified Ellora.

"It was just a figure of speech," defends Aparna.

"But you added your own colour to make it more colourful. No, correction, to make it off colour," says Ellora, before observing, "You do love taking liberties with your idioms don't you?"

"You're right. I love my freedom of idiomatic expression," says Aparna with a smile. They drive silently for few more minutes before Aparna breaks the silence by going back to their original topic of discussion.

"We don't get fresh *rui* and *ilish* here. I buy them frozen from Bangladeshi shops."

Ellora cannot help marvelling at her sister's determination and resourcefulness in finding the kind of fish her husband likes to eat. Husband or no husband, she cannot visualize herself going to the same lengths and taking the same amount of trouble over something as inane and insignificant as buying fish. But then, she is not like her sister who despite having a master's degree in chemistry has willingly made a career out of taking care of others. Just like their mother has done all her life.

"Maa was so particular about getting fresh fish for the day's cooking," says Ellora out of the blue.

"But she didn't have to hunt around for fish like me; the fish came to her doorstep," points out Aparna.

"You're right. The fish-vendor used to come with a basketful of fish fresh from the lake. I remember Maa inspecting the gills for redness before buying her daily quota of fish."

"She was like a Queen Mother choosing her gems for the day. It's sad that she's given up eating fish after Baba's death."

The GPS' female voice once again interrupts their conversation and as Aparna carefully listens to the instructions, Ellora looks out of the window. Outside, the sky looks vast and blue. As always, she wonders if the size of the country has anything to do with the vastness of its skies. Never before has she seen skies so magnificently vast and so brilliantly blue, but even as she admires the unhindered blue vista unfolding before her, there appears a very tall monument bisecting the open sky into two neat blocks of azure.

"Those are cherry blossom trees; they're not in bloom now, but you should see them when thousands collectively blossom to paint the town pink. It's a glorious sight. What a pity you were not here when they were all abloom a couple of months ago," says Aparna, as she looks for a parking place.

"May be, I can stand under one of the trees and coax it to bloom all over again," says Ellora.

"Not a bad idea. Only, you might have to stand for another nine months or so, before the tree obliges. But you know what, it's not such a bad idea. Instead of coming with me, why don't you take a walk under those trees and coax them to bloom, while I quickly go and finish the unpleasant business of buying fish?" suggests Aparna.

The view is so good and the offer is so tempting that Ellora does not need much coaxing to accept her sister's proposal.

Aparna looks for a parking space and stops when she finally spots a slot that is about to be vacated. She waits, but the driver of the car is taking forever to reverse.

"A watched car never reverses," Aparna theorizes in her typical Aparnian style, as she impatiently waits for the car to move. Ellora shakes her head and smiles, marvelling at her sister's capacity for coming up with gems like this.

After waving a temporary goodbye to her sister, Ellora stands under a cherry blossom tree. Bereft of its showy blossoms, the tree looks quite pedestrian. No flower-laden flourish to remind one of its springtime splendour. No budding signs of the elaborate makeover the tree undergoes every spring; a makeover so spectacular that the city celebrates a festival named after the blossoming trees. But alas! The magnificent flower-show lasts only for a few days.

"It's a fleeting season of blossoming delight and then, it is back to the same old humdrum existence, like my own love life," Ellora sardonically reflects, as she sits under one of the trees. However, she does not let her cynical reflections prevent her from enjoying the unhurried pace of the uncluttered urban space around her. She likes the fact that there are more leafy trees than people and vehicles on the streets. She also appreciates the fact that the monuments and the buildings, despite their imposing stature and magnificent hulk, do not overwhelm the senses or dominate the skyline. Even the tall and slim Washington Monument, though visible from everywhere, gives you enough room to ignore its towering presence. That is, if you wish to ignore its towering presence.

A skein of geese honk noisily, as they fly overhead in perfect formation. Ellora watches them contentedly until their resonant honks grow fainter and fainter and their formation fades away in the sky. The noise of the flying birds is replaced by the noise made by a group of boisterous high-school students, all laughing and joking, as they walk in small groups on the side-walk. Two girls lag behind their peers, because they are too engrossed in their own private conversation. Watching the two of them takes Ellora back to her school days, when Aditi and she had so much to say to each other that they often forgot the existence of everyone else around them.

"And then came a time when we had nothing to say to each other," recalls Ellora without feeling the sadness and bitterness that had overwhelmed her after breaking up with her best friend.

****

Chapter 30

December 2010, Delhi

They did not speak to each other for years. Even when Ellora visited Delhi to see her grandmother, she made no attempt to contact her once best friend. Aditi, for her part, was too stung by her friend's refusal to have anything to do with her to risk making any more attempts to contact her and explain her side of the story.

Not that there was much to explain. She had betrayed her dearest friend in the most callous and shocking manner and no excuses or explications could explain that away.

If truth be told, Aditi herself was clueless about how she had ended up falling for Rohinton Merchant. She was not the type to fall for guys, least of all, her best friend's boyfriend. Wearing her heart on her sleeve was too trivial a thing for someone as cerebral and goal-oriented as Aditi. And yet, when Rohinton Merchant began to seek her company after his dismissal from the national squad, she was unable to resist his persuasive and persistent overtures. She was flattered that he had chosen her as his sounding board to get things off his chest.

They both had known that it was a temporary thing. Before long, Rohinton would be leaving for England to play county cricket and she too would get too busy with her medical studies to have time for anything else. However, while they were still together, she cherished the moments she spent in the dapper batsman's company.

Of course, the fling (no matter how fleeting it turned out

to be) had lasting consequences. Aditi lost her only friend to this breezy summer romance. She had no idea where Ellora had suddenly disappeared. All her attempts to contact her friend were thwarted. Ellora's parents were civil, but cold. They refused to divulge their daughter's whereabouts. Even though they did not taunt or insult her, they made it very clear that they would like Aditi to leave their daughter alone.

It was not until many years later that Aditi and Ellora came face to face in a crowded shopping mall in Delhi. It was an emotional reunion; they both hugged and cried under the inquisitive eyes of Aditi's three-year-old son Arav, who was clearly puzzled why his mother was hugging a stranger and crying so loudly.

The long lost friends had a lot of catching up to do. Many things had happened during the years of long separation. Aditi was now married and lived in London with her doctor husband and son, whereas Ellora was still unmarried and lived in Delhi with her paralyzed grandmother and her arthritic housekeeper, Bela-di. There was so much to say, so much to learn and so many gaps to fill; however, a noisy shopping-mall was not a place where you could catch up on each other's lives and reminisce about the good old days, especially if your toddler had suddenly decided that he wanted to play video games.

"Let's meet tomorrow at my place," Aditi suggested and then, added quickly with a nervous smile, "We can meet at your place too, if coming all the way to Mehrauli is inconvenient for you." It was kind of strange to see her once domineering friend suggest something so tentatively and politely, as if she was afraid that Ellora would somehow find an excuse to refuse her invitation.

How could she refuse? If only Aditi knew how desperately she had wanted to revisit Balraj Uncle's farmhouse and how badly she had missed all the good times she had spent there in the company of her dearest friend. Regardless of all the dreadful and shocking things that happened afterwards, the place held many happy associations for Ellora. Not a day had gone by since the sudden parting of their ways, when she had not nostalgically thought of those fun-filled picnics under the Amaltas trees.

* * *

Balraj Uncle's farmhouse had not changed much even after so many years, however, those who resided there had. Balraj Uncle looked older and balder, Amrita Auntie looked prettier and happier and Roshan looked even taller and bulkier than before. Roshan still liked to crack juvenile jokes, but now that he had a decorous wife who frowned if his jokes were too puerile, his humour was less reckless and risky than before. He also winked a lot less, even though his hugs and handshakes were as bone-crunching as ever.

They all sat on the front porch and chatted. The garden had not changed much, except now it had more trees bearing mauve, pink and white blooms. The rose pergola under which Amrita Auntie's wedding had taken place still stood tall and blooming with pink and cream roses hanging down in masses.

"Let's take a walk in the backyard for old times' sake," suggested Aditi, eager to be alone with her friend. Arav wanted to accompany his mother and her pretty friend, but Roshan lured him away by bribing him with a hard-to-resist offer of playing video games with him.

Without realizing it, they both started walking towards the Amaltas grove, even though there were many other newly landscaped areas where they could sit and talk. The cassia trees were not yet in bloom but provided ample shade. As she sat on a cushioned chair, Ellora could almost visualize Rohinton Merchant standing at the bend and waving at them.

"He got married last year to an English girl," said Aditi, reading her thoughts.

"I know. I saw it in the news."

Ellora remembered being shocked but not disturbed when

she saw Rohinton's wedding picture in the sports section of the newspaper. Her first impulse had been to nervously scan the entire article accompanying the picture to make sure that her own name had been kept out of the news. Fortunately, the short paragraph only talked about Rohinton Merchant's 1995 debut at Colombo, in which he had made an important contribution to the team's victory by hitting a century against the Sri Lankans. It also mentioned how the right-handed batsman's career was abruptly cut short after he was unceremoniously dropped from the Indian squad because of poor form. Fortunately, the article did not go into the reasons for the batsman's poor form. Rohinton Merchant was no longer a big enough name in India for the journalists to dig up dirt from his past.

"He looks quite different now," said Aditi.

Ellora could not have agreed more. Like Aditi, she too had been dismayed to see Rohinton's picture. He was not yet middle-aged, but there were already signs of middle-age-spread all over. His face looked puffy with a down-and-coming double chin and his mop of curly brown hair was now a thatch of thinning grey hair. Gone was the spontaneous, boyish grin; the man who was smiling at her from the newspaper had a cultivated, plastic smile. Indeed, Rohinton Merchant was no longer a heartthrob by any stretch of imagination. He no longer made her heart skip a beat. Even if he were to still look like a heartthrob, Ellora doubted if he would have had any impact on her resilient heart that had stopped beating for him many years ago. When exactly had she got over him? She could not recall, but it must have happened a long time ago for her to forget all about it.

"He now runs a cricket academy in Derbyshire," informed Aditi in an attempt to break the uncomfortable silence.

"Does he live close to your place?" asked Ellora, wondering if her question seemed probing.

"If your question is, 'Do you meet each other in London?'

the answer is, 'No.' We lost touch soon after he left for England to play for Glamorgan County in Cardiff. We corresponded for a while, but then we both got too busy with our respective careers to have time for a long distance relationship."

There it was! Aditi had admitted to having had a relationship with Rohinton, no matter how short-lived and meaningless it had turned out to be.

They remained quiet for some time, both watching a pair of tiny green bee-eaters sitting on a branch with their backs turned to each other, as if they had had a tiff. The kohl- eyed birds reminded Ellora of her dancer mother's large brown eyes, made huger and darker by thick lines of black eye-liner before her performances.

"I'm sorry for everything that happened," said Aditi, after a long pause.

Ellora was not sure if Aditi was apologising to her for catalysing her breakup with Rohinton, or if she was sorry for the ordeals she herself underwent after the posters had come out. Not knowing how to respond to this vague apology, Ellora just looked at Aditi and gave her a reassuring smile, as if to say, it did not matter anymore.

Indeed, it did not matter anymore. She had forgiven Aditi long before she had fully gotten over Rohinton Merchant. She now knew that falling in love was not always a logical or ethical decision; people betrayed friends, broke promises, relinquished their loved ones, renounced kingdoms and did many other deranged things under the influence of a heady cocktail of chemicals. She now knew first-hand that it was possible to fall in love with someone highly unavailable against your own insistent voice of reason.

The pulls of heartstrings were often more powerful than the pangs of conscience.

* * *

The branches above whispered and nodded, as a breeze frostily blew over them, cold-shouldering their cheerful greetings. Aditi, who was feeling cold, moved her chair to a position where she could get direct sunlight. Her face glowed under the mellow rays of the December sun. She had put on weight, but marriage and motherhood had made her more attractive; her face now had a softer look about it. As expected, she had done extremely well even on the career front, acquiring all the professional degrees, fellowships, trainings and awards needed for working in a prestigious hospital in London as a consultant obstetrician and gynaecologist. As she listened to Aditi talking animatedly about her job, husband and son, Ellora tried to ignore the twinge of envy and regret she felt in her heart.

When a maid came carrying a tray of hot snacks and steaming tea, they were both transported to the days when they sat under those very Amaltas trees to eat *aloo parathas* and omelette.

As they sipped tea, Ellora told Aditi about her years in Gargi College in Nand Nagar and the reasons she had ended up getting a doctorate in environmental biology instead of becoming a doctor.

"No regrets, even though there're days when I can't help wondering if my father would've died a happier man, had I kept my promise of becoming a cardiologist," said Ellora with a sad smile.

Aditi remained quiet, not knowing what to say to her friend. She was ashamed that she had not been there for Ellora when her father had passed away.

"Was he sick?" she asked after a pause.

"He had a heart condition, made worse by the worries and pains I continued to cause him by saying no to all the prospective grooms he painstakingly chose. It was only a matter of time before his broken heart gave way to the pressures I put him through," said Ellora, trying hard to control her trembling voice.

"Don't blame yourself for things that were beyond your control," said Aditi comfortingly before asking, "Any particular reason for rejecting all the suitors?"

"Suitors, my foot. Most of them were more like prospective employers, who came with a list probing questions to find out if I had all the requisite qualifications and qualities they were looking for in their dream wife. Oh! I could write a book on those pompous fools!"

The topic then turned to Babu Shona's death that had happened a year after Ellora left for Nand Nagar.

"He was already ageing, of course, but I think he grew old overnight after my departure," said Ellora.

They talked some more about the people they had both known. By the time they went inside, most gaps had been filled and most distances had been bridged.

****

Chapter 31

July 2011,
Veterans Park, Virginia

It is just the kind of morning everyone was hoping for: bright and sunny, but not too warm.

"Wow!" exclaims Ellora as she gets out of the car and inspects the huge grounds surrounded by tall trees.

Two young men come running as soon as they spot Rahul's car. Rahul hastily introduces his sister-in-law to his young team-mates and then, without further ado, asks the question that is uppermost in his mind.

"Where's everyone?" It irritates him no end that despite his repeated reminders, most of his teammates have not yet arrived for the pre-match warm up.

As the three men get busy unloading heavy bags from the trunk, Rahul turns towards Ellora and says, "You can carry on but don't go too far. The match starts at ten sharp."

"I'll be there on time," assures Ellora before heading towards a stretch of shallow water bordering the road. It's quite a long walk, but she does not mind; she wants to have a closer look at the long-legged bird wading through the blue spikes of pickerelweeds.

Aparna was not happy with her sister's decision to go with Rahul instead of accompanying her to the match-venue a little later.

"What's the point of reaching the ground so early? You'll be all sweaty and sun-tanned by the time everyone arrives," Aparna grumbled.

"I promise I won't look like something the cat brought in," Ellora tried to humour her sister by using her kind of phraseology.

However, now as she stands there and takes in the view around her, Ellora completely loses track of time. She gets a shrill reminder of the minutes gone by when her cell-phone starts ringing.

"Where are you?" asks Aparna without making any attempt to hide her irritation. She softens her admonishing tone only to order her sister to come back without further delay. Ellora has no other choice except to retrace her steps to the ground as quickly as possible.

"Where were you?" asks Aparna, scrutinizing her sister's appearance.

"Trekking off the beaten track, I guess," says Jayanti, one of Aparna's close friends.

Ellora is acutely conscious that all eyes are upon her. The group of women sitting on folding chairs under a huge sycamore tree are regarding her with frank interest. She quickly sits down on an empty chair next to her sister to avoid being openly stared at. She is aware that many of these women are very close to her sister. They have been good friends ever since Aparna first arrived in this country after marriage. They may not share bloodline, but they have been sharing their joys, sorrows, problems, and confidences for years. That is why Ellora is uncomfortable in their presence. They probably know a lot more about her than they should be knowing and therefore take a lot more interest in her than they should be taking.

"You seem to have perfected the art of applying the no-makeup makeup," says one of the women, still regarding Ellora with open admiration and an affable smile.

"Ellora's idea of applying makeup is sweating in the sun and then wiping off all traces of the makeup she has been scolded into applying," says Aparna before her sister can reply.

"But it works. Look at her face. So flawless and fresh," says the woman and everyone nods in agreement.

Aparna knows that the unwanted attention is making her sister very uncomfortable, therefore, she quickly changes the topic by asking, "Why have the Bhallas not arrived as yet?

"Vicky and Sweety Bhalla always take her own sweet time to arrive, so what if he is the president of our cricket club? But looks like, her daughters and their friends are here," someone points out.

They all turn their heads to watch the new arrivals. Ellora squirms uncomfortably when she notes that two of the young women getting down from the car are the ones whom she had severely reprimanded at Vicky Bhalla's wedding anniversary bash.

"Why doesn't someone knock some dress-sense into Charu? That sundress with those huge sunflowers makes her look even more bulky," comments someone. It reminds Ellora of the mean title she had bestowed upon the poor girl just a week ago. She would rather not think about those silly titles, but now as she watches the dumpy damsel (who indeed looks very plump in her flouncy and flowery dress), she cannot help agreeing with her sister's friends. The young woman is indeed in serious need of some wardrobe counselling.

"Not that my own dress-sense is any better. Come to think of it, had it not been for Didi's continuous nagging, I'll still be in my dowdy casuals," Ellora reminds herself.

She had balked as usual when Aparna had taken her shopping the previous day, obstinately refusing to try on the clothes her sister had chosen for her.

"I don't do sleeveless tops, especially the ones trimmed with ridiculous ruffles in front. Agreed, I'm your little sis, but Didi, let me remind you just in case you've forgotten: I'm not exactly a spring-chicken anymore to be trimmed and dressed. Pun intended."

"Rubbish. You're in a country where you're as young as the clothes you wear. It's time you discarded those bagful of silly notions along with your baggage of baggy brown clothes you've brought from Delhi. These toned arms and those long shapely legs are meant to be flaunted in clothes that are little more flattering and fitting than your current set."

Her sister was right, as usual. Ellora feels taller, slimmer and younger in her new pair of blue jeans and white sleeveless top with ruffles that do not ruffle her feathers as much as they did when she first saw them.

"Looks like, we've won the toss. I wonder who's going to bat first," says Aparna, as she intently watches what is going on in the field. She gets her answer when her husband Rahul comes running towards them with a beaming smile on his face.

"We're batting," he informs them, as he hands his cell-phone and wallet to his wife for safekeeping. Then turning towards his sister-in-law, he asks, "Ellora, why are you sitting here? Come with me to the player's gallery. You'll get a better view from there. You'll also get better angles, in case you're planning to take some shots of your handsome brother-in-law in action."

Ellora does not need to be told a second time. She quickly gets up, happy to get away from the probing eyes and the boring babble of her sister's friends. She walks with Rahul to the so-called player's gallery, which is just a makeshift covered area with tiered rows of aluminium benches. Rahul quickly introduces her to his teammates before walking to the field with his batting partner Jai Sehgal.

"I'm happy you could make it," says Jai to her before departing.

As she watches Jai walking to the field with her brother-in-law, Ellora realizes that she too is happy to see him once again. Not just happy, but ecstatic. She is aware of a funny kind of floaty-fluttery-fuzzy-fizzy feeling inside her chest.

Vicky Bhalla brings her back to the ground by announcing

in his thundering pitch, "Mark my word Allora, Rahul is going to be today's Man of the Match. He's in great form."

Indeed, her brother-in-law is an absolute delight to watch. He looks all set to demolish the pace attack from the young rival bowlers with his brilliant hooks, drives and square cuts. Jai, on the other hand, looks slightly nervous after surviving an LBW appeal in the first over itself. However, once he starts hitting the balls, he does so with the complete ease and élan of an accomplished batsman, looking quite unruffled and suave as he tackles the bouncers aimed at his helmet. "A stylish batsman, not entirely without charm," decides Ellora, as she watches Jai play. Suddenly, she is transported to another place and time when she had been watching another match on television with Aditi and had been mesmerized by Rohinton Merchant's aggressive 'battitude.' However, the flash of memory fades as quickly as it came. The fleeting image of her past love does not come in the way of the current pleasure of watching another batsman batting with delightful and carefree battitude.

When the drinks interval is announced, trays of cucumber sandwich, cakes and cutlets magically appear on a makeshift picnic table. The players from the rival team (mostly students from various neighbouring universities) are also invited to join them. All eyes are on Rahul and Jai, as they walk back together. Charu runs up to Jai with a plateful of snacks, but he politely refuses to eat anything. Rahul, on the other hand, straightaway helps himself to his wife's fish cutlets, loudly declaring that they are sumptuous. Everyone seconds him, making Aparna beam with pleasure.

When the game resumes, Vicky Bhalla asks her to join him in the front row.

"Didn't I tell you that Rahul is going to be today's Man of the Match?" asks Vicky Bhalla. "But watch out for Jai too, for he's a fantastic finisher who likes to bat till the very end. Though the formidable Tigers have had a successful season so far, I'm sure today's match belongs to FCC," states the President of the Franconia Cricket Club with justifiable pride.

"Looking at the way our two openers are batting, that's a strong possibility," says Ellora.

"If we win today's match, I'm going to throw a party to celebrate our entry in the semi-finals," declares Vicky Bhalla loudly. His impromptu announcement is greeted with cheers all around.

Ellora is happy to note that her brother-in-law and Jai are looking well settled on the crease, steadily building up a partnership that could easily be a match-winning one. She crosses her fingers and hopes with all her heart that the two of them lead their team to a grand victory. She is in a mood for celebration. She wants a grand party. She wants an excuse to go back to the Bhalla mansion, where she can quietly slip away to the lily pond with its dazzling water lilies and swarming dragonflies. She wants to lose herself in the maze of those flower-edged paths all over again. She wants all this and more. And she does not want to get into the reasons for wanting these utterly silly things. There will be time enough for analysis and soul searching later; but for now, she just wants to remain with this funny floaty-fluttery-fuzzy-fizzy feeling that refuses to fizzle out.

****

Chapter 32

July 2011,

Mrs Morris's home in Edgewater, Maryland

Eventually, the floaty-fluttery-fuzzy-fizzy feeling has to fizzle out and so it does in due course. By Monday Ellora's high spirits have gradually given way to a sobering sense of sanity. The lingering fizz is not as flat as last night's champagne, but neither is it gushing with frothy abandon. However, decides Ellora, it is time to put a temporary tight lid to on all those bubbly feelings and bottle up those potent but potentially troublesome emotions. She must retreat to the quiet privacy of her room in order to meet some deadly deadlines.

But now as she types her field notes, Ellora's mind keeps going back to her exhilaration at Jai's presence on the cricket field. She has been romantically attracted to men before; she knows the symptoms quite well. She also knows the chemistry behind this temporary euphoria. However, she suddenly wants to know more and therefore, instead of working on her research paper she runs a search on "Love Chemicals in Brain." Within seconds she gets more than thirteen million results. She opens one of the articles and starts reading.

"Love originates and develops in the brain just like theories and theorems do. There is enough scientific evidence to suggest that when the Cupid's arrow strikes, it targets your brain rather than your heart. A tiny factory below your brain goes into production mode from the moment you are romantically attracted to someone. As you interact with this person, the pockets of your brain get busy producing a potent love potion and whoosh! You're crazily and euphorically in love."

Ellora quickly skims through the first few paragraphs before going back to typing her notes, but her mind keeps going back to what she has just read.

How old had she been, when she had first fallen in love with Rohinton Merchant? Which of her brain chemicals had been responsible for her besotted state? Had it been dopamine-drenched puppy love or had it been serotonin-starved obsession?"

Ellora closes her eyes and tries to recall the exhilaration she felt every time Rohinton's eyes furtively rested on hers. It is strange how vividly she can recollect those moments, given the fact that her love for the batsman died a natural death a long time ago. She can even smell the faint fragrance of the yellow blossoms that hung like chandeliers from the Amaltas trees, under which she and her friends were having a picnic when Rohinton Merchant first walked in and changed her world forever.

Had she felt the same degree of giddy elation when Jai's eyes had rested on hers the other day? No, how is that possible? She is not a teenager anymore. Besides, she has learnt her lessons from life. She knows better than to be euphoric over someone who is notoriously commitment-shy. But does her brain also know this?

It is evident to her that with her mind wandering so wildly, it will be impossible to focus on her work. She therefore goes back to reading the article.

"The chemical high of romantic attraction is transitory. The initial magic and euphoria go out of the window over a period of time. What cements and deepens this otherwise fleeting attraction, however, is the timely intervention by oxytocin. This so-called 'cuddle hormone' helps couples to stay committed to each other by replacing the short-lived passion with more enduring feelings like compassion and devotion."

That's interesting, thinks Ellora. She closes her eyes once again and starts wondering if her star-crossed romance with Rohinton would have blossomed into something more enduring, had it not been cut short so ruthlessly by that ugly scandal. The oxytocin ambulance never arrived. With no rescue-operation to resuscitate the dying flames, the love chemicals failed to sustain the fire they had started in the first place. Over the years, even the ashes were blown away, leaving behind only a few blisters and a lifelong fear of fire for the girl who had dared to play with the risky flames.

Looking back upon those incidents from a neurobiological perspective, Ellora has a better understanding of those unfortunate events.

Sooner or later I'd have discarded my rose-tinted glasses to see Rohinton for who he was, instead of magnifying his virtues and brushing aside his flaws. But what if we hadn't broken up so abruptly? What if we had eventually married? Would I have continued to find him handsome despite his expanding waistline and thinning hairline? Would I have continued to love him, despite his roving eye and self-absorbed ways?

Her eyes are tired so she decides to stop for the day. She goes to bed with her thoughts and memories; thoughts and memories that now keep her awake.

Was it Carl Jung who said that we love who we love because of how closely that person reminds us of our ancestors? But if she was so hardwired to like men who reminded her of her forefathers, then why had she rejected all the men chosen by her father? At least one or two of those Bengali men (each one of them a high-caste Brahmin, no less) should have fitted into the decisive love-map in her brain.

Night after night, her father had bent over the pages of The Times of India and The Hindustan Times and shortlisted suitable boys for her. And she had rejected each one of them for reasons that, according to her parents, were neither valid, nor solid. How could she have rejected those qualified engineers, doctors or bankers for being too short or too pompous or too immature? Why had she detested those men so much? Wasn't her brain genetically mapped and psychologically programmed to at least like them, if not fall in love with them right away? What had she been thinking defying the wishes of her parents and denying her own biological urges? By rejecting the boys (yes, men are often referred to as boys in some cultures) chosen by her father, she had not only dishonoured the time-honoured traditions of her forefathers, but had also disregarded her own ancient biological drive to find a mate.

What was it about her that prevented her from toeing the line, from being the kind of good girl most Bengali parents like to raise? A daughter they can dotingly call their Shona Meye, their Golden Girl. Like the prized metal, this good little golden girl is supposed to be precious and beautiful but her glowing beauty is not just ornamental; it shines from within, with unbeatable virtues (or should it be called beatable virtues?) like malleability and ductility thrown in for good measures. Malleability, submissiveness and obedience are considered to be the most desirable virtues in a daughter and indispensable, if she is to be lovingly moulded into the society's age-old concepts of a good girl; the kind who, when she eventually grows up, will fit into the love-map of an educated Bengali boy from a respectable family.

"I could not be the good girl my parents would've liked me to be," reflects Ellora, not ruefully, but with the helplessness of someone who cannot help being the way she inherently is.

"My brain probably has a highly warped love map that refuses to recognize any of the nice Bengali suitors who are supposed to fit into it snugly. Or am I like that dog in Pavlov's experiment in classical conditioning – too afraid to salivate over a potential mate, because of the painful shock I received the first time around?"

"What do you want? A prince?" Her mother had asked her angrily after she had rejected yet another suitable boy chosen by her father.

No, she does not want a prince, but then, she does not want a frog either.

Ellora ruefully smiles, as she recalls her widowed mother's

gentle face, nowadays perpetually fraught with frustration at failing to fulfil her late husband's dying wish.

What do I really want? Why am I being so finicky and fault-finding? Am I scared that these suitors, who are no princes to begin with, will turn out to be freaky frogs after marriage?

The questions take her back to a passage in the article, where the writer has quoted Dr Helen Fisher, an anthropologist at the Rutgers University. When asked, if her years of research on the chemistry of love has helped her to find a perfect romantic partner, the anthropologist quipped, "I kiss fewer frogs."

I too have kissed only one slimy frog in my thirty-three years of existence, thinks Ellora, as she sets an alarm for 4:00 a.m. She has to wake up early to finish her pending work. She must complete all her experimental analyses before December, if she wishes to have a relaxed holiday with her family in New York during Christmas.

****

Chapter 33

December 2011,
Springfield, Virginia

As she experiences the freedom of speeding along on an interstate highway not yet choked by the rush hour traffic, Ellora feels relaxed for the first time in months, despite being dead tired from lack of sleep.

It is a pleasure to drive on roads where everyone follows lane discipline. Back in Delhi, driving was always a series of close calls; she could never have let her guard down on the chaotic lanes where cars, autos, trucks, scooters, bullock carts and bicycles all jostled for space, honked for no apparent reasons and flouted all the traffic rules.

This is her first trip to Springfield since last August and Ellora is looking forward to meeting Aparna and Rahul after a gap of nearly four months. She is also looking forward to driving down to New York with her sister. Only the thought of meeting her elder brother Arnab is making her slightly nervous. Actually, neither Aparna nor Arnab is Ellora's real sibling; they both are her first cousins, but this has not stopped either of them from being overprotective towards their adopted sister; or from trying to change her, for that matter. While Aparna is determined to change Ellora's unmarried status to a married one, Arnab is more focused on changing his younger sister's personality and pronunciation.

"When in America, speak as the Americans do," Arnab had advised Ellora soon after she had arrived from India less than a year ago. More American than many Americans, Arnab frowns upon any kind of phraseological and phonological aberrations, especially the kinds made by newly arrived Indians.

"Don't encourage your sister to imitate the funny accent that you've picked up after coming to this country. Why should we change the way we speak just because we are living in a foreign country? Your father always used to say that your language shapes your identity. How you speak is who you are," Sumitra Devi had sternly told her son in her chaste Bengali.

"Maa, your language also shapes people's perception of you. In this country, if you wish to be understood, you've got to speak like them."

It all started with the ordering of tomato soup in a restaurant.

"It's not *te-MAH-toh,* it's *te-MAY-toh,*" her brother had primly pointed out.

"But I've called it *te-MAH-toh* all my life."

"Then it's time you started calling it *te-MAY-toh,* because when you're in America, you pronounce every vowel and enunciate every syllable the way the Americans do, unless you want people to gawk at you quizzically."

Ellora wanted to tell her brother primly that she had learnt her English from the Irish nuns in school. However, she did not retort, because she is too well brought-up to defy her elders, bumptious siblings included.

Arnab Chatterjee himself has lived in America long enough to have left behind the days when he had been gawked at by puzzled waitresses and clueless colleagues. He has worked on his accent to get rid of any inflections that will mark him as an Indian-American.

Blending in has been Arnab Chattrejee's chief motto from the time he first arrived in America as a graduate student almost twenty-five years ago. Since then, reflects Ellora, her brother has made a concerted effort to talk, act and behave like the people he now calls his compatriots. He openly admits that he has reached where he is today by speaking phonetically correct English and holding politically correct views.

"I made sure to tone down my fresh-off-the-boat accent and downplay my hyphenated identity," he boasts to all the youngsters who come to him for career advice.

Ellora understands her brother's passion for wanting to be an American sans the hyphen. He wants to be called an American and not an Indian-American. After all, he has lived with his Indian-American status long enough to have a strong desire to eliminate all traces of the superfluous dash that often hangs like a question mark to overshadow his identity. Yet, for all his passion for being an American without a hyphen, once he reaches home, Arnab Chatterjee slips into his Indian persona with the same ease with which he slips into the soft comfort of his draw-stringed, made-in-India kurta-pyjamas.

Ellora cannot help thinking that her brother is still trudging back and forth between his American and Indian identities, trying his best not to let the two overlap, even as he switches from one identity to another with the swiftness of a chameleon eager to blend in because it is afraid to stand out for the wrong reasons.

Whenever he calls Ellora to find how she is doing, Arnab Chatterjee goes back to being his American self.

As someone who has fulfilled his American dream by reaching one of the top rungs of the powerful corporate ladder, Arnab Chatterjee feels he is entitled to advise his newly arrived sister on how to put down her roots in American soil. He wants his brilliant sister to not just find her feet, but also to follow in his successful footsteps. Rung-by-rung, vowel-by-vowel, syllable-by-syllable.

It must be admitted though that for all his snobbish, opinionated, and overbearing ways, Arnab Chatterjee is a loving and concerned brother who cares deeply for his orphaned cousin. At times, bit too deeply perhaps, but he cannot help being overprotective of Ellora. He wants to make sure that his confused cousin knows what she wants in life and makes the right choice, instead of letting others push her into marrying the first eligible man who comes along. After all, he owes it to his late uncle Akshay Chatterjee, who had always encouraged him to pursue his dream of coming to America with passion and determination, instead of letting his parents talk him out of it.

****

Chapter 34

December 2011,

Springfield, Virginia

"Only one small suitcase?" asks Aparna, as she comes out to greet her sister.

"Come on Didi, I'm here only for two weeks," reminds Ellora.

"True, but don't forget that these will be two action-packed weeks," says Aparna with a beaming smile as they start walking towards the house. When her comment does not elicit any reaction from her sister, she prods, "Aren't you excited that we're travelling to New York?"

"I'm too exhausted to feel excited. Right now, all I want to do is to sleep, sleep and sleep," says Ellora, lifting her feet one at a time to take her shoes off before entering the carpeted foyer with her suitcase.

As they sit down on the living room sofa, Aparna notes that her sister indeed looks as if she could do with some sleep.

"You look thinner."

"And browner," volunteers Ellora.

"Browner too, but I'm more concerned about your being thinner. Have you been skipping meals? Maa is not going to be too pleased to see you like this."

"I'm not undernourished, just sleep deprived."

"In that case, let's have an early lunch. The birthday party doesn't start before seven, so you've got plenty of time to catch up on your sleep."

"Whose birthday party?" asks an alarmed Ellora, suddenly waking up to the fact that her sister had not been kidding when she had informed her that her two-week stay was going to be action-packed.

"My friend Jayanti turned fifty today. Her husband is throwing a surprise party for her and we all have been invited," informs Aparna.

"Didi, I don't think I'm up to attending any party tonight, least of all, a noisy birthday party. The previous evening, Mrs Morris shared her plum cake recipe and I nodded, nodded, nodded…and then just nodded off. If you insist on dragging me to this party, there's a strong possibility that I may repeat the nodding-off act once again. I may even snore in public, scaring away all the prospective grooms and ruining my marriage prospects in the process."

"That's not funny Ellora," says Aparna, trying her best not to sound too admonishing.

Ellora realizes that she has probably crossed the line by overstating her case and therefore, she tries a different approach.

"Even my jokes are falling flat, so now you know how sleepy I am. But jokes apart I've got a severe headache. In fact, my whole body is aching from lack of sleep."

"Your eyes are indeed red. You're probably coming down with flu. Let me check your temperature."

Aparna is back to being her caring Sister Aparna self. Within minutes, Ellora's temperature is taken and she is made to gulp down a bowl of nourishing soup before being tucked into bed and given medicine.

* * *

Ellora wakes up from her deep sleep to find herself alone in her room. The room is dark, except for the streetlight filtering in through the curtains. The house is very quiet, disquietingly so. Even the street outside is unnervingly silent. She can see parked cars, but not a single human being. Suddenly, she is depressed and homesick.

Homesick? But where is her home? This guest bedroom in Aparna's house? Or her rented room in Mrs Morris's house? Or her huge room in their Vijaypur home that is now unoccupied? Or her tiny room in her maternal uncle's apartment in Delhi that has closets with some of her clothes still hanging inside? Which of those dwellings can be regarded as her home?

* * *

They had all called her selfish for refusing to accompany her mother to the United States. Everyone had expected her to jump at the opportunity of moving to a new country and starting a new life. As if she had not been subjected to enough uprooting and relocation already! How many times was she supposed to relocate and start a new life all over again? But no one was willing to understand it from her point of view. They continued to blame her. It was because of her obduracy that her widowed mother was forced to live alone in Vijaypur, instead of being with her elder daughter and son in America.

In the end, of course, Sumitra Devi had had no other choice except to leave the country without Ellora. It had become impossible for her to live alone in that huge house after her husband's death.

Ellora had had her reasons for not wanting to leave Delhi. For the first time in many years, she was in a place that made her feel as if she belonged there. The city held so many cherished memories of her childhood. There was also a sense of contentment. She was doing things that made her happy. Besides teaching botany and environmental biology to undergraduate students in a girls' college, she was also actively involved in doing voluntary work for a non-profit environmental group.

Delhi Matters was a team of conservationists, scientific experts, social activists, educators, wildlife photographers and documentary filmmakers, all passionate about saving

Delhi's trees, forests and water bodies. Together, they explored the floodplains of the River Yamuna, discovered the wilderness hidden in the back-of beyond pockets of Delhi, surveyed the neighbouring forests and farmlands and worked towards creating environmental awareness through articles, documentaries and campaigns.

Ellora had started out as their tree expert and had gone on to become the scriptwriter for the documentaries they made. She also used to write articles for their monthly publication Urban Matters. Her work often took her to places outside the city limits.

Fortunately, she could disappear for days without having to answer any questions, because she was now living with her maternal uncle Sanjay Mama, who did not believe in asking questions.

Seven years ago, when Sanjay Sen had permanently moved to Delhi with his German girlfriend, he did so to be able to look after his dying mother in her last days. After his mother's death, he sold their Greater Kailash home and bought a luxury apartment in an upmarket residential colony in South Delhi. When Ellora had moved to Delhi after getting a job offer, he had invited her to stay in his house. He had wanted to make up for all the years he had not been there for his orphaned niece.

Sumitra Devi, however, was not at all happy about Ellora's living arrangements in Delhi. She did not like the fact that her daughter was living with her bohemian uncle and his German girlfriend who were forever partying and travelling, leaving Ellora alone in the house with Bela-di, who was much too old and too much of a couch potato to be a good guardian.

Sumitra Devi was also upset that her already brown daughter was browner than ever. She had worked extremely hard to banish all traces of honey from her daughter's skin, but thanks to all those day-long excursions in the sun, Ellora's complexion now had jars and jars of honey.

The browning of her wardrobe, on the other hand, had happened after she was stung by a bee during a field trip to the Biodiversity Park with a group of college students.

"Did it land upon one of the flowers on your kurta?" her editor Vikram Rathore had asked her the next day, when she was in his office to discuss an article she had been writing for the latest issue of Urban Matters. She looked at him in surprise. She could not believe that he had actually made that comment. Vikram never joked and he rarely smiled. He was too busy being a serious crusader to correct things that had gone wrong with his city to have time for frivolous activities like smiling or joking. But, he was joking with her now. He had even gone so far as to make a comment that was highly flippant and uncomfortably personal. When had he ever looked up from his pile of work to notice what others around him were wearing?

* * *

Ellora's train of thought is interrupted by the ringing of her phone.

"Thank God, you finally picked up. Where were you? Why didn't you answer my calls? Don't tell me you've been sleeping all this while," screams Aparna from the other end.

"As a matter of fact, I have. I just woke up," says Ellora.

"How are you feeling now?"

"I'm feeling much better.

"In that case, quickly change into something nice. Jai is on his way to check on you."

"What do you mean?" Ellora cannot believe what she just heard.

"I had to call Jai and ask him to check on you personally. You didn't leave me any other option, did you? I've been frantically trying to reach you for more than an hour and was extremely worried when you didn't answer any of my calls. Anyway, Jai must be already on his way, so get ready..."

Ellora cannot hear the rest of Aparna's sentence because the doorbell is ringing.

She catches a glimpse of herself in the mirror before rushing out to open the door. She decides she couldn't have looked worse; her tousled hair seems to be at its disobedient best. She quickly coils it into a tight knot before opening the door.

****

Chapter 35

"I apologize for turning up unannounced like this, but I'm here to check on you. Aparna's orders. I tried calling you, but there was no answer," says Jai, as he hesitantly steps inside.

"I was fast asleep and my phone was on silent mode as usual."

"Aparna was worried about you," says Jai, as they start walking towards the living room.

"That's an understatement. She was absolutely panicky, but knowing me, she shouldn't have panicked. She knows I don't always pick up my calls. My phone is either on silent, or switched off."

"Then it's a good thing that you're not a doctor," says Jai as they enter the dining area. He says it quite casually, but the comment somehow makes Ellora wonder if Aparna has told him about her brief stint as a medical student; she would not put it past her sister.

"Actually, I'm here on a mission. Aparna has asked me to make sure that you've had something to eat before you take your next dose of medicine."

"But I'm not hungry," protests Ellora.

"In that case, I'll stay back and give you company until you feel like eating something," says he as he pulls out one of the dining chairs for her before sitting on the chair opposite her.

"So how are you feeling now?" He smiles at her across the mahogany table that divides them.

"I feel wretched," says Ellora.

"Why? Are you still feverish?"

"No, I'm absolutely fine, but I feel wretched for getting you out of the house in this cold weather."

"Then stop feeling bad because I'm happy to have a legitimate excuse for getting out." Jai wants to add that he is also happy to have a legitimate excuse for seeing her again, but stops himself from saying it right in time, because he is not sure how the comment will be construed. Inwardly though, he cannot help admitting that he is indeed happy to have a chance to see her again. Proximity to this intriguing woman always gives him a feeling of pleasure.

However, he pushes the thought away by going back to making small talk.

"Aparna made it quite clear that I had to get in somehow or the other. She told me to barge in, break in, if necessary but not to stop trying until I found you."

"It's so like my Didi to send you on a rescue mission," laughs Ellora before getting up and asking, "I'm going to make myself some tea; what about you? What would you like to drink?"

"Why don't you just sit down and leave the tea-making to me? In fact, I insist that you sit down and relax," says he and then smilingly adds, "Doctor's orders."

Jai obviously knows his way around Aparna's kitchen, for he finds everything he needs without having to rummage through various drawers and cupboards.

He's neat, thinks Ellora, as she watches him roll up his sleeves and wash his hands, before proceeding to fill the kettle with water. Neat can mean so many things and all the definitions of the word apply to Jai, but right now, Ellora is admiring Jai's tidiness. Everything about the man, from his neatly combed hair, to his neatly clipped nails, to his neat, unfussy way of dressing is neat. As he brings the tea tray to the table, Ellora notes that he has left the counter spotlessly clean. Not a cookie crumb, a grain of sugar or a drop of milk left behind to show that someone had been making tea there.

Ellora cannot picture her late father making tea in the kitchen. In fact, she cannot even picture him pouring a glass of water for himself. There had always been someone willing to do those little things for him, leaving him free to do bigger things like curing illnesses and saving lives. Neither can she picture her brother Arnab in the kitchen of his New York apartment. For all his American ways, her brother has yet to shed his Indian inhibition for doing chores that a part of him continues to regard as a woman's job. Her brother-in-law Rahul, of course, is an exception; being a foodie, he loves to cook elaborate meals every once in a while, though Aparna dreads her husband's creative forays into her kitchen because she is the one who has to deal with all the mess he creates.

"Aparna tells me you've been quite busy these past few months," says Jai, as he places the plate of cookies in front of her.

"It's been hectic all right. I've been out in the sun all summer and fall, keeping tabs on tree saplings and tracking their growth. This project is a part of a broader study. We're searching for an answer to a deceptively simple question: is biodiversity good for plant communities?"

"Sounds interesting. So are you enjoying your work?"

"Very much, although it is physically draining. Most of our experiments are conducted outside the lab on experimental forest plots, but I'm used to working in harsh field conditions. Back in Delhi, my work with an environmental group called Delhi Matters was as physically taxing. We were out in the field most of the time."

She takes a sip of her tea before adding, "My brother thinks I'm wasting my time. He's quite disappointed that instead of pursuing my postdoctoral research, I'm whiling away my precious time on projects that will not lead to any worthwhile degree. But to be honest, I've done my share of research and am ready to explore other things."

"Such as?"

"Such as learning how to make films," answers Ellora without thinking.

Her answer takes Jai by complete surprise, but he makes sure not to show it. Instead, he asks casually, "Do you have any experience in filmmaking?"

"I've written scripts for documentaries produced by Delhi Matters but now I want to learn other aspects of filmmaking. I learnt a lot while working with a crew that made a feature-length documentary on the Yamuna River."

"Wow! That's impressive. Do you have the DVD with you?"

"No, but you can watch it on Delhi Matters' official website. It's called Dammed, Doomed and Dead. Our team traced the path of the Yamuna from its pristine source in the Himalayas to the plains where this so-called sacred river collects industrial runoff, untreated sewage, garbage, carcasses, corpses and many other foul offerings to become the dirty stream sluggishly snaking across the heart of Delhi"

Ellora pauses briefly to twist her hair into a knot at the nape of her neck, but within minutes, the knot unfurls on its own to tumble down her shoulders and back.

Like a river in spate, thinks Jai, as he watches the movement of the cascading brown waves in fascination. He is amused by the simile he just used; he is not the type who makes such absurd poetic observations. Is it possible that he came up with that silly simile because Ellora is talking about a river? But then, she is talking about a river in distress rather than in spate.

Ellora is conscious of her unruly locks. She is also conscious of Jai's eyes resting on them. She quickly restrains the tumbling brown waves by twisting them back into a knot, this time more severely and more tightly than before. Her mane is the bane of her day-to-day life; it invariably curls into wayward wisps and waves, instead of following the straight course she would like it to follow.

As she goes back to talking animatedly about the documentary, Jai finds himself regarding Ellora with greater interest. He is suddenly aware that the woman sitting in front of him has a good deal more than just an attractive face. She is no longer the dazzling beauty he first saw at Vicky Bhalla's party; – her face is leaner and browner but it now has a natural radiance and serenity that are soothing to the eye. Her eyes, however, are anything but serene and soothing. Unlined and undefined by any pencil or shadow, they appear disconcertingly larger and greener. He has never seen such green eyes on so brown a face. Why hadn't he noticed that she has flecks of green in her eyes before? *Is it the light reflecting from the lamp above that is making them appear greener than they actually are? Or is it her bluish-green top that is doing the trick? Gosh! How do you take your eyes off a fascinating face like that; a face that is so guileless and yet so beguiling?*

****

Chapter 36

After returning home, Jai switches on his laptop. A quick surfing of the Delhi Matters website yields the documentary he is looking for. He does not have any surgeries scheduled for the next morning; therefore, he does not mind staying up past his usual bedtime to watch the entire documentary titled Damned, Doomed, and Dead. After a short introduction to the fabled Yamuna's mythological history, the documentary follows the river's journey from the foothills of Himalayas to the plains of Northern India. As the landscapes change, so do the narrators and Jai is pleasantly surprised to see Ellora take over the final part of the narration. He rewinds the portion in order to watch her again.

"For a city that claims to be one of the greenest capitals in the world, Delhi also has the dubious distinction of having one of the blackest rivers on earth," says Ellora, her voice powerful, but not overpowering to detract from the graphic visuals that support her strong statement. The camera now moves from her serene face to cover things that are disturbing and ugly.

"The Yamuna is black with the sewage and garbage dumped into it daily. As you view its banks from a moving boat, you can see the stretch of fetid sludge strewn with Styrofoam and plastic debris. There is no sign of life here; no birds, no fish and yet the river is teeming with faecal coliforms that ferment a malodorous soup bubbling with foul gases. You can smell the stink from miles away."

The camera now captures a bird's eye view of the murky

black stream that looks more like a drain than a river. "As you view miles and miles of this apology of a river that is so laden with raw sewage that many call it a putrid black ribbon, it hits you that you're actually looking at miles of red tape, miles of crippled infrastructure, miles of criminal neglect and miles of corruption."

At this point, the camera pans over the garlands and coconuts floating on the viscous black sludge. Ellora faces the camera once again to say, "Rivers are revered in India because they bring the gift of life to us. Unfortunately, our sacred rivers pay a heavy price for being revered too much and respected too little. We worship them and yet treat them as a dumping ground for our sacred offerings and not-so-sacred waste. This particular holy river has literally taken a lot of unholy shit. No wonder the Yamuna's dissolved oxygen levels are so low that the river that once supported life is now gasping for life support. Is there any hope for this dying river? Or have we already choked the Yamuna to death?"

As he watches Ellora interview a rag picker rummaging through piles of rubble on the banks, Jai wonders what makes a seemingly delicate and beautiful woman like her take on tasks that are certainly not for the faint-hearted. His own job requires him to deal with unsightly sights and unsettling situations on a daily basis, but his environs are sterilized and clean, even beautiful, with sage-green walls, brightly lit corridors and rooms overlooking gardens. He knows that he is finding the visuals highly disturbing, because he has led a sanitized existence cut off from the grubby ground realities back home. He was only ten, when he accompanied his parents and siblings to the United States and since then, his visits to India have been limited to occasional trip. Even those infrequent trips stopped once he joined medical school. Now his hospital schedule is so tight that he cannot even make time for visiting his family in Florida.

There is one more reason for not visiting his family often enough. They invariably broach the unpleasant topic of his remarriage, as if marrying once was not good enough. His parents insist that he will be truly happy only after he remarries. According to them, without marriage, his life is not complete enough for him to feel completely happy.

"Am I completely happy?" Jai asks himself. The answer is, 'No.' He revises his question and asks, "Am I unhappy?" The answer is 'No' once again. He looks at Ellora's calm face on his computer screen. She has a placid smile on her suntanned face, as she walks back with the gangly boy, carrying a sackful of garbage on his back. "Is she happy?" He does not know the answer, but she certainly seems to have made peace with whatever has caused her to be unhappy in the past.

Jai knows about the horrible car crash that had killed Ellora's biological parents. He also has some vague idea about the unfortunate events that had adversely affected her marriage prospects. There was a time when Aparna used to confide to him a lot. She had often invited him for informal dinner in those days and Ellora's name would invariably crop up during their after-dinner conversations. That is how Jai came to know all about her; well, not everything, but enough for him to be able to add two and two.

Ellora's story had baffled him a lot. It still does. He has spent far too many years away from India to be able to comprehend fully the complexities of Indian society, the nuances of Indian culture and the intricacies of Indian mind-sets. Aparna's attempts at matchmaking, on the other hand, had not just baffled him but had also irritated him quite a bit. He had been peeved when it became clear that Aparna's ulterior motive for frequently inviting him for dinner was to prepare him for the marriage proposal she was ultimately going to spring on him.

"There is no hurry; you can take your time and make up your mind only after you've met her. Ellora is going to be here very soon. Once you two get to know each other, you can take things from there; hopefully to the next level," Aparna had assured him.

The next level, Aparna had obviously been hoping, would be marriage between him and her sister. Jai had not even met this woman (who had yet to arrive from India) and he was expected to date this stranger at a future date with marriage firmly in mind. How could Aparna have expected him to consider this ridiculous proposal?

As much as he hated hurting the feelings of someone who reminded him of his own exuberant and overbearing sister, Jai was left with no other choice except to answer with a firm and unequivocal 'No' to Aparna's preposterous proposal. He had made it clear to her that marriage was not on his agenda anymore; he had been there and done that and did not want to go down that road again.

Of course, that had not been the first and the last time he had rejected a marriage proposal. Even now, friends and acquaintances are constantly trying to set him up with their sisters, daughters, cousins, nieces or even neighbours. It is strange the way he has been fielding so many proposals as well as propositions ever since his divorce from Nina. Doesn't the fact that he has a failed marriage behind him deter these people from viewing him as an eligible match? Or are they so desperate to somehow marry off their relatives (on the verge of becoming unmarriageable by crossing the marriageable age) that they are willing to overlook this significant flaw in his personal profile?

Thankfully, things have considerably quietened down, now that most of them have realized that they were barking up the wrong tree and trying to catch the wrong groom. Nowadays, instead of coming to him with a marriage proposal, they shrug their shoulders and rationalize:

"No point pinning your hopes on Jai: he's commitment shy."

"It's a case of once bitten twice shy."

Such tittle-tattle is common. Even those who do not know him very well, nod their heads knowledgeably and make such personal comments with complete authority.

They are right, of course. When was the last time he took a serious interest in a woman; serious enough to want to court her? All the accusations flung at him by his disappointed dates and their disillusioned relatives are true. He is afraid of commitment, afraid of falling in love and afraid of marriage.

Nina, his ex-wife had had other accusations to make. She had called him a prisoner of his own personal space. She had wanted to occupy every inch of that space and had been frustrated and angry enough to leave him for another man when he did not let her. They had met through mutual friends. He had been drawn to her easy laughter, her bubbly, fun-loving personality, her habit of clapping her hands when excited. He had been fascinated by the way her eyes twinkled, the way they refused to stay still and constantly darted from one face to another while she talked.

And how she talked! Nina could go on and on and on, without giving anyone a chance to speak. He had been charmed by her gregarious and garrulous personality, enchanted by her vivacious beauty; enchanted enough to propose. After marriage, the same nonstop, juvenile prattle that had amused him once, started getting on his nerves. Nina wanted to celebrate every moment of their togetherness and he was not in the mood for celebration after performing long and complicated operations that often left him physically and emotionally drained.

Looking back, he takes his share of responsibility for the things that eventually led to their divorce. However, he is not too sure if he wouldn't repeat the same mistakes, were he to marry again. He likes women; he enjoys their company but not enough to let them invade his inner world that craves silence and peace when he comes home after a long day at work. If anything, he is now more set in his ways than ever. Living alone somehow grows on you after a while. He has made peace with his single status. He enjoys the solitude and freedom that come with it. He is now free to spend his weekends playing cricket without any guilt, free to head for the nearest mountains on his bike without being answerable to anyone. But, the thing that really keeps him going is his work. He enjoys nothing more than figuring out complex medical problems and how he loves fixing them! Ever since he can remember, he had wanted to be a surgeon and today he is living his dream.

Jai no longer goes through the unbearable pain that he went through after the first few years of divorce. He still suffers from occasional bouts of loneliness, but his life does not seem incredibly empty anymore. In some ways, he was lonelier when he was married to Nina. There is nothing more isolating and estranging than a bad marriage.

"I don't mind being alone. I enjoy my own company," he often tells himself when the craving for companionship becomes strong enough to make him feel lonely. Of course, there are days when he delays leaving the hospital because he does not want to come home to an empty house.

Fortunately, today was not one of the days when he had to come home to an empty house. He was on his way to home, when Aparna called and asked him to check on her sister, making the whole thing sound like an emergency.

Jai is glad that Aparna thought of him instead of calling someone else from the neighbourhood. Ever since his refusal to consider her proposal, things have cooled down considerably between the two of them. Aparna no longer invites him informally for impromptu dinners. Nor is he the trusted confidant with whom she used to share everything. They are still friends but no longer close friends. The last time they ran into each other at a supermarket, Aparna had smugly informed him that she was taking Ellora to New York to meet the family of a bright young investment banker. "I saw his profile in one of the matrimonial sites. He's a very good prospect for Ellora. If everything else works out, there could be wedding bells soon."

Jai has no doubt that things will work out exactly the way Aparna wants them to work out for her sister. Who can refuse to marry someone as beautiful and intelligent as Ellora?

Well, he did.

Had he been wrong in dismissing the marriage proposal without even giving it a second thought?

No. Given all the circumstances, he had done the right thing.

Would he give it a second thought, if Aparna were to make that suggestion once again?

He is not too sure. He likes Ellora and he enjoyed being with her this evening. He found her company pleasant, even soothing; but then, he probably enjoyed her company mainly because there were no strings attached to that meeting.

Does he want to see her again?

Yes, very much.

Is he going to call her now that he has her phone number?

He cannot rule out the possibility.

Will that be a wise thing to do?

He is not too sure.

****

Chapter 37

December 2011,
Manhattan, New York

"Try this poached lobster. It's so creamy, it melts in your mouth," says Arnab.

"What melts in our mouth usually solidifies on your thighs and remains there forever," says Aparna, as she accepts the bowl from her brother.

"Nonsense," dismisses Arnab.

Ellora has not heard the above exchange because she is busy keeping an eye on her mother, who is currently struggling to spear a slippery chickpea with her fork. Why does her brother, Arnab, invariably choose fancy restaurants where the choice of food is very limited for their vegetarian mother and where eating with one's hands is not an option?

Sumitra Devi, however, is not overtly concerned about the fact that the menu has practically nothing that she can eat without qualms. She is pretending to eat the mixed salad of artichoke, tomato, goat cheese and chickpeas, but it is not difficult to guess from her expressions that given a choice, she would rather leave her plate untouched. She dislikes the strong whiff of the vinaigrette drizzled on her salad. For someone who has never used anything other than the juice of freshly-plucked fragrant limes from her kitchen garden to dress her salads, the unfamiliar aroma of vinegar is highly off-putting. However, instead of worrying about what she can eat, Sumitra Devi is more concerned about what Neil is eating. Every now and then, she throws an anxious glance in

Aparna's direction to remind her to refill his plate.

"They all like him," reflects Ellora. Even she cannot help liking Neil Banerjee, whom she is meeting for the first time. He is a nice enough fellow with pleasing manners and refined taste, at least in clothes. He has come straight from work and is wearing a dark suit. He is not strikingly handsome, but there is something about his regular features and ready smile that pleases the eye. She would have probably noticed him in a room full of people because of his immaculate clothes and his friendly smile, but yes, Ellora acknowledges that he is indeed very likeable once you start paying attention to the little things he effortlessly does to make people like him. She likes the fact that although the conversation is mainly carried out in English, he turns to her mother from to time and says something in Bengali just for her benefit. At one point, when her mother spills her orange juice, Neil hastily reaches out for a napkin and wipes the drops that have fallen on her sari. Ellora is sure that his clients and co-workers also must like him a great deal. He is the kind of man who wins your trust and approval not only because he seems to care, but also because he seems capable of taking care of all your needs, no matter how small or big, trivial or crucial they might be.

"Call me Neil," he tells Sumitra Devi, when she calls him Neelkanth for the third time. He says it with an endearing smile that he must use quite often on some of his difficult but important clients.

"Is that what they call you at home?" enquires Sumitra Devi

"Everybody calls me Neil. Only my late grandfather who gave me that name, insisted upon calling me Neelkanth. But after his death, nobody called me by that tongue twister of a name anymore."

"But it's such a beautiful name. Do you know the meaning of Neelkanth?"

"I think it means the Blue-Throated One," says Neil.

"Right. It was the name given to Lord Shiva because his

throat turned blue after drinking the poison that emerged from the churning of the oceans. And who says it is a tongue twister of a name? Neelkanth is so simple to pronounce," says Sumitra Devi, not entirely convinced that a name that belongs to Lord Shiva himself should be changed into something as insignificant and ordinary as Neel, which just means blue.

"But Mashima, don't you like the shorter Neil? It's so much easier to pronounce?" asks he, putting an affectionate arm around the elderly woman sitting next to him. He addresses her as Mashima (maternal aunt) to show respect. If things go the way he is hoping they will, she will soon be his mother-in-law and he will have to start calling her Maa, just as her son, daughters and daughter-in-law call her.

Neil looks into Sumitra Devi's eyes and adds, "In this country, people like to keep things, particularly names, simple. Even my brother Joydeep decided to simplify things for himself by shortening his name to Joy."

"Now let me guess, Joydeep must have grown tired of seeing the amused expression on people's face when he told them his name," says Aparna with a knowing smile. She knows at least two Joydeeps who decided to change their name to Joy for the very same reason.

"Absolutely right, but he was getting even more tired of seeing their surprised expression when he informed them that Joydeep means a victory lamp and not deep joy."

They all laugh. Ellora identifies with Joydeep's plight. She knows what it is to have a name that elicits all types of surprised reactions and funny questions. She has done her share of answering endless questions for being named after the famous caves. She has to thank her archaeologist grandfather for naming her after the beautifully sculptured caves in Aurangabad, Maharashtra.

* * *

By the time Neil gets up to leave, he has charmed every member of Ellora's family. Even her hard-to-please brother

Arnab is pleased with the smart banker. Nevertheless, he has a word of caution for his younger sister after Neil's departure.

"He's a bright young man. He'll go a long way, no doubt, but don't let this fact influence your decision. It's your life, so don't let anyone pressurise you into marrying him in a hurry. Take as much time as you need to make up your mind. No hurry and no pressure," Arnab tells his sister privately when they walk together towards the car park.

"No pressure? You must be joking Dada," Ellora says to her brother.

"No, I'm serious. You're now in a country where you have choices – You only have to make the right ones by learning to stand your ground. Remember I'm with you, always," says Arnab, as he gives his sister an affectionate hug before walking towards his car. Like Neil, he too is in a hurry to get back to work now that he has performed his brotherly duty.

* * *

The pressure comes into play sooner than Ellora had anticipated.

"Such a level-headed fellow and so charming," says Aparna as soon as her car hits the road that heads home.

"He's indeed a bright and pleasant young man," seconds Kajol, Arnab's wife. She is the quiet one in the family and never praises anyone, unless the person is truly deserving of praise.

Sumitra Devi, who sits with Ellora in the backseat reaches out for her daughter's hand and holds it in hers before asking, "He's such a nice and well-bred boy, don't you like him?"

"I do, but that doesn't mean I'm ready to marry him on the next available auspicious date suggested by your astrologer. I need more time, Maa. I think, both Neil and I need to spend some more time with each other before we make any major decisions regarding our future," says she. Ellora has gone through this entire exercise enough times to feel embarrassed about putting her point across so frankly and firmly.

"I saw your father only once before our wedding and look how happy our marriage turned out to be," says Sumitra Devi, still holding Ellora's hand.

"You just got lucky, Maa," says Ellora with an indulgent smile. She has heard it before, not just once, but many a times.

"What about Rahul and Aparna? What about Arnab and Kajol? They too met each other only once or twice before they got married. Do you think all four of them got lucky?" asks Sumitra Devi.

Ellora chooses not to answer the question but Aparna jumps to her sister's defence by quickly answering on her behalf, "Yes Maa, all of us got lucky. Or rather our husbands got lucky that they found wives like us. But times have changed. People no longer want to leave a life-changing decision like marriage to parents or to chance. Ellora is right. She needs to spend more time with Neil in order to get to know him better. Don't try to rush her into marriage. Let her take as much time as she needs to make up her mind."

"Let her take all the time in the world to make up her mind! That's what she has been doing for the past ten years, hasn't she? Taking her own sweet time. And while she was still making up her stubborn mind, the father who desperately wanted to see his daughter married and well-settled in life before his death, died without being able to perform his last sacred duty." Sumitra Devi uses the corner of her sari to wipe the tears that have started flowing at the mention of her husband's name.

Everyone remains silent. However, she has not finished yet.

"Even the night before he died, your father was frantically searching for a suitable groom for her in the matrimonial columns. But no, how does it matter if he died without being able to find the man who was good enough for his wilful daughter? You're right. Where's the hurry? Let me also die before she makes up her mind. I'm not even her real mother, so how does it matter if I die without seeing her settled in life?"

"Maa, please don't cry," says Kajol, as she turns around and hands a tissue to her crying mother-in-law. Ellora also wants to comfort her mother, but instead, she looks out of the window to hide the tears welling up in her eyes.

However, now that she has started, Sumitra Devi is determined to speak her mind loudly and clearly, even if it breaks several hearts, hers included.

"Have you noticed her face lately? Don't you see the lines and the sunspots that are visible even to my ageing eyes? You say times have changed, but I say nothing has changed. To this day, men, even men old enough to be grandfathers, like to marry women who are youthful and attractive. A man can marry in his forties, fifties, even sixties and seventies, but a woman cannot afford to delay her marriage after the age of thirty. With each passing year, her face loses its natural glow, her eyes lose their brightness, her hair loses its sheen, her hormones start dwindling, her womb starts shrinking, her eggs become fewer and fewer and her capacity to conceive and raise children becomes lesser and lesser."

"Spoken like a doctor's wife," says Aparna when she finally recovers from the bout of speechlessness that her mother's blunt speech has caused her.

"You don't need to be a doctor's wife to know that a woman's body has been created for procreation. A woman is born with a womb so that she can carry children and the womb cries, protests, even rebels by malfunctioning, if you don't let it perform its preordained biological function properly. Unlike men who produce millions of seeds daily, a woman produces just one egg every month and has a limited number of years at her disposal to get those precious eggs fertilized. These are the facts of life. Even my late grandmother knew this and she never went to a school. Nor was she married to a doctor."

****

Chapter 38

December 2011,

New York

Arnab Chatterjee's riverside condominium has floor-to-ceiling windows that offer a magnificent view of the Manhattan skyline. But the view is rather dull this morning. Everything is covered in a hazy mist with no sign of any sunlight peeping through the grey clouds that are holding the sky hostage. Lying in bed, gazing at the gloomy sky, yesterday's disturbing conversation comes to Ellora's mind.

Her mother, with her limited knowledge of science but her unlimited conventional wisdom, had stated things that indeed made scientific sense. She had neatly summed up in two precise paragraphs the complex biological principles that she herself had learnt from thick textbooks in school and college.

It was through those biology textbooks that Ellora had first discovered that reproduction is not an equal equation; that men and women invest different amounts of energy and effort to beget offspring. Men produce countless cheap sperms daily in their built-in factories in an assembly-line fashion, whereas women produce only one egg each month; and if that precious egg is not fertilized within hours, it goes to waste and has to be discarded, along with the blood and tissue that the uterus had been happily building up in anticipation of a future pregnancy.

Her mother had rightly implied that men are like cavemen. They are still driven by their ancient craving for women who are curvy and youthful. They are still drawn to women who display the outer signs that they have functioning ovaries and fertile wombs. Even when they are past the age of producing their own children, men still like to scatter their ageing seeds on grounds that are fertile and moist.

Her mother is right. By refusing to marry, she is not just letting her family down, but also letting her body down. A body designed and programmed for procreation. A body that has its demands and needs, physical as well as emotional. A body that wants to fulfil all those needs one way or another. Love, lust and marriage, are all roads leading towards the same destination, the act of procreation. Selecting the mate may be her prerogative, but she cannot postpone making that crucial choice forever. Evolutionarily speaking, she has been a failure because despite being thirty-three, she has failed to deliver on the innate biological promise of passing on her genes through the act of procreation. She has let her eggs go waste month after month and years after years by refusing to marry any one of the suitable men chosen by her father; the suitable mate, who would have provided the much needed sperms with the right DNA to fertilize her waiting eggs.

As she watches a tall clock tower in the distance, Ellora is acutely aware of her own furiously ticking biological clock. Time is ticking away quite fast. Has the countdown already begun? Will she miss her biological deadline by the time she makes up her mind? Will she be able to conceive when she gets married eventually? She loves children, she would love to have her own one day. She cannot pass a pram without wanting to pick up the baby sleeping inside and cradling it in her arms. She has felt this way for quite some time now.

There is one more urge simmering latently; it is something she does not feel comfortable thinking about, but it is there nevertheless. She wants to feel the thrill, the joy, the ecstasy of a man touching her body. She wants to be cuddled, she wants to be held, she wants to be loved, caressed and kissed by a man. Not just any man, but the right man.

"The right man?" she asks herself. The question jolts her enough to make her come out of her sleepy inertia. She gets up and goes to the window and gazes vacantly at the sky outside. The sun is still paying hide and seek, but the clouds are decidedly less grey and less gloomy.

How could either of the two men she had once desired intensely have been right for her? Rohinton, of course, had been the wrong man from the word go. And as for the other man, he was so wrong that Ellora is not willing to acknowledge even to herself that she ever desired him.

"Stop, Ellora. Stop thinking about him," she tells herself, careful not to take Vikram's name even in the privacy of her thoughts.

****

Chapter 39

Delhi, 2010

Vikram Rathore is one chapter in Ellora's life she would rather forget and yet that is one thing she has not been able to do, despite her best efforts to block him out of her memory.

When Vikram invited her to join Delhi Matters, Ellora did so gladly because she had seen enough of his documentaries and had attended enough of his lectures to have great respect for the kind of work he was doing. After working with him for some time, her open admiration turned into a secret crush but the knowledge did not bother Ellora greatly. Every single woman, young or old, working in the Delhi Matters office had a crush on Vikram Rathore and she was no exception. There was something about his intense deep-set eyes and his lean, angular face, perpetually covered by the five o' clock shadow, which attracted women to him. No woman was immune to his inexplicable appeal. He had a strange vulnerability about him, as if he badly needed a hearty meal and could do with a good night's sleep to get rid of that haunted, sleep-deprived look on his face.

The scion of an aristocratic family with political muscle and financial clout, Vikram Rathore had chosen to branch out at a very young age from his illustrious family tree to start his own business of designing eco-friendly homes. Simultaneously, he founded Delhi Matters because his city and its inhabitants mattered to him. He was serious about saving the creatures that his cousins hunted for fun on the weekends.

It was difficult not to admire a man who stood for all the things Ellora herself believed in. It was even more difficult not to let that admiration turn into a powerful attraction.

It had started innocently enough. A light touch on the shoulder, an unintentional brushing of hands, an accidental meeting of the eyes; thrilling accidents that made her giddy with joy and set her heart racing. However, she was not content with those fleeting accidental touches. She wanted more. She wanted the innocent unintended touches to become naughtily intentional. She wanted the brief moments of surreal intimacy to become tangibly real. And with her womanly instincts, Ellora knew that Vikram wanted them too.

However, it is one thing to have a secret crush on a married man and quite another to let that crush develop into something more serious. When it became clear that this was no longer a harmless, one-sided crush and that Vikram was taking more interest in her than she had bargained for, Ellora started avoiding going to his office when he was alone. To his credit, Vikram too left her alone. They started discussing the ideas for her articles and the scripts for his documentaries over the phone and through email. There was this tacit line they were both trying very hard not to cross.

And then, Vikram invited her to be a part of the crew for the documentary he was making on the River Yamuna. Ellora had had her compunctions, yet she decided to accompany Vikram and the rest of the crew for the three-week shoot. It was too good a chance to say no to.

They travelled by car, by bus or on foot most of the time, staying in the hotels that were nearest to their shooting locations. At night, they all assembled in Vikram's room for brainstorming sessions after dinner, sharing ideas, discussing details and working on the scenes they were going to shoot the next morning. It was a hectic and tiring outdoor schedule; however, she was glad that despite the long hours of proximity, they were too preoccupied with their project to think about anything else.

It was during the last week of the shooting that Vikram

asked her to stay back after others had left. He wanted to discuss the script they had jointly written. He had few changes in mind. It was not an unusual request; the script often needed to be rewritten on location to meet the demands of the changing visuals. They sat side-by-side for over thirty minutes, incorporating the changes he wanted in the script. Not once did their hands touch, shoulders rub or eyes lock, accidentally or otherwise. Nevertheless, being alone in a hotel room with Vikram made Ellora extremely uncomfortable and nervous. She could see his bed from where she was sitting; it was just a few feet away. Suddenly, it felt terribly wrong to be in the same room with him at an hour when no one was likely to disturb them.

Even though, Vikram was still in the middle of making an important point, she got up suddenly, saying she must leave because she was too sleepy to concentrate. He got up too and walked her to the door.

"Please don't go," he pleaded, without any preamble, without any warning, without any attempt to touch her. There was just a hint of tremor in his voice.

Ellora was too shocked to say anything except mumbling a barely audible, "Good night," before hurriedly leaving his room. She went straight to her room and burst into tears.

Since that night, Ellora has often lain awake, night after night, thinking about those moments. She still feels a deep sense of shame, when she realizes that a part of her had desperately wanted to stay in his room. A part of her had wholeheartedly wanted to spend the night with Vikram in that austere hotel room.

"How could you, Ellora Chatterjee, how could you?" she asks herself even now, after more than a year. Now that she can view the whole episode more dispassionately and without emotion, she realizes how wrong she had been to have feelings for a man who was not only married but was also the father of two little girls. How could she? She used to see his two adorable daughters almost daily. They would often come to her desk to find out the names of the flowers that grew in the garden outside. She could tell from the way the girls invented excuses to spend time with her, that they were very fond of her.

She could also tell from the way Vikram's wife pretended to see through her when she visited the office, that Tara Rathore was not at all fond of her. Mrs Rathore went out of her way to greet everyone in the office. She made it a point to stop at their desks to chitchat for a while, but she never stopped at Ellora's desk. She never attempted to make any small talk with her, except for saying a perfunctory hello and that too rather imperiously.

Ellora now understood why married women like Tara Rathore perceive unmarried women like herself as threats.

Her decision to come to the USA had been made immediately after returning to Delhi from the outdoor shoot. It was not an impulsive decision: Ellora had thought about it carefully and with a clear head. She wrote to her sister Aparna, informing her of her decision. She wanted to get away from Delhi. She was ready to join her family in the United States. She was even willing to give marriage a chance.

Ellora now knows that she was not running away from Vikram, she was running away from her own shameless and uninhibited self; the self that was capable of breaking a marriage, wrecking a home and destroying lives. Now that she knew what could have happened that night, she was not going to take any further chances. She was scared of her latent passions that were waiting to be unleashed. She was afraid that the next time around Vikram asked her to stay back in a hotel room with him, she would not have the willpower to say no to him. It was just a matter of time.

Now, as she stands near the window of her brother Arnab's riverside condominium and watches the slow-moving cars and the fast-walking pedestrians on the streets below, a thought suddenly comes to Ellora's mind.

Was it her cavewoman instinct that protected her from her own risky passions? Wasteful passions that could never lead to procreation? Had she really run away from Vikram that night because she had not wanted to hurt his children and his wife? Or had she run away from him because he could never have been the father of her own children? At least, not legally.

It's a new insight. However, Ellora neither has enough conventional wisdom nor enough scientific knowledge to test her untested hypothesis.

****

Chapter 40

December 2011,
New York

"Neil should be here any minute," says Aparna, as she clicks some more pictures of the giant Rockefeller Centre Christmas Tree.

Ellora stands in one corner, watching people around her. Most of them are tourists and Christmas shoppers. The place is bustling with them at this time of the year. She can also spot a couple of bankers among the sea of shoppers and the sightseers. Not only do they dress differently, but they also walk differently. There is nothing casual about either their clothes or their pace. Even as they talk on their cell phones, they cross the street with the long, purposeful strides of someone with a mission to accomplish. Watching these men, it strikes Ellora that Neil is also perhaps one of them; he too would be crossing the street in the same purposeful manner. He too would be in a great rush to get a pedestrian task like crossing the street quickly out of the way, so that he could get down to the exciting business of sealing deals. She does not have to wait for too long to test her assumption, for she can now see Neil taking long strides towards them, looking like any other smart and dynamic finance guy with an appointment to keep.

Aparna does not waste any time in making polite conversation.

"Listen, I've some serious shopping to do at the Saks Fifth Avenue, so you know where to find me," she tells the two of them before waving a temporary goodbye.

After Aparna's hurried departure, Neil and Ellora go to a cafe inside the plaza. It is crowded and noisy but a smiling waiter appears from nowhere to lead them to their reserved table that offers an excellent view of the ice rink and the Christmas tree.

"Even if our conversation is punctuated by long, awkward pauses, we can pretend to watch the action in the rink," thinks Ellora, as she gazes at the novice skaters merrily gliding and wobbling under the watchful eye of the recumbent Prometheus, the gilded statue of the Greek legend. However, she need not have worried about them having nothing much to say to each other. When you are with someone as articulate as Neil, you do not run the risk of running out of conversation. In fact, he has so much to say, mostly about his work, his clients, his ambitions and his dream for the future (which includes her), that she hardly gets a chance to speak much. He does all the talking for the two of them.

Ellora is not too hungry. She just wants to order a salad, but Neil insists that she must try the seared Mahi-mahi with braised beans and tomato. He orders buttermilk-fried chicken for himself. As they eat, he tells her that a typical workday for him starts at 7 am and often ends well past midnight.

"There's no typical day as such. Every day brings new challenges and you've got to do whatever needs to be done and finish what you've started, even if it means pulling an all-nighter, sometimes, pulling several all-nighters in a row. But I love the pressure. Quite often, I don't know what's around the corner, but that's part of the fun. I love the unpredictability. It's never quiet, it's never boring. "

Neil stops because his phone is ringing. He puts his fork down and gets up.

"Sorry, but I've to take this call," he excuses himself and steps out, leaving Ellora alone to deal with the seared fish that she has neither the inclination, nor the appetite to deal with. When Neil comes back after about fifteen minutes, he apologizes profusely and then, goes back to talking about his work. His conversation includes words like merger, acquisition, equity, pitching; words that are vaguely familiar, but are not exciting enough for Ellora to ask questions and find out more. Instead, she asks something totally unrelated, just to change the boring course this conversation is currently taking.

"Do you like reading books?" she wants to know.

"Oh yes, I love to read books on trading and financial crises, especially the ones that tell the inside stories of the dramatic upheavals that have changed investment banking forever. I find these behind the scene narratives more thrilling than the crime thrillers. I also read motivational, self-help books whenever I'm on a long flight."

"Do you like watching movies?" Not that she really wants to know. Nevertheless she asks, just to steer the conversation in a direction where she too can contribute.

"Where's the time? I saw my last movie almost a year ago. I remember the movie though. I think it was called Transformers: Dark of the Moon. My friends and I enjoyed it thoroughly. Have you seen it?"

Ellora has, but she does not have the heart to tell Neil that she found the movie painfully noisy and incredibly inane, so much so, that she walked out of the hall to escape from the collective auditory, visual and cerebral assault. Even now, just thinking about the noise and the mindless plot gives her a headache.

They now switch to talking about music. His eclectic taste in music does not include songs from Hindi movies and if there is a genre of music he simply cannot stand, it is Indian classical music.

"My parents once persuaded me to accompany them to a concert of a renowned classical singer from India and I can't tell you how painful the whole experience was. I just couldn't sit through it. How can you sit through a recital where the performer takes almost an hour to come to the point?"

Our tastes in music and movies are poles apart. I wonder if our views on life are also as diametrically different, wonders Ellora, as she takes a sip from the cappuccino that the waiter has just brought. Neil is drinking black coffee to remain alert for the meeting he is going to attend shortly.

He pays the bill; the waiter seems happy with the generous tip. Together, they step out into the cold December afternoon. Neil says a hurried bye to Ellora at the entrance of Saks. He is already a couple of minutes late for his meeting.

* * *

"So how did it go?" asks Aparna as soon as they come face-to-face.

Ellora has been dreading this question, because she does not have an answer to it. Did she like Neil? Of course, she did. There is no denying that Neil is an extremely well-mannered, intelligent and articulate man. But had she enjoyed his company? If truth be told, she did not. It was more of a presentation than a conversation: he was presenting himself to her by talking about his high-powered job, his high-profile clients and his high-flying ambitions. She was duly impressed, but that's about it. She wanted to know the kind of man Neil Banerjee was, but instead, she ended up discovering the kind of dedicated and driven investment banker he was.

"You didn't answer my question," says Aparna.

"I like him, but not enough to want to marry him. Not yet," replies Ellora.

"Don't worry, it'll happen. You'll discover enough reasons to like him, once you get to know him better. And for that you'll have to spend as much time together as possible during the next few days. I'm at your service. I'll be happy to be your chauffer-cum-chaperone."

* * *

They meet again the next day. Neil takes Ellora and Aparna to his two-bedroom apartment on the Upper East Side. The sisters are pleasantly surprised. It is an airy, spacious and well-lit apartment with plush carpets and plenty of rugs, cushions, paintings and artefacts everywhere to make the place look like a family home rather than a bachelor pad.

"The credit goes to my mother – she's chosen the furniture and the artwork. You can see that she's left her feminine touch all over the place. And that's not all. Being who she is, my mother comes every week from New Jersey to ensure that my plants are watered, the bed-sheets are changed and the floors are vacuumed," informs Neil.

"How wonderful! So when are we going to meet her?" says Aparna, without beating around the bush. It was originally her idea that they would meet Neil's parents only after Neil and Ellora had seen and liked each other.

"I was about to come to that. I spoke to my mother last night. She has invited all of you for lunch on Sunday," informs Neil.

Things are moving fast, much too fast, thinks Ellora.

****

Chapter 41

"My mother is an anglophile. She's a penchant for all things British. But don't let her intimidate you," Neil had warned Ellora before bringing her to his parental home in Hillsborough, New Jersey the following Sunday. Neil could not have been more right. His mother indeed turns out to be an incorrigible anglophile and despite all his assurances, it is impossible for Ellora not to feel intimidated in her imposing presence. A tall and well-built woman, Leela Banerjee wears her supercilious smugness like a second skin. She talks about her elite upper-class upbringing all the time.

"My father was an eminent barrister during the British times." He made sure to send all four of his daughters to Loreto House in Calcutta so that we could learn to speak English the proper way," Leela Banerjee tells them as soon as she serves her guests freshly brewed Darjeeling tea with cake. As she deftly slices the Christmas cake she has especially baked in their honour, she smugly adds, "He was a pucca brown Sahib."

Ellora looks at her sister Aparna with a puzzled expression, not too sure if her potential mother-in-law is praising or deriding her anglophile father. In college, 'brown Sahib' had been a derogatory term, frequently used by the students for an anglicised English professor, who wore tweed jackets and tie-pinned silk ties to college even at the peak of summer. Ironically, despite the professor's penchant for all things white, his surname (like his skin colour) was Brown. They all jokingly called him Dr Coconut Brown: Brown on the outside and white on the inside

Now, as she listens to Neil's mother, Ellora wonders if she too belongs to the same category.Thankfully, instead of going on and on about her privileged upbringing, Leela Banerjee, decides to change the topic. She now shows an interest in knowing more about Ellora's late parents. Sumitra Devi, who has been unusually quiet all this while, is only too happy to provide all the details. It is now her turn to boast about her highly educated and cultured family. However, even as she enthusiastically describes the accomplishments of her cardiologist brother-in-law and his dancer wife, Sumitra Devi waits for the right opportunity to talk about more important matter such as the wedding date. But she hesitates to broach the delicate subject for fear of annoying her son Arnab.

"Please don't put any kind of pressure on them. There's no hurry to fix the date. Let them take as much time as they need to make up their minds," Arnab had firmly told his mother the previous night. Therefore, despite all her anxiousness and desperation, she has to act calm and remain quiet.

Eventually, of course, Sumitra Devi gets her own way, but only after four months of anxious waiting. And that too after she falls critically ill with acute bronchitis. Ellora, who has to rush to New York after getting the news of her mother's illness, has no choice except to give in to her tearful demands. Surprisingly, the moment she agrees to the engagement, Sumitra Devi's alarming symptoms magically disappear. It would not be wrong to say that Ellora is practically pressured into getting engaged (emotionally blackmailed is more like it), but then, how else could she stop her mother from shedding those copious tears; tears that invariably lead to nonstop coughing, wheezing, and breathlessness?

Post engagement, Ellora's only consolation is, now that she is officially engaged to Neil, she will never have to go through the humiliation of being paraded before the prospective suitors and their relatives. Never again.

****

Chapter 42

April 2012,

Mrs Morris's home in Edgewater Maryland

They came, they saw and they commented. Sometimes they came alone and sometimes they came with an inspection team. Sometimes they commented without even waiting for her to leave the room and sometimes they sent their post-inspection comments by post.

They commented on her gawky height, her green-brown eyes and her honey-brown skin; trifling defects that they were magnanimous enough to overlook in view of her excellent qualifications and her illustrious family background.

The lists too came by post along with those comments: lists, itemizing pieces of gold jewellery, furniture, refrigerator, silk saris etc. to be given as wedding gifts in order to make her light eyes and not-so-light skin easier on the eyes.

"It's a good thing that they have yet to discover my major flaw: my scandalous past, otherwise who knows what else they would have liked to extract from my parents," wonders Ellora, as she flips through the thick folder labelled 'Ellora's Marriage Correspondence.'

When she had found the folder among papers belonging to her late father, her first impulse had been to throw it away: the thick file was a grim reminder of the things gone so wrong that they had caused her father's death.

Eventually, of course, she could not bring herself to throw the file. How could she throw something that contained the last letters written by her father, even if reading those letters evoked memories that were excruciatingly painful? She always intended to read the correspondence one day but had not found the courage to do so until today.

As she flips through the pages, Ellora marvels at the meticulousness with which her father had filed the clippings of matrimonial ads, photocopies of his correspondence with various prospective grooms or their fathers and the dowry lists that some of the greedy but pragmatic fathers had sent along with their letters. One such list contains items like a Godrej almirah, a sewing machine, an electric toaster, a colour television, a four-poster bed, a dressing table and two chests of drawers (all in rosewood). There are thirty such household items on the list. There are two more lists for gold ornaments and silk saris separately.

She cannot help being amused as she reads the ads placed by her father in two popular English-language newspapers published from Delhi. The first ad reads:

> *A well-to-do Bengali Brahmin family seeks suitable alliance from highly qualified doctors for their beautiful and intelligent 26-year old daughter currently doing her PhD in Botany. She is slim, tall (5 feet 6 inches) and has a wheatish complexion. The boy must belong to a Bengali Brahmin family of similar status.*

In the second ad placed after a gap of six months, her father had relaxed his rather strict and narrow prerequisites considerably by seeking not just doctors but also engineers and other qualified professionals. In the third ad, he had lowered the bar further by stating "Sub-caste no bar," instead of rigidly insisting upon a Bengali Brahmin match. It must have been an agonizing decision for someone who had been raised with the belief that his Brahmanical lineage automatically made him genetically superior to those who did not share his illustrious bloodline.

There is one particular letter that captures Ellora's attention at once because of the red marker her father had used for crossing out the entire page and writing a footnote that declares the man to be an 'impudent imbecile.' The letter is from an agricultural scientist working for Indian Agricultural Research Institute. In response to the second ad placed by her father, the 'impudent imbecile' wrote:

"You mention that your daughter has wheatish complexion. Could you please elaborate on that? I would like to know which particular species of wheat you are referring to, so that I can visualize the colour of your daughter's skin a little more accurately. You see, the adjective 'wheatish' by itself is not quite helpful, because the wheat grown in India comes in various shades. It can be dark red, light brown, yellow, cream or white in colour, depending on the species and the cultivars. The kernels of Triticum aestivum, for instance can be red or white. The kernels of Triticum durum are yellowish, the kernels of Triticum spelta are dark red, whereas the kernels of Kalyan Sona and Sonalika (our home-grown varieties) are amber in colour. So, Dr Chatterjee, could you please specify which particular species of wheat precisely matches the colour of your daughter's skin?"

Ellora cannot help smiling. She can imagine how furious those comments must have made her father; nevertheless she wishes that he had not dismissed the 'impudent imbecile' so categorically. He seems like an interesting man, albeit with a weird sense of humour. But at least he was funny instead of being stuffy like most other men who came to meet her.

She now goes through the set of letters that her father had exchanged with the father of an eligible neurologist who had worked in the United States for many years before joining his father's private hospital in South Delhi. She reads the entire correspondence carefully to find what exactly went wrong. To start with, the father of the neurologist, (himself a urologist) seems very keen on the alliance. He ends every letter with, "Please give my love to dear Ellora." His tone is always polite and warm. However, the friendly warmth suddenly changes to frosty coldness after receiving the letter in which her father informed him about the scandal shadowing his daughter's past. The gentleman is still quite polite, but he is also quite firm about not wanting a girl with a tainted past for his son. He ends his letter with, "I hope you understand," instead of his usual, "Give my love to dear Ellora."

There are several such rejection letters with tones ranging

from chilly coldness to fuming outrage at the gall of her father for wanting to marry off his unworthy, characterless daughter to their worthy sons. It goes to her father's credit that he never let those rude letters stop him from trying even harder. He, the highly respected family doctor whom the townspeople worshipped for his honesty and dedication, was literally begging these disdainful, rude people to reconsider their decision; pleading with them to meet his daughter at least once before assuming such an irrevocable stand.

Unfortunately, her father was trying to sell damaged goods in a buyer's market that placed great emphasis upon perfection and purity. Purity, as in chastity and modesty.

One of the pompous fathers of a highly eligible son had responded by sending an alternative proposal. He had come straight to the point by stating, "I am afraid, as far as my son is concerned, the negotiation is closed. However, I have a nephew who is ready to forgive your daughter and marry her despite her scandalous past. My nephew, who is a clerk in the Ministry of Foreign Affairs, lost his father last year and is looking for a beautiful but homely wife who will be a companion to his bed-ridden mother and a loving guardian to his two teenage brothers."

Her father had sent his reply in two terse sentences, saying "I think your nephew needs to search the want columns of The Times of India, instead of the matrimonial ones. He is looking for a nurse-cum-housekeeper and not a wife."

However, Dr Akhilesh Chatterjee was not always curt. Most of the time, he ended up sounding like the helpless father of a daughter with a tainted past; a father so desperate to see his daughter well-settled, that he did not mind writing long, pleading letters to those callous men in a last-ditch attempt to appeal to their better nature. Getting her married had become her father's sole mission in life; a mission that remained unaccomplished during his lifetime. And even five years after his death.

****

Chapter 43

April 2012,

Mrs Morris's backyard, Edgewater, Maryland

"Spring is here," Mrs Morris cheerfully announces. She is all dressed up for church, teaming her pale purple two-piece dress with matching purple shoes and a large brimmed purple hat trimmed with ostrich feathers.

"You look wonderful," says Ellora, admiring the elderly woman's formal yet flamboyant style.

"I know I look out of place in this casual age, but I so love to wear a hat. I feel like the Queen Mum, but it's a beautiful spring day worthy of dressing like a queen. I think you too should go out and enjoy the sunshine," she beamingly tells her young tenant before leaving.

Ellora marvels, not for the first time, at Mrs Morris's capacity to remain in high spirits always. Her own spirits are perpetually low these days, despite the fact that she is now officially engaged to Neil and should be feeling happy and relaxed instead of being depressed and worried.

They had become engaged two weeks ago when she and Aparna had to rush to New York to see their seriously ill mother.

The marriage date has not yet been finalized, but it is understood that they will get married sometime in June. It is also understood that she will give up whatever she is currently pursuing to start a new life in New York after marriage. Everyone including Neil presumes that she will pursue her postdoctoral research at New York University to keep her mind gainfully occupied, even though her main occupation after marriage will be to look pretty and be a supportive wife to her brilliant husband with a bright future.

Ellora decides to take a walk in the backyard to get away from the inchoate chaos brewing inside her brain. As Mrs Morris had declared, the spring is indeed here; the azaleas, the crocuses and the jonquils are peeking out of the soil. However, the grass is not yet fully green nor have the trees budded yet.

It has been fascinating to witness the greening, the bronzing, the baring and the budding of the American trees in a quick succession over a short period of time. Ellora, with her subtropical tree-sense, can only marvel at these rapidly changing arboreal moods. In India, most trees remain monotonously green for the best part of the year, but in this country, they go through dramatic transitions with each change of season. When they were green, they were too green, when they were bronze, they were too bronze. And then suddenly, one fine morning, they decided to drop all their dressy foliage to become all too bare. Thankfully, the buds are back and the branches are no longer starkly naked.

Sitting on a branch that is not yet fully clothed, a male cardinal bird looks redder than ever, now that there is no green cover to hide the vivid plumage. Ellora always wondered why a bird that is as flamboyantly red as this one, has a name that is as sombrely dull as cardinal, until Mrs Morris informed her that the bird gets its name from the red cassocks worn by Catholic cardinals.

She can also see a tiny brown bird sitting on the ledge of the kitchen window. From a distance, it looks like a sparrow.

Passer domesticus: she recalls the house sparrow's scientific name, the specific name signifying the domesticated bird's fondness for human habitats.

* * *

So many sparrows came to their garden in Vijaypur every morning. Her childhood companion Kusum (their gardener's daughter) invited the birds by scattering seeds on the ground in the hope of reaping a good husband. She had been told by an astrologer that if she wanted a decent husband, she first had to get rid of all her bad karma by feeding birds. Ever since, Kusum had religiously fed those perky sparrows, which came in huge flocks the moment she started scattering fistful of millet and sorghum seeds on the ground.

As she watches the dull brown sparrow still sitting on the ledge, it strikes Ellora that the bird is truly homely in every sense of the word: homely as in plain and ordinary and homely as in domesticated and docile. However, in the matrimonial ads she found in her father's file, the word homely implies anything but plain and ordinary. In the context of those ads, to be homely is to be a good homemaker. When they advertise for, 'a beautiful and homely girl,' they basically want a girl who will keep their homes, cook for the family and look eminently presentable on top of being homely.

Now that she is to be married very soon, she too will have to look beautiful and be 'homely'. She too will have to look ornamental, dust the shelves, arrange the flowers, do fancy cooking and nod her head knowledgeably when her husband's colleagues and clients talk shop during their office parties. She too will have to attend art exhibitions with her mother-in-law, sip champagne and pretend that she is enjoying the inane small talk. She too will be required to learn the intricate etiquette, follow the tedious protocol, cram the clever key-words and incorporate them smartly in her conversations to prove how well-bred and well-read she is and how wisely Neil has chosen his wife.

If there is one thing she will not be required to do after marriage, it is to be herself and follow her own dreams.

"What am I doing? What am I getting into?" Ellora asks herself every day first thing in the morning. She likes Neil, there is no doubt about it; but she does not like him enough to even look forward to his phone calls, let alone look forward to spending the rest of her life with him.

"Follow your heart," that's what Aditi told her to do when she had called her last week to seek her advice. It was not what she had expected her forthright friend to say. She had wanted Aditi to shake her out of her complaisant, people-pleasing mode by telling her bluntly that she was making a huge mistake. The Aditi she had known in school would have severely reprimanded her by saying, "You're picking your husband for God's sake and not your nose, so stop being so casual about it." However, marriage has mellowed Aditi. She is no longer the brash girl who bluntly spoke her mind. This mature and calm Aditi does not believe in making decisions for others.

But how can you follow your heart when it is going in ten different directions?

Mrs Morris had been a bit more helpful when she had said to her, "Do what you think will make you happy in the long run."

"What will make me happy?" Ellora asks herself. Will she be happy sharing her life and her bed with a man with whom she shares so little in common otherwise? Will she be happy assuming a new identity and playing new social roles? Will she be happy hobnobbing with the who's who of the New York social circle?"

Ellora knows the answers to these questions, but then, what are her other options?

To stay unmarried forever?

No, that is out of question. It would break her mother's heart. She cannot escape marriage; it is her sacred Hindu duty, just as giving her away in marriage was her father's sacred Hindu duty which he was prevented from fulfilling because of her own obduracy.

Like Indian Independence, marriage is her ultimate

'Tryst with Destiny,' and it is not in her hand to escape her preordained and compulsory fate. A marriageable daughter is the lowest common denominator in the giant scheme of things.

How about postponing the entire thing indefinitely by insisting that she needs more time to sort out her feelings? She has real concerns and she knows that they are not merely pre-marriage jitters. But no, she cannot back out at this stage, no matter how cold her feet are and how burning her concerns are. It is too late to vacillate or use delay tactics. She is aware that someone as goal-oriented as Neil, who has now made marriage one of his main goals, will not wait endlessly for a bride who takes forever to make up her mind. Besides, she is already thirty-three. If she has to get married, it has to be now. In the Indian marriage market, a thirty-plus woman is like a perishable good with a short expiry date and given this slim deadline, her marriageable status has either already expired, or is on the verge of doing so. No, she cannot put off her inevitable tryst with destiny.

In any case, what's wrong with Neil? Why is she being so pernickety? Why is she trying to invent excuses not to marry him? He is intelligent, open-minded, suave and rich. Not to mention that he's Bengali to boot; a Bengali Brahmin, no less. Just the kind of perfect groom her late father would have chosen for her. Neil looks so right for her on paper: right job, right salary, right age, right upbringing, even right caste and sub-caste.

One thing she really appreciates in Neil is the fact that despite knowing everything about her scandalous past, he has not broached that unpleasant topic even once during their long telephonic conversations. Ellora respects him for that. She also appreciates his clarity of intent. He is so unlike all those appalling men who came to see her in India: the condescending man who was 'ready to forgive all her past sins', the bumptious IT guy who blew smoke in her face, the balding midget who had more hairs sprouting from his earlobes and nostrils than growing on top of his head and the lecherous lout who took great offence when she angrily thwarted his determined attempt to hold her hand. The last one had even sneeringly told her, "I was under the impression that you were a modern girl with modern notions. I'd no idea you would have such crusty, out-dated notions. What's wrong with holding hands? You've done it before, haven't you? Or do you only allow famous cricketers to take liberties with you?"

Obviously, her father's painstaking efforts to screen those men were not fool proof enough. When she thinks about those riffraff ruffians and the pompous morons who came to see her, she cannot help thinking how fortunate she is to have an urbane and mature person like Neil seriously interested in marrying her.

But again, she is back to the same old questions. Is she doing the right thing by agreeing to marry Neil? Will she be happy after marriage?

She is not sure. The answer depends on what one's definition of a happy marriage is.

Five years ago, when her childhood companion Kusum had come to see her after her father's death, Ellora had asked her the same question.

"Are you happy?" she had asked the woman with whom she had once played for hours in the garden. Kusum, who had married at the age of sixteen, was already a mother of three, so it was a bit late to ask her such a question; nevertheless, Ellora asked, because she had really wanted to know the answer. Kusum had just smiled in reply, exposing the gap left by two of her missing front teeth. It had been difficult for Ellora to believe that the emaciated and malnourished woman with the deeply wrinkled face sitting in front of her was her once lanky and beautiful childhood friend.

"So tell me Kusum, are you happy that you got married at such a young age?" Ellora had repeated her question, rephrasing it.

"Yes I am," Kusum had once again smiled, this time, hiding her missing teeth by covering her mouth with her calloused palm. "My husband is a good man. He drinks every night, but then they all do. At least, unlike other men from our community, he doesn't beat his wife and children every night after his drinking. I'm very lucky to have a kind-hearted husband like him. I'm very happy."

So all said and done, feeding the sparrows had indeed done the trick. Kusum's good deeds had paid off. She now had a husband decent enough not to beat her.

That had been Kusum's concept of a good husband: a husband who did not beat her, despite being drunk every night.

That had been Kusum's definition of a happy marriage.

What are mine? Ellora silently wonders.

****

Chapter 44

April 2012,
Springfield, Virginia

Jai is sitting in his office, phone in hand, debating silently whether to call Ellora or not. He would have made this call a good deal sooner, except that he had not been able to stop debating with himself about the propriety of calling her. Every time he was about to dial her number, he let his better sense prevail. Even now, he is not sure if calling Ellora is a good thing for either of them. But he must make this call. He has news that might interest her. He glances at his watch. He still has a few minutes before his next appointment. Perhaps, he better make that call now before he changes his mind once again.

Ellora answers the call after the third ring. Listening to her soft, mellifluous voice, Jai has a sudden vision of her sitting in Aparna's kitchen with her wavy brown hair cascading down her brown shoulders. Until this moment, he had not realized how much he enjoyed her company that evening and how much he wants to see her again.

"How wonderful to hear from you," says Ellora, when she recognizes his voice. As usual, she has picked up the call without reading the caller's name.

"Are you busy?"

"Never too busy for someone who gets out of the house on a cold December evening to make me a wonderful cup of tea," laughs Ellora.

"It was a pleasure," says Jai. He wants to add that it is

always a pleasure making tea for a beautiful woman, but decides against it. He has to remind himself that the woman he is talking to is soon going to marry an eligible banker from New York.

"Actually, I'm expecting a patient in the next five minutes, so let me come to the point straightaway. Are you interested in attending a filmmaking workshop?"

"Wow! Where, when and by whom?" Ellora can hardly contain her excitement.

"Phew! Let me try to answer all your questions one by one. You must have heard of Kevin Miller. He is an award-winning wildlife documentary maker. His film on Alaskan bears won him an Oscar nomination last year. Well, Kevin happens to be a good friend of mine. We studied in the same school, until he left for New York to study filmmaking." Jai pauses, waiting for Ellora to say something.

"Wow!" says Ellora, wondering if she is sounding like a gushing schoolgirl.

Assured that Ellora is all ears, Jai continues. "The good news is, Kevin is in town. In fact, he came over to see me yesterday. I took the liberty of showing parts of your documentary on Yamuna to him. He liked it very much. In fact, he went so far as to suggest that you should join the filmmaking-workshop he's going to conduct shortly in the Chesapeake Bay area. Presuming, you may not have time to attend an intensive outdoor workshop, you can at least meet Kevin in person and get some valuable tips from him."

"What makes you presume that I may not have time for a filmmaking-workshop?" She knows the answer, but still wants to probe. She has no doubt that Jai knows about her engagement to Neil. Thanks to her ecstatic and overexcited sister, by now, the entire East Coast Indian community knows about it.

"Well, Aparna told me that you're in the final stage of writing your research paper," says Jai. And then, after a brief pause, he adds, "She also gave me the good news. I'm sorry, I should've congratulated you first on your engagement."

"You can still do it," says Ellora.

"Yes, of course. Congratulations."

There is an uncomfortable pause. Jai does not know what else to say. Ellora rescues both of them from this awkward silence by going back to the original topic.

"So tell me, when can I meet your friend Kevin Miller?"

"He lives in a remote and isolated place. It's quite far from Springfield. You'll never be able to find the place on your own. You'll have to come with me. You've got no other choice."

"Don't make it sound like a punishment. I was hoping that you'd offer to drive me there," says Ellora, her face lighting up with unconcealed joy. She cannot understand why she is feeling so elated all of a sudden.

****

Chapter 45

Late April, 2012,

Springfield, Virginia

Jai and Ellora drive down to Kevin Miller's place the following weekend. It is a pleasant drive, filled with casual chitchat and easy laughter. The trip itself is quite fruitful; Kevin invites Ellora personally to join his week-long filmmaking workshop and she is only too happy to accept the offer.

Her state of euphoria continues when she accompanies Jai to another excursion a week later, this time a trip to the nearby mountains on their bikes.

However now, as she feels the full blast of the cold mountain wind in her face, Ellora feels like an errant schoolgirl who has played truant and has lied to everyone in order to follow her heart.

"Aditi didn't tell you to follow your wayward heart and leave your brain behind," she chides herself, even as she reminds herself not to let the guilt weigh her high spirits down. She is indeed high, literally and exhilaratingly so. From the moment she put her feet on the pedals, she knew she was going to enjoy every moment of this uphill journey on her rented bike. She had almost forgotten how much fun one could have riding on two wheels. There is an utter sense of freedom. There is also a rush of excitement that is strangely tranquil. It is difficult to decide if the cause of this Zen-like euphoria is psychological, physiological, physical or physiochemical in nature.

It was during the drive to Kevin Miller's home that Jai had

asked her if she would like to accompany him on a mountain biking trail. She, of course, had jumped at his suggestion (of late, she had been jumping at a lot of his suggestions). She should have politely refused, but instead, she found herself saying, "I'd love to."

It all started with a simple question she asked him during that long drive.

"What do you do on days when you're not operating on your patients?"

"I like to swap my surgical gloves for riding ones," Jai told her with his trademark playfulness before elaborating his statement. "I'm an avid mountain biker. Whenever I can, I head straight for the mountains on my bike, weather and time permitting, of course. It's an altogether different feeling. Very liberating indeed."

"I know what you mean. I've done my share of biking on mountainous trails during my college years."

"Really?" Jai could hardly conceal his excitement and joy.

"You cannot be a botanist without being a bicyclist. Most botanical excursions are made either on bike, or on foot," she told him, thinking nostalgically of the days when she had cycled with Dr Maya Bose and other research scholars to remote tribal areas in search of indigenous medicinal plants.

As she looks at the cloudless sky that somehow seems bluer than ever from her elevated position, she is glad that she accepted Jai's invitation despite all her compunctions.

"I'm sure my sister and mother are not going to be too thrilled when I tell them about this expedition," she had told Jai this morning when they were at the bike rental shop.

"Then don't tell them. I'll also make sure not to say anything to Aparna or Rahul. So that makes me your partner in crime," he told her with a conspiratorial wink.

Despite her Zen-like elated state, Ellora cannot entirely silence the nagging voice inside her head. She cannot completely shake off the feeling of guilt for being absolutely tight-lipped about this pre-planned outing with Jai. As she braces herself to absorb the shock from the bumpy ground ahead, she tells herself that there was no way she could have told her family members the truth. They would have never understood. They would have never approved of the idea of her accompanying Jai on an adventurous outing that was risky in more ways than one.

"What am I doing? I shouldn't be here in the first place." She wrestles with her conscience, as she carefully negotiates a narrow, weaving dirt trail closely behind Jai.

The burden of her guilt is double because she had not told Neil either, when he had called her last night from London. Not that she had an opportunity to do so. It had been a short call and as usual, they had talked about his work most of the time. She was surprised to have received his call so late in the evening. A quick mental calculation told her that it must be two o' clock in the morning in London. She just had to ask Neil why he was still awake at that unearthly hour and he broke into a long monologue, full of financial jargon about the presentation he was working on for an audience comprising some of the top investors and economists in England. She wanted to tell him about this biking trip with Jai. It was important for her to be able to tell her fiancé everything, but he went on and on about his presentation and somehow, the moment was lost. After a while, she even stopped listening to what he was saying.

"You seem distracted. Is everything alright, sweetheart?" Neil wanted to know when he finally realized that she was unusually quiet. She assured him it was nothing; just stress. Neil at once understood. "Don't work too hard. Take it easy. You'll be fine my precious, I promise," he assured her before ringing off.

Neil, of course, is good at reassuring people; as a successful investment banker, that is part of his job. He also happens to be an open-minded person. And that is why Ellora feels doubly guilty about cycling alongside another man without her fiancé knowing about it. She promises herself that the next time Neil calls, she is going to tell him everything: about her trip with Jai to see Kevin Miller, about her plans to join Kevin's filmmaking workshop and last but not least, about this day-out on a hilly trail with Jai.

"A penny for your thoughts," Jai tells her, when they complete the loop and stop at the bike rental shop. He takes out a shining penny from his wallet and holds it in front of her.

"Thank you. I'll keep your penny as well as my thoughts." Ellora teasingly smiles, as she swiftly takes the coin from his fingers.

As he looks at her smiling face, radiant with a healthy post-cycling glow, Jai thinks, not for the first time, how guilelessly attractive her beauty is. Her face has a lack of artifice that is so unlike the artfully made up faces he sees around him all the time. Deliberately, he forces himself to look away, switching his thoughts to things that are less distracting.

"I'd no idea that I could do it," Ellora tells Jai, as they start walking towards the car park.

"You were pretty good, in fact. It's quite a challenging track. Certainly not meant for beginners. To be honest, I didn't expect you to last for more than twenty minutes," says Jai.

"Well, don't forget that I've had plenty of practice cycling on dirt roads full of potholes," reminds Ellora.

Once inside the car, Jai turns towards her and says, "I'm hoping all this exercise has made you hungry, because I'm going to take you to a wonderful restaurant that serves excellent Southern cuisine." He then hesitantly adds, "But if you're in a hurry to get back to your work, I'll drop you home."

"I'm in no hurry to get back to work. Between you and me, my work is almost over. I'm just pretending to be busy."

"Why?" Jai is more amused than surprised.

"To avoid going to Springfield. My mother has already reached from New York. They're all waiting for me to pack my bags and join them. But I'm not yet ready to go. I need some more time to process my thoughts. I need time to come to terms with the fact that I'm going to be married a month from now." The words are out before Ellora can stop herself. She is grateful to Jai for absorbing this inadvertently given information without asking any probing questions.

As she looks at his smooth and long-fingered surgeon's hands on the steering wheel, Ellora realizes, again not for the first time, how much she admires the man sitting beside her and how much she enjoys being with him. She is aware that he too is attracted to her, that he too enjoys her company; but obviously not enough to attempt to force the pace and let the strong attraction between them become something deeper and more solid.

Sitting beside her, Jai too is thinking along the same lines. He wonders why he has thought so much about Ellora of late. The truth is, he is seriously interested in pursuing this relationship, but is not sure if it would be a good thing for either of them. Seeing her alone like this on three consecutive occasions, however, has set him wondering about the wisdom of holding back from this intriguing woman. Has he been foolish? Why didn't he do something to stop her from becoming engaged to another man? Why is he still not doing anything about it? What is he afraid of?

* * *

The restaurant is everything Jai described it to be: authentically Southern with an old country feel.

As they wait for their spicy grilled catfish, turnip greens and corn muffins with maple syrup, Jai finally brings himself to ask Ellora the question he has wanted to ask her for some time.

"Are you happy about your engagement with Neil?"

"Depends on what your definition of happiness is," she says cryptically, not wanting to elaborate further. Then suddenly, without any warning, she looks into his eyes and asks sharply, "Why should I be unhappy? Neil is a good man, a very good catch, as some of my sister's friends would say. The whole Indian community from Washington DC to New York is already talking about how lucky I am to have snared a good catch like him. So why shouldn't I be happy?" The flecks of green in her eyes are now flashing brilliantly.

"That still doesn't answer my question," says Jai, quite surprised to see this new volatile side of the serene woman sitting opposite him.

"I'll answer all your questions, but some other time. Not now. In any case, you're always making me talk about myself. Don't you think it's time we talked about you for a change?"

"What do you want to know? I'm a busy surgeon leading a rather boring and routine life that revolves around round-the-clock appointments, operations and administrative work. You'll be very bored if I start talking about my work."

"Then talk about your personal life," says Ellora, stirring her iced tea.

"What do you want to know?" asks Jai solemnly, looking directly into her eyes.

There is a moment's silence before Ellora speaks and when she does, she tries to choose her words carefully; but there is only one way of phrasing the question she wants to ask, so without further ado, she asks him directly, "Tell me about your marriage. What went wrong?"

To her relief, Jai smiles. Then, after a brief pause, he says, "It's been quite some time since someone asked me that question, but since you want to know, I'll tell you everything you're interested in knowing. But first, let's eat our food, because it's already here." He smiles at the waitress who has returned with a huge tray laden with steaming dishes.

They talk about all things other than his marriage. They

talk about the dogs they once had. She tells him about Babu Shona, the Golden Retriever that came to her as a posthumous birthday gift from her biological parents and he tells her about Bolto, his German Shepherd that died two years ago.

* * *

On the way back, Jai keeps his promise: he tells Ellora all about his failed marriage. Without going into all the unpleasant details, he tells her everything from beginning to end: how things turned bitter when he could not give his ex-wife the time and the attention she constantly demanded and how she took the extreme step of leaving him for another man. He takes his share of the blame. He admits his own failure at filling in the widening cracks in his troubled marriage with togetherness that would have cemented their relationship.

"Now it's your turn," says he, after several moments of silence.

"What do you want to know?" asks Ellora, not sure, if she wants to talk about the things she has on her mind.

"You hardly know Neil. How can you agree to marry him?"

This is a concerned man talking, a man who had made the same mistake of making an impulsive and hasty decision of marrying someone he did not know very well.

Ellora remains quiet, composing her thoughts.

"You've met Neil only a couple of times. How can you make up your mind about marrying him in such a short time?" Jai persists.

"Because I really like Neil. Because he's the only decent man in recent years who has asked me to marry him. Because I'm already thirty-three. Because time is running out and I'm running out of options. Because it will make my unhappy mother very happy. Because I'm a good girl and a good girl is only happy when she makes her loved ones happy."

Ellora looks at Jai, sitting silently beside her, focusing on the road ahead instead of making any comment. They drive in total silence. A lot has been said. They have both said a good deal more than what had passed in words. Now it is time for silent reflection. However, before she gets down from the car at the metro station, Ellora decides to breaks the long silence by having her final say.

"So Jai, now that you know my reasons for marrying Neil, do you have any solution to offer? Do you have any alternative proposal in mind? Because, if you do, I'll be glad to hear it. Who knows? I may even consider it seriously. You have my phone number, so please call, if you've got something concrete to say to me. But otherwise, don't call, because I'm getting married shortly and am answerable to my future husband."

****

Chapter 46

Mid May 2012
Hillsborough, New Jersey

"My husband is a Phileas Fogg. Nikhil is methodical to the core. Everything has to be just so, down to the temperature of his morning tea and I, as his honorary Passepartout have to constantly run around to satisfy his high standards of perfection and punctuality," says Neil's mother Leela Banerjee to the group of women she has invited to high tea to introduce them to the young woman her son has chosen to marry. Everyone laughs. They have all read Jules Verne's classic novel Around the World in Eighty Days and are familiar with the characters of Phileas Fogg, the highly punctual and slightly eccentric Englishman and his obedient French servant Passepartout.

This is Ellora's fourth meeting with her future mother-in-law and she is still as uncomfortable and nervous in her presence as she was when she met her for the first time during her visit to New York just before Christmas.

Sitting in Leela Banerjee's garden, as she listens to the women gathered here for high tea, it is not difficult for Ellora to guess that most of them are also born coconuts like her anglophile college professor Dr Brown. Now in their mid-sixties, many of these women were once a part of a rigid hierarchical society where proficiency in English often determined who was placed where in the pecking order.

Despite living in America for many years, these women refuse to adopt American ways: they continue to follow English traditions and continue to speak the Queen's English with the fawning faithfulness of subjects who believe that mastering the tongue of their colonial masters is the best form of flattery. They continue to pucker their stiff upper lips when they hear someone speak English with a vernacular accent. A part of them still resides in those high-ceilinged, airy bungalows in the erstwhile British neighbourhoods in Calcutta, now Kolkata. A part of them still longs for those exclusive clubs where the walls had been Georgian, the dress code had been colonial and where they sat with their friends and drank sherry served by uniformed waiters. Even those who secretly acknowledge that the Great Britain is neither that great, nor that British anymore, tenaciously cling to the cherished memories of their post-Raj life in Calcutta.

The woman sitting next to Ellora, however, is slightly less nostalgic and considerably more pragmatic when she candidly admits that her recent visit to Kolkata was a complete disaster. "Everything has changed and yet nothing has changed. The traffic is worse than ever, the air is more polluted than ever and the mosquitoes are more resolute than ever in extracting their pint of blood from your veins."

As she listens to this tête-à-tête over cups of Darjeeling tea and bites of cucumber sandwiches and fish croquettes, Ellora feels like she has walked into a parody set in the Edwardian era. The props are all in place: silverware polished to perfection, tables covered with the finest linen, a tea trolley complete with bone china teapots, cups and saucers, doilies and napkins. Only the actors are all brown and instead of wearing full-length skirts, tight corsets and sun hats, they are all dressed in summery chiffons and flowery silks.

Ellora herself is wearing a delicate French chiffon sari in pistachio green. Her mother wanted her to wear her heavy emerald set for the occasion, but Aparna made sure that her sister wore nothing flashier than a fine gold chain with a solitaire diamond pendant. Her sister, as always, was right. Leela Banerjee's old school friends, despite their fixation for all things colonial and dated, are quite contemporary in their tastes, especially when it comes to clothes and jewellery.

"I wonder what Kate is going to wear to the Queen's Diamond Jubilee lunch," wonders someone aloud, her voice as screechy as chalk across a blackboard.

"I loved the blue lace dress she wore to her friend's wedding recently," says another woman as she takes a dainty bite of her watercress sandwich.

Ellora and Aparna furtively exchange smiles. They cannot help being amused by this conversation. These women obviously have a great fondness for the House of Windsor: they are talking about Kate Middleton, Princess Diana and Sarah Ferguson between sips of tea, as if they are talking about their next-door neighbours.

When they are not exchanging notes on British royalty, they are discussing vintage porcelain. As she listens to this conversation peppered with words like Queen Mother, Beatrix Potter, Wedgewood, Dresden and Arthur Sullivan, it occurs to Ellora that these women are trapped in a colonial time warp. The settlers they so adore have gone back to settle down in their own country. The party has been over for more than sixty-five years. However, these intoxicated, nostalgic women are still nursing a colonial hangover like a cherished drink.

"These scones are splendid," says a double-chinned woman, as she spreads generous layers of clotted cream and strawberry jam across Leela Banerjee's homemade scones.

"This clotted cream is so high in calories that I won't even attempt to count them," Ellora hears someone else say.

Leela Banerjee, now that she has overseen all the arrangements, sits down next to Aparna and Kajol.

"Where's Mr Banerjee?" asks Aparna.

"Oh! It's four o' clock, so he must be in his music room practicing his sitar. My husband is very particular about doing things at mathematically fixed hours. I asked him to join us, but he refused, saying he'd feel like a baffled rooster in a noisy henhouse." Everybody laughs and they all nod their heads understandingly.

"This butterfly fairy cake is delicious. Did you bake it yourself?" Kajol, the usually quiet sister-in-law of Ellora and Aparna breaks her long silence to ask.

Leela Banerjee is quite happy to share her recipe with Kajol, who takes out a pen and paper from her purse and starts jotting down the recipe quickly, looking more like a competent secretary taking down dictation than a professor of law that she actually is.

Ellora envies these women. They are all fine homemakers who have made a fine art out of homemaking. Unlike her, their dreams and ambitions are not in conflict with their current vocation in life. She wonders if she can ever be one of them, hosting parties, exchanging recipes and learning to bake spongy sponge cakes.

Not surprisingly, the topic eventually turns to cricket. A young mother, who has recently arrived in the US after living in England for many years, laments the fact that the otherwise sporty Americans are so unsupportive and unsporting when it comes to a sport like cricket.

"My son is miserable that no one in his school plays cricket. Back in Derbyshire, he was training under Rohinton Merchant. You must have heard his name. He used to play for India."

Aparna shoots a look at Ellora who is looking stunned like a deer caught in headlights. Even their mother, despite her limited knowledge of English, has turned white.

However, there is more to come.

"Of course, we've all heard about Rohinton Merchant. Who could forget the magnificent debut he made against Sri Lanka in the mid-nineties? Ellora, isn't this Merchant fellow the same dashing batsman who was smitten by you when you were still in school? I think the two of you were dating each other and all the newspapers in the country had a field day talking about your budding romance." This is Leela Banerjee, making a public announcement in her booming voice about the scandal that nearly destroyed Ellora's life.

Surprisingly, there is no stunned pin drop silence and no sharp intake of breath following this shocking announcement, just a chorus of, "Really?" from most of Leela Banerjee's incredulous friends. They all look at Ellora with new eyes and renewed interest. All this time, they thought she was just pretty, but all of a sudden, they reassess her looks and decide that she is uncommonly pretty. Within seconds, Ellora has gone up a notch or two in their estimation by scoring an unexpected Brownie point because of her past romantic association with a well-known cricketer. A cricketer who once played for India and is now living in England. A cricketer who now has an English wife and English children.

What irony! Suddenly her shameful past has become something to be proud of, something to flaunt, something to boast about, something to discuss between sips of Darjeeling tea.

Ellora earns her next Brownie point when Leela Banerjee lets everyone know (once again in her booming voice) that Ellora is the daughter of famous Elina Chatterjee. The name does not ring an immediate bell, but many nod their heads, nevertheless. Others look at their hostess like clueless children waiting for the quizmaster to give them their next clue. Leela Banerjee promptly obliges by helpfully providing them with some more information.

"Elina Chatterjee: the famous Odissi dancer," she announces with the zest of an enigmatic magician pulling a rabbit out of his hat.

Some more heads nod, this time, a bit more vigorously.

"She was featured in Vogue," informs Leela Banerjee with justifiable pride.

The other shoe finally drops and all heads start nodding vigorously and appreciatively.

"Splendid," they all say, almost in chorus.

****

Chapter 47

June 1, 2012,

Edgewater, Maryland

Ellora connects her cell phone to the charger to stop it from beeping annoyingly every two minutes to remind her that it is running on low battery. It is hard to ignore the pathetic beeps that sound more like muffled moans from an instrument breathing its last.

Ever since her last conversation with Jai five weeks ago, she made sure to charge her phone every morning in the hope of receiving a call. She put everything, her wedding preparation, her visit to New York and her feelings for Neil on hold, waiting for that one call. Finally, as the days turned into weeks and the weeks into a month, Ellora stopped waiting for the call that was never going to come, just as she stopped charging her phone first thing in the morning.

What kept her going through this frustrating phase of endless waiting were the phone calls from her fiancé. To his credit, Neil never failed to call her even when he was in a different time zone.

Now that he is in Singapore, he calls her every morning after he is done for the day. Most of the time, he talks while she listens to him talk about the strategies he is chalking out for turning pitches into live deals. In between all this shop talk, Neil manages to convey how much he is missing her and how eagerly he is looking forward to the day when he can finally hold her in his arms.

Ellora needs to hear him say all these romantic and

reassuring things. She needs to know that she is loved, cherished, desired and not all that unwanted. However, this morning, her need for solitude and silence is far greater than her need for any reassuring words. She has woken up with a dull headache and is not up to listening to Neil's long and dull conversation. Besides, there are matters, serious matters, which she needs to sort out in her head before she discusses them with him.

As a matter of fact, a discussion with Neil is overdue. There are questions she needs to ask him and there are answers he must provide.

As she heads for the kitchen to make herself a much-needed cup of tea, Ellora recalls a conversation that has been replaying over and over in her mind for over two weeks now. She has yet to come to terms with what Neil's mother had to say to her on the day of the high tea. She has not been able to shrug off the sense of unease she felt at the time.

She had been alone with Leela Banerjee in her kitchen. The two of them were hand-washing the delicate bone china crockery that had once belonged to Leela Banerjee's grandmother and was therefore, too precious to be put in the dishwasher. Before letting Ellora handle her prized family heirlooms, her future mother-in-law showed her how to wipe them gently with a soft dishtowel.

As she now washes her sturdy mug under running tap water, Ellora recalls how nervous she had been about handling those delicate cups and saucers: her focus had been fully upon doing her assigned task correctly but her concentration had been broken when Neil's mother had casually inquired, "So I hear you're planning to join a filmmaking workshop."

The question took Ellora by complete surprise. Only three days ago, she had finally managed to tell Neil about her decision to join Kevin Miller's workshop and the news, it seemed, had already reached Leela Banerjee. Her fiancé certainly had not lost any time in passing on the information given to him in confidence to his mother who, in turn, did not lose much time in grilling her about it.

Ellora stopped washing the soapy and slippery saucer in her hand to brace herself for what was coming. Actually, she already had an idea what was coming because, despite the casual tone, there was an unmistakable undertone of disapproval in Leela Banerjee's comment.

"I do hope you're planning to take it up just as a hobby. Or are you, by any chance, seriously considering filmmaking as a career option?" she asked, taking the saucer from her future daughter-in-law's hands to demonstrate to her once again the correct way of washing her precious china.

"It's a bit premature for me to be able to say anything right now, but yes, someday, I'd love to make documentaries if I get the opportunity," replied Ellora. She could not help wondering if Neil's mother was asking her that question of her own accord, or if Neil had asked his mother to do his dirty work for him.

Ellora braced herself for a long lecture, but instead, received a long explanation.

"I'm sure you're aware that Neil has had two broken relationships. He must have told you about his previous two girlfriends. His first girlfriend worked with him in the same office. They broke up because they both were too busy with their respective careers to have time for a meaningful relationship. His second girlfriend was the editor of a fashion magazine, but once again, she was too busy with her fashion shows, photo shoots and deadlines to have time for a boyfriend."

Leela Banerjee paused briefly to smile at Ellora, before adding, "So now you know why I'm concerned when Neil tells me that you're planning to join a filmmaking workshop. And if you're wondering if Neil also shares my concerns, the answer is yes. Don't get me wrong, my son doesn't have any problems with his wife working after marriage, but he would prefer her to have a job that doesn't require her to work at odd hours. He's thirty-six after all. He now wants to settle down, he wants to have children right away, he wants stability in his life; which I'm sure you're going to provide, provided you pursue a career with regular work hours, instead of dabbling in things that will get in the way of your being a good homemaker and a supportive wife."

Leela Banerjee paused and waited for Ellora to say something. Fortunately, Ellora did not have to respond to her immediately. Their conversation was interrupted when Neil's father entered the kitchen to make himself his five o' clock cup of tea.

* * *

Now, as she stands near her window and sips tea from her mug, Ellora remembers how disturbed she was for days after coming back from New York. She could not discuss her misgivings and anxieties with her sister, because she already knew what her reaction would be. She has not been able to broach the subject with Neil either, not yet. But it is high time the two of them had a serious discussion. While she understands Neil's apprehensions, she is not at all happy that instead of discussing his concerns with her, he asked his mother to do so. Why hadn't he said anything to her when she first told him about her plans of joining the workshop? If the idea had disturbed him so much, why hadn't he said so? Would he do the same thing even after they were married? Discuss things with his mother first, instead of talking to her directly about his concerns?

"I'm already getting a taste of what marriage is all about. I'm not even married yet and my dreams are already under scrutiny, my choices are already being questioned and my wings are already being clipped," reflects Ellora rather cynically. But then, she has been through all this and more. Life has trained her well for situations like this, hasn't it?

In any case, filmmaking might have been on her bucket

list, but it was never on her list of career options. She may be passionate about making documentaries, but taking it up seriously as a profession had never crossed her mind before, at least, not until she had had that conversation with Jai in Aparna's kitchen, when he made her talk about her future goals. Jai always had that effect on her. He made her think aloud, he made her talk about things she herself did not know she wanted to do. She herself had had no idea how much she wanted to learn the techniques and the technicalities of making films, until Jai told her about Kevin Miller's workshop.

And now she must forget all about Jai as well as filmmaking. What's the point of moping over something that is unachievable and someone who is unattainable? She is getting married in ten days' time and her biological clock is furiously ticking away. Like her fiancé, she too would like to have children right away. Neil and his mother are right. Filmmaking will have to take a back seat. It will have to go back to being on her bucket-list. Someday, in the not so near future, she will make documentaries that the BBC and National Geographic channels would like to broadcast. But all that will have to wait till her children start college.

"You do have a fertile imagination Ms Ellora Chatterjee. You're not even married and you're already dreaming about your brilliant future as a filmmaker after your future children with your future husband start going to college," she scoffs at herself.

****

Chapter 48

4th June, 2012, Edgewaters.

Her cell phone is ringing. It must be Neil. Good that the battery is not yet fully charged; he cannot go on and on and on about things she is not up to hearing right now. She has once again woken up with a dull headache.

Ellora picks up the phone and waits for Neil to ask perkily, "How're you doing this morning, my precious?" But instead, she hears a voice that she had waited to hear for more than a month and had given up on hearing ever again.

"Remember me? I won't be surprised if you don't, because it's been a while." Jai's voice does not give away much, but Ellora can picture him smiling his dimpled smile and looking very amused.

"How can he joke after putting me through all this," thinks Ellora, but aloud she says, "How nice of you to call, even though I must admit, I wasn't expecting it."

"I had to call, because I've some exciting news for you."

It is a good thing that Ellora does not allow Jai's comment to raise her expectations too much; otherwise, they would have come crashing down after hearing his next sentence.

"I know of a place you'd love to visit."

"I'm not up to any mountain biking," says Ellora rather sharply and drily.

"Who's talking about mountain biking? I'm planning to take you to a scenic town called Floyd. I've an elderly friend called Mildred, who lives there with her husband and her hummingbirds. She has invited the two of us to spend the weekend with them. I'm sure you're going to love it. You can sit on her deck for hours, watching those tiny birds dart in and out with supersonic speed."

Jai pauses, anxiously waiting for Ellora to say something, but she remains silent, leaving him with no other choice except to continue.

"Those fidgety blink-and-you'll miss them birds are impossible to photograph. They vanish before you can say, "Hummingbirds." All you can capture is the blurred movement of those furiously flapping wings. Mildred hasn't been able to get a single good shot of her dear hummers till date. She's absolutely thrilled to know that I'll be bringing a friend who can click some good pictures of her feathered friends."

"Jai, why're we talking about this? You know very well I can't accompany you to this place. Why are you even suggesting this trip? Don't you understand that with my wedding just around the corner, I've no time for any such silly outings?"

Her cutting and icy tone cuts no ice with Jai, who riles her further by responding cheerfully, "All the more reason for you to accompany me. When will you get a golden opportunity like this again? I'm sure your banker fiancé will always be too busy to take you for such trips."

Ellora is aghast at Jai's brazen brashness that borders on audacity. How can he talk to her like this? What right does he have to say such preposterous things? No, she is not going to dignify his cheeky comments by responding. In any case, going by the pathetic beeps being emitted by her cell phone, the battery is about to run out any moment now. Thankfully, this annoying conversation is going to come to an abrupt end very soon.

"So have you taken something for your headache?"

"Who says I have a headache?"

"You do sound like someone with a headache. Another good reason for you to accompany me to this town. Watching those tiny hummingbirds is just the cure for you. They will hum away your headache. Besides, you always wanted to make a film on them, so how can you say no to this tempting offer?"

Ellora is stumped. Does he have a secret camera to spy on her head and the thoughts inside it? How could he have guessed that she has a throbbing headache? And how on earth does he know about her desire to make a film on hummingbirds?

Then it all comes back to her.

The topic had come up during their long drive to Kevin Miller's place. They had been talking about Jai's penchant for outdoor activities like mountain biking. After telling her how eagerly he looked forward to swapping his surgical gloves for riding ones, he had turned towards her and had asked, "And what about you? What do you like doing when you've got nothing else to do?"

"I like to take pictures. I find it therapeutic. In Delhi, I used to sit for hours on my balcony filming sunbirds that visited our terrace garden. I could spend an entire Sunday shooting those tiny little shiny birds flitting from flower to flower. As a matter of fact, now that my project is nearly complete, I'm longing to go someplace where I can shoot hummingbirds. I've always wanted to make a film on them."

The conversation had taken place only few weeks ago and yet she had forgotten all about it until Jai brought it up. She has been quite disoriented and forgetful of late. It has been a month of unbearable silence, a month filled with hopes, insecurities, desperation and frustrations. A month of agony, shame and regrets for saying things that were better left unsaid.

A month ago, when she got down from Jai's car, she had told him very bluntly and very unequivocally that he was not to call her again, unless he had something important and concrete to say to her. She could not have been more candid and more explicit than that. And yet, here Jai is, calling her again to discuss things that are anything but concrete. What's wrong with this man? Why is he calling her to discuss, of all things, an inconsequential film she is never going to make?

"How about the coming Saturday, say at around ten o' clock? I'll pick you up from the Springfield metro station like last time. It's about a six hour drive to Floyd."

"And what are we going to talk about during those six long hours? I'm afraid I've nothing more to say to you, Jai. Not anymore. I've already said enough." Ellora hopes her tone is cold enough to convey the icy message she is trying to convey. She does not know why she is even continuing with this conversation. She only knows that her cell-phone battery may die on her any moment now and she wants to say something, just anything, to keep this inane conversation going before it finally dies.

"But I've a lot of things to say to you. Concrete and serious things. Things that might interest you. Things that could change everything for the both of us. In fact, I've so much to say to you that six hours are going to fly just like that."

Jai waits, but there is no response.

"Ellora," he repeats, "I'll be waiting for you at our usual meeting place outside the metro station. Don't forget the day and the time. Saturday, 9th June, at 10.00 a.m. sharp"

Another long silence follows. Jai can hear the chirping birds in the background. The pause is getting considerably long but Jai waits patiently at the other end for her to say something, anything. Finally, after what seems like ages, she breaks the prolonged silence.

"Jai, do you even realize how absurd and crazy you're beginning to sound? I'm getting married in six days' time and you wish to take me out to a remote village just a day before my wedding? Are you dumb or are you nuts?"

"I'm nuts. I'm absolutely nuts about you Ellora. I've tried my best not to feel this way about you, but I've failed miserably in all my attempts to resist you. You're simply irresistible. In the past few weeks, I've done nothing much except thinking about you and about us."

Ellora gasps audibly. What is he saying and why is he saying this? And that too now, just days before her wedding? No, she cannot go on listening to this utter nonsense anymore.

Thankfully, she does not have to listen to Jai anymore. Her phone dies at that precise moment without any warning.

****

Chapter 49

In the days that follow, Ellora walks in a daze, unaware of Mrs Morris's anxious glances and questioning eyes as they both pack her things. Her state of numbness continues even after reaching Aparna's house where the wedding preparations are already in full swing. She mechanically goes through the motions of playing the bride-to-be, but her unhappiness is written all over her face for everyone to see, read and draw conclusions.

The house is teeming with guests. Rahulda's brothers and their wives arrived last night from Chicago. However, most other guests are going to stay in a nearby hotel. Arnab and Kajol are also staying in the same hotel to be able to oversee the arrangements and look after the guests, especially the ones from the groom's side.

Despite being dead tired, Ellora is not able to sleep at night, not because she is now sharing her bed with her niece Ananya (the original occupant of the room) but because there are too many disturbing thoughts and distracting memories keeping her awake night after night. If only she could get some sleep! If only she could run away from all this madness!

But how can she run away? Well, she can, if she really wants to. She can still run away with Jai, it's not yet too late for that. No, that's out of the question. How can she even think about it? How can she cause so much pain to so many people? People she loves, people she intends to love, people who love her back so fiercely, so oppressively and so conditionally that she wants to break free. But how can she break free, especially now? No, there's no way she can do it.

It's too late to back out. It's too late to break free.

Unable to keep her eyes closed any longer, Ellora gets up. It is only five in the morning. She quietly gets into her jogging pants and goes out for a long run. She takes a route that goes via Jai's house. She has been covertly doing this for the past three days: spying on Jai's house from a distance to find some sign of his presence inside, but the empty driveway and the pile of newspapers outside the front door tell a different story.

Hopefully, this hopeless prying is going to come to an end today itself. Neil and his relatives are arriving from New York this morning and henceforth, things are going to get only too hectic to leave her any time for such pointless pursuits. She must go home and start getting ready. She has to be at the airport to receive her groom and his party of relatives and friends.

****

Chapter 50

9th June 2012, Springfield.

"Ellora is coming with me in my car."

There is something about Arnab's tone that warns everybody not to argue or ask questions.

Altogether, there are five cars, they are all going to the airport to receive the groom and his party. Arnab waits for the other cars to disappear from sight before he parks his in the first vacant parking spot he can find. He then turns towards Ellora and says, "Now tell me what is bothering you. I'm here to listen."

This time, Arnab's tone is that of a caring elder brother who wants to help his distressed sister. Ellora says nothing, but her tears say a lot. Three sleepless nights in a row have made her vulnerable and weak.

Arnab puts an affectionate arm around her heaving shoulders and says, "You obviously don't want to marry Neil, it is written all over your face. You look more like a frightened calf being readied for the slaughterhouse than a happy bride getting ready for marriage. Now let me ask you a straight question and I want a straight answer. Do you like someone else? Let me be more specific: do you like Jai?"

Ellora is dumbfounded. How does he know about Jai? Who could have told him? It must have been Mrs Morris, who else? No one knows how deeply she feels for Jai except her landlady who arrived yesterday and has been spending a lot of time with Arnab and Kajol ever since. Her brother, of course, has a way of extracting information, as he is doing now.

Before she knows it, Ellora has told her brother everything, from beginning to end, even about the phone call she received from Jai five days ago.

'Today is the day I was supposed to meet Jai outside the metro station," she informs him wistfully, her eyes automatically checking the time on her wristwatch. It is not yet eight, but how does it matter what time it is?

"Ellora, it's not yet too late to change your mind. We can still go to the metro station instead of the airport. So tell me now: where do you want to go?" asks Arnab.

"To the airport. Going anywhere else is out of question. We're already late, so let's get going." There is a finality to her statement that tells Arnab that the subject is closed to any further debate or discussion.

They drive silently for a while and then, Arnab breaks the silence by saying, "We just left behind the road that goes to the metro station. Do you want me to take a U-turn?" asks her brother.

"No," replies Ellora quite firmly. It is too late to take a U-turn. It's too late to veer off to roads leading towards Jai. From today onwards, all her paths should only lead towards Neil and all her thoughts should only revolve around her husband-to-be.

* * *

As they wait in the hotel lobby for the elevator to arrive, Aparna dictates the order in which the wedding guests will go to their respective rooms. She also decides which member of her family will accompany whom.

"There's no room inside the lift. You come with Neil," says Aparna to Ellora before getting into the elevator with Neil's parents. Ellora has no other choice except to comply with her sister's command, especially because the elevator door has already closed. She gets a feeling that they have all connived together to leave the two of them alone. She is furious with her sister for trapping her into this awkward situation.

As she walks in the corridor behind Neil and the bellboy, Ellora is not sure if she wants to be alone in a hotel room with her fiancé. She steps inside the plush room with great trepidation. Her fears are not misplaced. After the bellboy leaves, Neil wastes no time in taking her in his arms and planting kisses all over her face and neck. She meekly submits to his wild kisses. This is a new Neil. A man with male desires. A man with his manhood now pressing against her body. She is uncomfortably aware that the next time they are alone in his bedroom in New York, his kisses will be wilder and deeper, his maleness will be more insistent and much more invasive. Her heart sinks at the very thought of it, not because she is not woman enough to respond to male desires, but because the woman inside her desires someone else, even at this very moment when she is being fervently kissed by a man who is going to be her husband by tomorrow night. Thankfully, a timely knock on the door cuts short the unwanted kisses.

"Did I interrupt something?" asks Aparna with a mischievous grin as she enters the room. Then looking at Neil, she smiles some more and continues, "Sorry to have interrupted the two of you, but I'd no other choice. Neil, I'm here to abduct my sister. We have to leave now. Ellora must get ready for the afternoon rituals and so must you. But don't look so dejected. You'll be seeing her soon in the evening during the *Sangeet* ceremony," says Aparna in a consoling manner, as she takes Ellora's hand and steps out. Then, looking at the cardboard sign hanging from the door handle, she turns towards Neil and says, "The next time you two are together in a hotel room, you will be officially allowed to hang the Do Not Disturb sign outside. So cheer up."

Neil smiles, but there is something missing from his smile, notes Ellora.

* * *

As they all start walking back towards their cars, Aparna

reminds Arnab that he has to drop their sister to the beauty salon.

"Ellora's appointment is at ten, so you better get going," commands Aparna.

"Yes, ma'am," says the brother with an elaborate army salute and a broad smile.

However, neither Arnab, nor Ellora is smiling during the drive to the salon. Ellora is too shaken up with what just took place in Neil's room a few moments ago. It was a rude awakening for her. She now knows first-hand that the pleasant and mild-mannered banker is not going to talk just shop after marriage. What was she thinking when she got herself into all this? That their marriage would smoothly transition from his boring shop-talk to pleasant pillow talk and no further interaction or intimacy would follow? Of course, she knew all along everything there is to know. She had been preparing herself for months for all this and more. And yet, she couldn't handle it when her fiancé started kissing her all over. How would she handle it when he progresses beyond kisses?

Ellora stares vacantly ahead, not aware, how forlorn and wan she is looking now. She is also unaware of her brother's worried expression, as he takes his eyes off the road frequently to glance in her direction.

Arnab drives quietly for several minutes and then, just before approaching a signal, he turns towards Ellora and says, "The next traffic signal could be the most significant turning point of your life. If we turn left, we will reach your salon and if we turn right, we will reach the metro station. Now which way do you want me to turn?"

"Right," says Ellora after a brief pause, still in a state of utter confusion and shock.

"Right it is," says Arnab as he quickly changes lanes without further ado and without giving his sister any chance to change her mind. For the first time during this whole drive, he looks happy and relaxed.

Neither of them says anything as they drive towards the new destination. Ellora is the first one to break the long silence by asking, "What if Jai is not at the station?"

"Then we'll go back to the same signal and take a left. We'll be late for your salon appointment by an hour or so, of course" says her brother matter-of-factly.

A part of Ellora is certain that Jai will not be waiting for her at the station. How can he be? He is out of town. Even this morning his car was not in the driveway and his mailbox was still overflowing with uncollected mail and parcels. But what if he has come back? Would he be foolish enough to come all the way to the station and wait for her there after what she had told him?

I hope not, thinks Ellora silently. This is absolute madness. Why had she let her brother talk her into doing something so outrageous?

She is going to be late for the beautician's appointment. They were going to do her hair, nails and face. They were going to fix her dark circles, thread her eyebrows, polish her skin, paint her nails, scrub her feet, wax her legs and arms and style her hair. She was going to be dressed in a pink Banarasi that has arrived all the way from India. She was going to be decked out in rubies and diamonds belonging to her dancer mother.

Everything is going to be delayed because of this sudden unplanned detour. Today is her Ai Buro Bhat, her last meal as an unmarried daughter of the house, to be eaten with her unmarried niece Ananya and her friends. She herself does not have any cousins or friends who are still unmarried. Aparna has planned an elaborate menu that includes fish head curry, prawn malai curry, shukto, mango chutney, payesh, roshogolla and so many other items. Her sister has been cooking and preparing for this ceremony for the last three days.

What is she doing? How can she do this, knowing what it entails? Does she know the financial, social and emotional consequences of her selfish action? The caterers have been paid in advance, the marriage hall has been booked, the photographers have been hired, the hotel rooms have been confirmed, the invitations have been accepted, many of the guests have already arrived. A whole lot of money has already been spent; money painstakingly saved for her marriage by her loving father before his death.

And what about Neil? How can she do this to him? He is all set to build a dream future with her and here she is, all set to destroy his dreams. This wedding is an important occasion for him to showcase his rich culture to his American colleagues and bosses, most of whom are arriving tomorrow. Their flights and rooms have already been booked. His immediate boss has even cancelled an important meeting in order to be here on the day of the wedding.

And how can she subject her mother and sister to the humiliating disgrace that will inevitably follow? How can she cause a scandal all over again? Thanks to social networking sites, the whole world will come to know in no time that the bride-to-be has run away with someone else. The news of her elopement will reach far and wide, even as far as Vijaypur. She can picture some of Aparna's friends with their mocking smiles. She can visualize her mother's friends shaking their heads in total disbelief and saying, "She's done it once again. She's brought shame on her family and disgraced her dead father's good name."

"Don't think too much. Don't agonize over your decision," says Arnab, as they approach the station. He is using exactly the same words his uncle Akshay Kaka had used to encourage him to stand his ground and stick to his decision of coming to America for further studies, instead of giving it all up in order to please his parents. Had it not been for his uncle's moral and financial support, he would have never made it to this land of opportunity.

Today, it is his turn to repay his debt to his late uncle by making sure that Akshay Kaka's daughter pursues her own happiness instead of trying to make everybody else around her happy.

"Dada, do we have to do it this way? I can't bear to think what this is going to do to Maa. She is going to be devastated."

"Unfortunately, this is the only way to do it. If you don't run away now, even I can't save you from the collective pressure and the joint emotional blackmail you'll to be subjected to from the united mother-sister front. They won't let you change your mind now. Running away is your only option. There will be consequences, of course, serious consequences. It is going to be utter chaos for a while. There will be waterworks, hysterics, high drama, hunger strike, shouting, screaming, even fainting. But don't worry. I'll handle everyone. They will all listen to me. Even Maa and Aparna will. The important thing is for you to be happy. You can't sacrifice your happiness at the altar of family duty."

"But how can I be sure that I'll find my happiness with Jai?"

"Happiness does not come with a guarantee or warranty. You have to take your chances. You're an intelligent woman. Marriage shouldn't be the be all and end all of your existence. Being unmarried is not all that tragic. Come on, Sis, get a life. A life that you want to live rather than what others expect you to live. We can still go back, if that's what you really want. Nothing has changed, yet. You still have all your options open. So make up your mind and while you do that, I'll go out and get myself some coffee," saying this, Arnab gets out of the car.

Sitting alone in the car, Ellora carefully weighs all her options. Finally, she reaches a decision. It is the memory of the disappointed look on Neil's face when she failed to respond to his shower of kisses that helps her make up her mind. She knows that their future kisses are also going to be equally disappointing, not just for her but for him too. Try as she might, she will never be able to fake passion that she does not feel for Neil, no matter how likeable she finds him.

Feeling at once lighter and better, she now looks out of the car window, her eyes frantically searching for the one man who sets her heart racing faster than the metro rails. One man for whom she will never have to fake passion. But where is he for heaven's sake? It's already ten past ten and he is nowhere in sight.

She hesitantly gets out of the car, not sure if she can go through the agonizing ordeal of waiting forever for Jai all over again. To add to her woes, there is no sign of the sun, either. It is a gloomy morning.

She looks around, her eyes impatiently searching for Jai. And then, she spots him, as he emerges from the crowd, taller than everyone. He walks towards her with his hands in his pockets and a smile on his lips, looking absurdly handsome in a green and blue plaid shirt. Suddenly the morning is no longer gloomy and sunless.

As they come face to face, she waits for him to smile his playful dimpled smile or say something teasing and naughty, but instead, he sombrely holds both her hands in his and brings them to his lips, kissing them tenderly, closing his eyes, as if in silent prayer. He keeps holding her hands, now in a tighter grip, as if he does not want to let go of them ever again.

"I've left behind everything and everyone to be with you," says Ellora when he finally releases her hands and looks at her.

"Good girl," says a beaming Jai.

Ellora smiles, a bit sadly. This is the first time someone has called her a good girl for not acting like one.

****

Acknowledgements

I am enormously grateful to:

Ravinder Singh, my publisher, who believed in the book from the word go and treated me like an established author from day one. Not many debutant authors are lucky enough to have a publisher who is also a friendly mentor and a thoughtful editor. He, in his gentle persuasive ways, challenged me to dig deeper and fill all the gaps, connect all the dots, and add little more drama to the ending to make it more impactful. No matter how busy he was, he always had time for answering all my mails and addressing all my concerns. Thank you Ravin for treading so softly and so courteously around my fragile writer's ego to make some great suggestions - suggestions that have taken the book to another level. Working with you has indeed been a delight.

Neha Mathrani, my editor, for helping me to say things in a simpler and clearer manner. There is no doubt that she is extremely thorough. She went through the entire manuscript with a fine tooth comb and came up with a list of careless mistakes, redundant phrases, probing questions, and valuable suggestions that have improved the narration tremendously without interfering with the actual narrative.

Dilip Roy, my husband, who made it possible for me to write without having to worry about mundane matters like money and who gave me my space to write, no matter how much he disliked being shut out from there.

Aniruddh Roy, my son, who never let me forget that besides being his mother, writing is my true calling in life. He also gets an extra helping of thanks for taking me to all his cricket matches played in Virginia and Maryland – thanks to those long afternoons watching him and his teammates play, I was able to create authentic settings of cricket grounds in America.

Phyllis Randall, who generously opened her home to me during all my annual visits to Blacksburg, Virginia. Those long leisurely afternoons spent chatting with her in her bustling kitchen, picturesque deck and sprawling backyard, have been a significant source of inspiration for some of the characters and settings in the book. I have even taken the liberty of lifting few sentences from her emails and using them verbatim as dialogues in the book. Thank you, Phyllis, for your wonderful hospitality, erudite eloquence, intelligent inputs, and priceless friendship.

James Walters, our friend from Fairfax, Virginia, for patiently and painstakingly going through many of the chapters taking place in and around Washington metropolitan area, and for getting back to me promptly with a list of tracked corrections, invaluable suggestions and insightful comments. Jim, how can I thank you enough for helping me to get the language and the geography right?

Bobu George, my former colleague and friend, who came to my rescue every time my moody computer with mercurial mood swings decided to crash. Not only did he retrieve the lost chapters (including the last one), but also revived the seemingly dead computer in no time with his resuscitating touch.

Ms. Shobhaa De, the well-known Indian author and columnist, for taking time out from her busy schedule to encourage a first-time author like me, and that too without knowing me personally or through any reference. Ms. De, I am deeply indebted to you for forwarding my manuscript to your publishing contacts and for helping me to take a rejection slip with a shrug of the shoulders and a smile. Thank you for lifting my sinking spirits with your heartening emails at a time when I desperately needed someone to believe in my work.

And finally, a huge thanks to all my friends and family, especially my five siblings, nieces, nephews and their respective spouses for their prayers and good wishes. Nandini didi, Tapan-dada, Mohan-da, Chandan-da and Bandana-di, thank you for everything. Khushi, Meeta, Atula, Hricha, Padmini and Neeta, thank you for listening to my woes and seeing me through the lows. Thank you, Chor-di (Mrs. Leena Chatterjee) and Mamu (Dr. Souren Ghoshal), for your encouraging emails that invariably started with the inescapable question, "When is your book going to get published?" Well, I'm happy to announce that thanks to all your prayers, A Good Girl is finally here.

****